MAYBE BABY

POETRY BY TENAYA DARLINGTON

Madame Deluxe

MAYBE BABY

A NOVEL

Tenaya Darlington

BACK BAY BOOKS

Little, Brown and Company

New York   Boston

Back Bay Books / Little, Brown and Company
Time Warner Book Group
1271 Avenue of the Americas, New York, NY 10020
Visit our Web site at www.twbookmark.com

First Edition

The characters and events in this book are fictitious. Any
similarity to real persons, living or dead, is
coincidental and not intended by the author.

The author is grateful to Thames and Hudson
for permission to reprint the epigraph by Michel Nedjar from
Outsider Art: Spontaneous Alternatives, by Colin Rhodes.

Library of Congress Cataloging-in-Publication Data
Darlington, Tenaya.
    Maybe baby : a novel / Tenaya Darlington.
        p.   cm.
    ISBN 0-316-00075-2
    1. Problem families — Fiction. 2. Parent and child — Fiction. 3. Infants — Fiction.
I. Title.
PS3554.A723M39 2004
813'.6 — dc22   2003024864

10   9   8   7   6   5   4   3   2   1

Q-FF

Book design by JoAnne Metsch
Printed in the United States of America

For Anevay

"We know what we are,
but know not what we may be."

— WILLIAM SHAKESPEARE

"One is not male, one is not female,
one is a substance."

— MICHEL NEDJAR

MAYBE BABY

Chapter 1

BREAKING AND ENTERING

Amazing — there is no sound during conception. No chimes. No fizzing. No horns along the uterine turnpike honking as one swift cell drives headlong into another. Life begins in total silence, a microscopic He or She forming instantaneously, quick as a stereotype, even in its spiritlike simplicity. It dances in limbo. It hugs the shore, developing quietly. It is, first and foremost, its own secret, the date and time of its first trembling completely unknown, an indeterminable factor. What a phantom beginning. What a glorious moment to become Occupant X and nothing more. A ghost pulse, a comma amid the silence.

And yet.

Rusty opened the front door and stood for a moment in his wet loafers, eyeing the dark foyer. He sensed something in the air had changed. He paused, glove on the knob, and peered down the familiar hall, following the lines of the yellowed walls to where the evening light had gathered in the kitchen doorway. Where was the hum of the fridge? The routine clank of the furnace? The house felt too quiet. It seemed almost unnatural, stillness itself muted, as if all the furniture lay under snowfall.

"Judy?" he called, pushing back the sleeve of his gray overcoat to check his watch. "Hello?"

He cocked his head toward the basement, thinking he heard voices, then touched his ear to make sure his new hearing aid was on. From the kitchen came the sound of the northern oriole. The singing bird clock above the sink struck six, sending off its percolating forest call. It was followed by the sound of the furnace, the fridge joining. And so Rusty did what he always did after a long day at work. Too tired to plod down the hall to his closet, he hung his pants on the hook by the front door, dropped his suit coat and gold tie on the chair. Loafers squeaking, he padded into the kitchen, where he opened the fridge and stood wearing nothing but his shirt and underwear before a heavenly host of condiments and soda. There he raised his arms and let the cool air dry his sweat stains.

Had he flipped on the stove light, had his eyes swept across the braided rug before the sink, he might have noticed a pair of snowy boot prints slowly melting, the last of a trail that wound through the house, leaving wet marks on top of the wine-colored carpet. Had he given thought to the canister where his wife kept coffee-flavored candies next to the blender, he might have noticed the lid was slightly askew, a wrapper left in its shadow — something his wife, a tidy and thorough woman, would never do. It might have raised his suspicions then that he was not alone in the house, that something was about to happen.

In the basement, in a room below the kitchen, two beings huddled together on top of a ruffled bedspread for warmth, Rusty's adult daughter, Gretchen, and her boyfriend, Ray. They cocked their ears, held their breath. "Beer," whispered Gretchen, lying next to Ray on her old bed, their hands clasped through orange mittens, the last glimmer of daylight shining through the blue curtains. "Now he'll take it to his chair and flip on PBS."

Upstairs, Rusty shuffled across the living room, set the six-pack on the coffee table, and flipped open the red cooler he kept next to his recliner. Inside, the snow from yesterday was slushy yet still firm enough to hold the cans upright. He popped the tab on one and planted the rest firmly in the slush, burying their tops with a ginger sweep of his hand as if they were flower bulbs he'd planted in real earth. He liked his MGD just shy of frozen, and he relished the moment of lifting an ice-covered can out of the cooler, just like in the commercials.

When Judy came through the door, depositing her faux beaver coat on the banister, she could hear the distinct voice of David Attenborough coming from the living room, followed by the squawk of migrating birds. She kicked off her rubber boots, tiptoed toward the kitchen in her stockings, and knelt down to open the cupboard under the sink, only to step in a puddle of something cold and wet. She frowned, pursing her red lips fiercely together. "Rusty!" she called. "Did you track snow into the kitchen?"

No answer. She closed her eyes, gave a quick sigh, and pulled out a pair of mauve heels she kept in their original box under the sink by the cat food. She liked the sound of lifting the shoes out of rustling tissue paper as if they were brand new, and since she had been reassigned to teach gym class instead of home economics at Fort Cloud Middle School, she missed the power and pride she had once felt while storming down the hall in a good pair of heels.

"Cocktail," Gretchen whispered to Ray as the two stared at the glow-in-the-dark stars on the ceiling. Thousands of them that Gretchen and her two brothers had put there — and planets, too — Jupiter and Saturn and tiny Pluto, a personal favorite, her ATM password. Ray, silent in his bulky snowmobile suit — so silent he might have been sleeping or meditating — squeezed her hand. The little ring he'd placed on her finger at breakfast that morning pinched her skin, and she squealed, then quickly clapped a hand over her mouth. The ring was made from a nail that Ray himself had hammered into a circle.

Upstairs, Judy — reaching for the butterscotch schnapps she kept behind the Crock-Pot — cocked her ears. "Rusty?" she called. Then louder, "Rusty, did you say something?"

Rusty, who hated hearing his named yelled, especially after a long day on the lot, picked up the remote and increased the volume of the television by two notches. Rusty sold cars. All day he practiced being friendly, driving little old ladies around in Caprices, only to have them say, "That was such a nice ride, Mr. Glide. Let me think about it." There was one for whom he'd bought numerous cups of coffee as she labored over the financing, pushing manicured nails into her powdery temples. Could she afford it? she kept asking. Of course she could, Rusty thought, and he would have told her flat out that anyone who bought her dead husband a stone vault could certainly afford to drive an '82 white Cadillac Coupe De Ville. But she was a member of their church and a friend of Judy's besides, and he couldn't risk showing his temper.

Judy peered over the shutters that separated the living room from the kitchen and clucked her tongue. He was already on his third beer, watching a flock of geese fly in formation across the screen. It was bad enough that she had to listen to seventh graders shriek for six straight hours of dodgeball — did she have to come home to geese honking at near concert volume? If not geese, then whales. Last night, hyenas. Couldn't she, for once, just come home to some quiet, stretch out on the couch, and watch the sun set beyond the yard?

She crossed the linoleum, heels clicking, and flipped on the little black-and-white TV she kept next to the coffeemaker. Laughter flooded the room as Lucille Ball ran around, fanning her burning apron strings. A few seconds later, as Judy was giving her schnapps and water a stir with her little finger, the birds came louder from the living room.

But why bother migrating? boomed David Attenborough. *It costs most birds half their total population in casualties.*

Judy uncrossed her legs, fluffed the hair by her ear with a vague sense of drama, and turned the little TV to full volume so that Lucy and Ricky buzzed and crackled.

Above the sink, the mourning dove struck seven, its somber cry muffled by a distorted laugh track. "Cuckoo, cuckoo," warbled Judy as she raised her heavily penciled eyes and took a swig.

Below, Gretchen — the quietest and most sensitive of the Glide children — furrowed her brow, while Ray, who had a performance art degree from the University of Massachusetts, said simply, "Wow," as the universe above them trembled and shook, sending a few crusty stars raining down on their hooded shadows.

"Let's make love," Ray said, swinging a leg over her bundled torso. He tossed his mittens onto the floor and sat up on one elbow to kiss the side of her cheek. He could tell that she was biting her lip, and, sensing her resistance, he unzipped his brown snowsuit down to his shins. Underneath, he had on a leotard and tube socks.

"I don't know. This seems so weird," Gretchen said. She took her scarf off just as Handel's *Messiah* emanated from the upstairs. Handel was followed by the vacuum cleaner and, soon after, a stomping, which sounded vaguely like someone trying to tap-dance in high-heeled shoes. The basement was dank and cold, with a faint mushroomy smell that suggested hairline cracks in the cement, damp carpet pads. Gretchen wondered, as Ray un-buttoned her shirt, how she and her brothers had survived the winter nights down here, though that had been part of their re-bellion as, one by one, they vacated their warm, happy rooms on the first floor for the privacy and grit of the basement, with its thin, paneled walls and cold cement floors, its cobwebby corners and crickets that lived under the stairs.

Her oldest brother, Henry, had been the first to leave his bed-room, at age fourteen. He began with his record player and Ra-mones posters. He wanted to create a listening lounge, he told their mother, starting with two lawn chairs and a turntable propped on a wicker hamper. Soon the hamper was full of cracker crumbs and empty soda cans, and before long, a sleeping bag was found behind the dryer, along with some stuffed animals and a pillow.

"Fine," Rusty said. "You want to live like a rat, sleep next to the sump pump, I don't care, but don't leave any more Ho Ho wrap-pers on the ironing board."

"You have such a nice room," Judy tried to insist. "What about your airplane wallpaper?"

Henry shrugged, pushing past her with paper sacks of markers and comic books.

"Aren't you going to take your Golden Books? Or your tooth-fairy box? Don't you want your baby teeth?" asked Judy, wringing her hands in the hall outside his old bedroom door.

Henry scowled and closed one eye, his way of saying no. Down-stairs, by candlelight, he ripped his jeans — a slow, methodical process involving a dull steak knife and a comb — then safety-pinned them back together. Though his parents would not let him wear the pants to school, he wore them around the house, along with a pair of green elf shoes he'd found in the ravine across the road.

By fifteen, he was stealing *Playboy* from Little's Drugstore and rolling his own cigarettes. He blew the smoke into a roll of pink insulation propped behind the water heater and stored the *Playboys* in an old cello case that had Judy's name stenciled on it in faded yellow block letters — it was from back when she was Judy Wolfe. She found the stash one afternoon when she was looking for her Christmas wreaths, and that ended it. No more living in the basement. Judy stood at the bottom of the stairs with a ruler while Henry toted all his belongings back up to his old room.

For three days, over the first weekend of Advent, Henry sat up in his room with the door closed, howling like a wolf. He'd been named by his father, after the late Henry Ford, and when he put his mind to it, he knew how to invent new forms of subtle domination. At last — at the risk of fleeing to the basement for good herself — Judy agreed to let him return to his dark grotto, but she insisted that Rusty and Henry lay down carpet (orange shag) and make the place livable (wood paneling). They sectioned off the basement into three rooms, making a laundry area, a storage room for Rusty's hunting gear, and a bedroom for Henry.

It was only a matter of time before Carson, the middle child, followed his brother's example and vacated his room. He appeared at his mother's door one morning with his belongings packed in a suitcase. It was either downstairs, he proffered, or out the door. Judy knew better than to argue with Carson, who had shown himself to be fearless by hitchhiking to school on several occasions, while her other children waited for the bus.

"But you have such a nice room. Isn't it cozy?" Judy protested.

"It's painted in camouflage," Carson said flatly, his neck looped with beads, his tennis shoes covered in peace signs and slogans.

"Your dad worked so hard to make it nice for you." Judy held out her palms, remembering how eager Rusty had been to fix up the nursery for their second child.

"I'm against hunting," Carson said. "Plus, I'm thinking about becoming a vegetarian."

And so Judy let him take over the storage room in the basement as long as he promised to keep eating ham sandwiches and Sunday-night pot roast for the rest of his life. Downstairs, away from the camouflage, which he would later claim stunted his artistic side, Carson discovered he had a beautiful falsetto voice. He spent his free time harmonizing with the Beach Boys and working on latch hook, hour upon hour, until blocks of fuzzy yarn images covered the walls, soundproofing his room completely and allowing him to wake up at dawn singing like a little bird.

He was the star of the Fort Cloud Lutheran Church Choir and of the show choir at St. Bernadette's. When his voice changed at the late age of fifteen, it was a crushing blow. He stripped the room of his latch-hook rugs and sold them on the side of the road to raise money to attend a performing arts camp at NYU. There, mocked by kids who could flawlessly sing everything from *Hair* to Wagner, he skipped out of his classes and spent his remaining days with the Hare Krishna, singing all afternoon in Washington Square Park and peddling small paperback vegetarian cookbooks. He came back to Fort Cloud a vegetarian, wearing a bedsheet dyed cinnamon orange.

Disgusted, Rusty forced him to resume sleeping under camo in the upstairs bedroom, and a few weeks later, Carson — who was named after the famous late-night television talk show host Rusty so admired — was gone without a word. He took only his robe and his mother's good handbag, her favorite: black patent leather with a rhinestone clasp.

Rusty dearly lamented losing his youngest son, who, of all his children, showed the most business savvy. He'd observed the way Carson had wheeled and dealt with the old ladies for his latch hooks, and Rusty had already entertained a series of daydreams in which his little used car lot blazed with a great neon sign that read CARSON'S CARS. He'd pictured sitting in the back room, wearing a white suit and fedora, filling out paperwork from to time while Carson hovered around the lot and cut the deals. Rusty had already set aside a '67 Malibu convertible for his sixteenth birthday.

Though Carson sent an occasional message to his parents, saying he would stop through Fort Cloud again, he never returned. Several times a year, his mother made mysterious trips to Milwaukee, where she claimed to be taking cello lessons, though some believed she was visiting Carson, stealing off with her old cello case stuffed full of clothes and dry goods and money.

Rusty eventually took Carson's photo down off the wall and buried it in the yard.

That left an empty room in the basement. At age twelve, Gretchen claimed it as her scientific laboratory, and because she held promise as a young astrophysicist (her teachers said her understanding of the big bang and her ensuing diorama were unprecedented by anyone her age), her parents finally agreed. They spent the weekend she was away at science camp in Ogden decorating it for her thirteenth birthday. Judy painted the walls pink and hung blue daisy-patterned curtains while Rusty built her a study carrel with a special display case for her collection of moon rocks and micro scopes.

"I wanted a black room," Gretchen had moaned upon her return. Across the hall, Henry's space-age lair was lit up with red lava lamps that played off dark walls. He had started a rock band by that time, the Brother of Carson Glide, much to his mother's cha-grin, but because of Carson's widely publicized disappearance, the band enjoyed quite a following, at least regionally in southern Wisconsin and northern Illinois.

"You're a little girl," Judy had said, throwing up her arms, as if that explained everything. Gretchen, who by then had developed a healthy skepticism toward cheerleaders and ballerinas, scratched her head. Later that night, she scrounged around in the laundry room until she came upon some black Rit dye with which she planned to adjust her bedroom's color scheme. But just as she was preparing to mash her bedspread and curtains into the washing machine's gaping mouth, the toilet flushed upstairs and her father appeared at the top of the stairwell in his underwear, demanding to know why the lights were still on. When her subversive plan was discovered, there was a family intervention.

Gretchen and Ray lay tangled in their many limbs, some real, some just hollow sleeves made of padded nylon, and gazed at each other in wonderment. They had made love in nothing but their earmuffs, which only vaguely muffled the cacophony coming from above. They had made love undetected and unprotected, Gretchen gasping in the middle of it as she caught sight of the saucer-shaped smoke detector on the ceiling above her, similar in shape to the diaphragm she had left on the dresser of their apartment back in Chicago.

Upstairs, all was now silent. Ray scratched at his chest hair and uncurled himself from Gretchen's warm body to take stock of her old bedroom. "Wow," he said, stretching. Feeling newly aware of his surroundings, he began to make out small oddities on the shelves around him, his eyes having finally adjusted to the dark. Was that really a row of Barbies on the dresser? Was that saran wrap sealing the pink bookshelves from dust? Was that face opposite him on the wall really Strawberry Shortcake, in latch hook? And the ruffly pillow shams, covered with small raised dots — had these things really once belonged to Gretchen, the same Gretchen whose hair he'd neatly shaved that morning while sitting on the back of the toilet?

"Don't," Gretchen said as she saw him craning to make out an inspirational saying at the top of a florid poster. Ray had spent much of his childhood in an intentional community outside of Viroqua, Wisconsin, where his parents, who were anarchists, had homeschooled him in a wing off the abandoned post office where they lived. Later, his mother had developed an experiential high school curriculum for him by dragging him from commune to commune in an ongoing attempt to find herself.

"Ray," Gretchen said quietly, placing a hand on his shoulder blade. She moved toward him, her chin bearing down on the soft tissue between his neck and shoulder. She ran a hand down his back and let it rest on his hip. "It's cold down here. Let's leave."

"What about them?" he whispered, pushing a finger up toward the ceiling. He rolled over to face her, the part in his hair appearing like a white line drawn down the center of a dark road.

"Now may not be a good time for introductions." Gretchen

studied Ray's face, tracing his square jaw with a finger. His hair, which was dark and waist length, was out of its braid, falling in waves along his temples and down over his muscular shoulders and upper arms. His mustache and thick beard concealed any expression she might have read on his lips.

"What do you think about babies, Ray?" She leaned in close, tucked her nose up by his ear, and before he could answer, drew back, clenching her teeth. She drew in a breath so fast it whistled. "We may have just —" Her voice rose and then broke off.

Ray studied her small breasts, ran a hand down the length of her body, then let his eyes survey the other side of the room. Moonlight coming in through the window lent Gretchen's old pink desk a sickly glow. "You're right," he said, sitting up. "Let's go."

Dancing around on the cold floor, they struggled back into their clothes, Ray into his leotard, Gretchen into overalls. While Ray fluffed the pillows, Gretchen got up on her desk chair and peeled Pluto off the ceiling. They left as quietly as they had come, using the basement door, which brought them up by the side of the house.

When they entered the dark yard, they saw that a fresh layer of snow had fallen. The air, windless and still, seemed to encapsulate the neighboring houses, all pastel in color — like bits of fruit set in blue gelatin. Arms linked, they skirted the side of the house toward the back, hugging their bodies close to the yellow siding, until they came upon the kitchen window, through which they could see Judy framed by fruit-patterned curtains, legs crossed at a barstool by the counter, eyes glued to the television. In one hand, she held a can of green beans with a fork in it, in the other, a liter of 50/50.

She sat motionless against the olive cupboards, like a wax figurine — made only slightly more realistic by the gray roots of

her neatly combed golden hair, which stood out like a shelf mush-
room just above her neck and ears. Her face was pale with powder, her dull red lips parted in a partial frown. Ray stood close
enough by the sill to reach in and touch her elbow had the window been open.

"She doesn't look a thing like you," he marveled, surveying
Judy's maroon sweaterdress, which tied at the waist and had a
huge cowl neck that billowed down over her chest like hoops of
hoary skin. She was thin-boned but softly padded, with nubby
features and small, girlish hands that looked as if they probably
practiced perfect penmanship. When she sipped from a plastic
cup on the counter, she shuddered a little.

Gretchen shook her head and rubbed her mittens together.
"That's her," she said. "The womb." She stepped back and gave a
little laugh at her own sense of disconnect. Lately, she'd been
thinking about bodies, particularly mothering bodies, how easy it
was for them to develop something inside of them, something
that might grow up to become unrecognizable. Did birds, kanga-
roos, badgers, ever experience such alienation from their young?
she wondered. Did a mother titmouse ever look at her brood and
think, *Who are you?*

Maybe, Gretchen thought, it was a purely human phenomenon
for parents to push their children to become mirror images, and a
purely human phenomenon for parents to become estranged from
their children when they don't comply. Did a mother ostrich, for
example, ever scold her female chicks: "Cross your legs!" "Watch
your weight!" "Hush your mouth!"?

"Come on," Ray whispered, turning away and thrusting his arm
over Gretchen's dark form. As they stepped around the side of the
house, making for Ray's truck parked on the next block, the double glass door on the back of the living room slid open. Ray and

Gretchen drew back as a man in cotton briefs emerged and hob-
bled around in the snow wearing loafers, dragging what looked to
be a red cooler with wheels and a short handle. He drew it up by
the woodpile, where there was a gaggle of cement ducklings, and
tipped his head back to study the sky.

He stood for a moment, legs slightly bent at the knees, his arms
positioned stiffly away from his body, fingers spread. He looked as
if he might lift off the ground, take to the sky. Gretchen and Ray
hunkered down in the shadows of meatball-shaped shrubs along
the back of the house. Slowly, Rusty began to spin. He stopped to
lift one leg and scratch briefly at his calf, his eyes still raised to the
sky. Cold air flared from his nostrils. His silvery hair, usually
neatly swept back with pomade, stuck up around his ears like
spines. After a few moments, he resumed spinning, the soles of his
shoes scraping against the snow. His arms were almost entirely extended now, positioned slightly back. They flapped a slow, arrhythmic pattern.

Ray pressed his face into his sleeve to conceal his amusement.
Gretchen tucked her head behind the bushes, drawing her arms
in against her chest. "Drunk," she said frostily.

There was a clomping sound, then a muffled thump as Rusty,
whose shoe must have hit the side of the cooler, toppled to the
ground.

It was Ray who jumped up, despite Gretchen's whimper of
protest. He waded out into the snow, then paused a few feet away.
Rusty lay faceup, immobile.

"Ray!" Gretchen called in a hoarse whisper.

Ray crept closer, digging around in his pockets for his mittens,
and was soon peering into the face of Gretchen's father, a face he
had never seen but which bore a slight resemblance to the woman
he planned to spend his life with. Something about the heavy

eyebrows, the hard line of the nose. Rusty's mouth was slack, his eyes closed.

Ray swept his hair back into a ponytail, securing it with his right hand, so he could press a clear ear to Rusty's heart. He listened for a motion behind the damp T-shirt, then heard it, the slow but sure *thump-thump*, distant and heavy-sounding, like a lone fish flopping in a tub.

Rusty gave a little snort. Ray sat back on his heels, then rejoined Gretchen by the house. A good minute passed before Rusty's body stirred. Then his tan loafers began to spread, and his arms rose slowly from his sides, swooshing snow up around his head in great arcs. He was making a snow angel.

Chapter 2

THE CHIMP

Three months later, when the crocuses were up along the medians and what remained of the snow was strung across lawns in elongated patches like windblown lingerie, Rusty received an unexpected phone call from Gretchen at work. The call came in around noon, just as Rusty was about to start for the bank. He had a shirt pocket full of checks. With spring on its way, sales were up. People were eager for trade-ins, happy to cut quick deals that would launch them into top-down plushness. A jeweler had just dropped off a fat red Pontiac Grand Prix and in the next breath walked away with a gold Chrysler convertible with only the tiniest cigarette burn on the backseat.

"I know you must be busy," Gretchen said, her tone concealing any hint of excitement. "But I have something to say —" Here she paused, and Rusty could hear her swallow. He licked his lips, ran the tips of his fingers nervously along the edge of the blotter on his desk, and wondered if he'd missed her birthday.

"I'm pregnant." Her voice came at him in a way that was so pragmatic, so professional, that he found himself responding as if it were a business deal. "Okay, then," he said curtly, beginning to doodle on some registration papers lying on his desk.

"I'm due in October. Tell Mom she can call for details."

"It's a deal," Rusty said, loosening his tie.

"I'll talk to you later then."

"Righty-oh."

Rusty was so caught off guard, he even ended the call with his customary "Thanks for calling Glide's Autos." When he hung up, he sat for a moment, staring through the window at a pair of pink flamingos he had duct-taped to the antennae of two CRXs that flanked the lot's wide drive. He gulped some cold coffee, then tossed the cup into the trash under his desk, cocking his ear as the liquid trickled satisfyingly over some cellophane candy wrappers and down around the plastic liner.

It wasn't until he sat squarely behind the wheel of the Grand Prix that it dawned on him: he didn't even know who the father was. In the few times he'd talked to his daughter in the last year, she had, on occasion, mentioned a partner. And she had used the word *partner* — that very disconcerting modern term that made couples sound like they were in a law firm rather than a relationship. If Gretchen was going to couch her love interests in business lingo, Rusty had decided he would keep a professional distance. What he realized, though, was that he had no idea what she was up to and that the exact date of her birth had slipped his mind.

Like his other two children, Gretchen had become an enigma. Always good at kitchen chemistry, she had gone off to school to study science and nutrition, a useful-sounding major, whatever it was. Four years later, he'd driven a white Sunbird, with just the most minor rust around the front right fender, down to her graduation at the University of Illinois, only to discover she had majored in women's studies. She walked across the stage for her diploma with pink hair and a ring in her nose, and Rusty had sat next to Judy, holding the day's program with white-knuckled rage.

It was the only graduation they had ever attended. Year after year, they watched their neighbors congregate on summer lawns with their college-age children in cap and gown. Rusty, who kept a pair of binoculars by the front window for just such occasions, had always quietly observed these family gatherings — the fluttering mothers; the stiff-shouldered fathers, beaming with well-scrubbed pride; the graduates, like eaglets, looking dignified despite having to stand around in unflattering black housecoats.

With each of his children, Rusty's disappointment had mounted. To lose his sons — to what? what had he done? — and then to watch Gretchen, their most promising one, make a mockery of him — that's how he saw it, a mockery — had been more than he could take. He had driven the Sunbird straight home, parked it in the lot of an abandoned rifle range he'd once frequented, and left the car to rust and blister in the sun.

Now Rusty replayed the conversation with Gretchen in his mind as he drove to the bank and then home. It was early afternoon, prime sales time, but he couldn't face the idea of pasting on a smile and swaggering between the rows of bright hoods as if nothing were wrong. He parked the Pontiac in the drive and entered the house through the garage. What he wanted to do was put on his dungarees, grab his 30-06 rifle, and go out to shoot something.

He went for the closet, thrashed around among the hanging slacks for the feel of the gun barrel, and eventually got down on his knees to crawl way to the back, where he always propped it behind his wedding suit. He didn't hunt much anymore, didn't have the aim that he used to. His eyes were bad from squinting. If there was one thing he had learned about business, though, it was that people looked for honesty in the eyes. Obstruct them with a pair of glasses, worse yet bifocals or trifocals, and people were less likely to buy. When they scrutinized your face at that crucial moment before the close, they didn't want to catch sight of themselves. It confused them. It reminded them that they were the same people who had set foot on the lot just two hours before.

Rusty had also found that by squinting at his clientele, they felt he was more understanding. They read his bad vision as something genuine, a face fraught with concern. And so his bad eyesight had become both a selling point and an occupational hazard, no different, he always reasoned to Judy when she fretted over his driving, than the two times she had been thrown back onto the sprung-wood floor of the junior high gym by an erratic volleyball. Swerving around such hazards was part of living in the world.

Rusty batted at the back of his closet, overturning shoes and slippers, kneeing a box of Judy's old letters he kept there, but the gun was gone. He was sure he hadn't put it elsewhere, unless maybe he had mistakenly put it on Judy's side. The closet, with its two sets of shuttered doors, was one continuous passage. He squeezed around a footstool and was soon pushing his hunky form through a miasma of double-knit pants and floral wraparound skirts. At the far end, he found his nose embedded in a floor-length turquoise negligee he had given Judy after Carson's birth. He inhaled along its hem for the scent of her. It smelled only faintly of night cream and fabric softener.

He felt lost for a moment. Judy was, at times, still a complete mystery to him. She had secrets — not big ones, he felt, not big enough to confront — but, from time to time, he noticed things: the odometer on her Datsun would be two hundred miles ahead of the day before, though she'd claim to have gone nowhere but work. He'd find a ticket stub on the floor in the hall, though she would not have mentioned going to a movie. Who knew what she did with her time? He couldn't remember the last book she had read or even what she ate for breakfast.

If he thought seriously about it, he began to despair. He'd find himself, on a day like today, in her closet, sniffing her clothes for some scent, some trace of what she was like. But he'd find nothing there, just a generic female sort of smell, the way all the Realtor trade-ins stank of perfume and baby aspirin. And he'd end up sitting on the corner of the bed at the end of the day, trying to imagine her in the doorway, facing him with her neatly aligned limbs, her little belts that cinched her waist just below her bosom, the little pear-shaped rose-quartz earrings she liked to wear, her narrow feet in their good shoes making ruts in the carpet. He could always picture her when she was away — her presence hung about like a specter — but he was at a loss to conjure anything more, the texture of her hair between his fingers, the sound of her breath by his ear, the scent of her wrists, her neck.

It had been different once. When they were young, he had loved the smell of her sweat after a tennis game. It reminded him vaguely of decomposing lilacs, a fond memory from his youth of the great lilac bushes outside his bedroom window. Then there was the smell of her sleep and her waking, like damp mittens. It was her own morning smell. Even his children had smelled distinctly when they awoke. Henry of Wheaties. Carson of something earthy and sweet, like a new potato. Gretchen, whose name meant "little pearl," had always smelled vaguely of the sea, especially when she sat on his lap as a child and he had rested his face by her barrette.

It was impossible for Rusty to imagine this daughter having a baby, not because she was thin and birdlike, but because the news had been delivered in a fashion that was so compulsory it exaggerated the rift that Rusty felt between himself and all his children, between himself and Judy. Years ago, he might have imagined the conversation with Gretchen in other ways. She had been his little shadow. She had been the image of his own mother, with her toothy smile and long, sloping forehead and streaky blond hair. He remembered the way Gretchen loved to ride around with him in the old cars that came in, how she would clamber around the seats for pennies, digging with her fingers between the cushions, where she might find a lady's compact, a book of matches, a cigarette. She liked to sit up front like a grown-up, with her legs crossed and her hands in her lap.

Nothing in his life had prepared him for his children's mockery, for the distance they imposed on him later, as if his usefulness had expired. He had raised his children as he had been raised, guiding his boys with a firm hand and instilling in them a sense of what the world wanted from men: protection, fearlessness, devotion. Gretchen had been more Judy's concern. She had taught Gretchen to cook and to take care of little details. Gretchen had taken these things up with ease and was, by nature, reserved and fawning. It wasn't until she moved her room to the basement that she'd begun to slip from them. Was that even it?

One night, he'd descended the stairs to check the furnace, only to find Gretchen in Henry's bed and Henry in Gretchen's. They'd swapped rooms. Rusty had shot through the roof. It set him off to see his children readjusting their worlds — cagey Henry, who loved male singers in makeup. Rusty had rousted him from Gretchen's pink sheets and dragged him by the ear across the hall. Gretchen he had shooed back to her room. She'd been wearing Henry's *Star Wars* pajamas, and Henry — well, Rusty didn't like to think about what Henry'd had on. It still caused every muscle in his neck to spasm.

Unable to locate his rifle in either his or Judy's closet, Rusty spent the rest of the afternoon chasing the remaining snow from the yard with a small garden shovel and scooping it into his ice chest. When it was full, he squat-thrusted it, carried it with shaking elbows through the house and down the basement stairs to dump it into the empty Deepfreeze. All summer, he would have fresh snow.

The next day, an April Saturday, he caught Judy as she was about to head to a cello lesson in the afternoon. "Come sit," he said. She drew in her red lips, widened her small gray eyes. She was wearing pale blue pants and a ribbed coral sweater that accentuated her form. Rusty liked the whispery sound of her slacks as she made her way across the living room to the couch. He searched her face for some clue to how she might react to his news, but she wore the pert, concerned look she always wore. He had spent much of the morning preparing to tell her about Gretchen's phone call and had almost confided in his neighbor Donald over the fence but had decided the risk was too great.

Judy might not want the neighbors to know. She was sensitive to how she was viewed on the block, and attending the graduation parties and weddings and christenings of everyone else's children in the neighborhood was hard for her, Rusty knew.

"Gretchen called me yesterday at work," Rusty began, pursing his lips. He leaned forward sharply over his knees and pressed his hands together, lining up his fingertips. He could hear Judy's breath catch. Gretchen rarely called, never visited. It would seem strange to Judy that Gretchen had revealed her news to him.

"Is she okay?"

Rusty waited a moment before turning to face his wife, to offer his deferred lament. "She's pregnant."

Judy's irises floated in wide-open white space. After a few moments, her darkly lined lips bled into a shimmering smile. "A baby?" she whispered. Then, daring to raise her voice, "You're not pulling my leg, Russ, a baby?"

She stood up, drove her fists into the air with a cheer, then dropped back and threw her arms around Rusty, who was still anchored to the couch, studying his palms.

"I don't get it; you've known since yesterday, and you didn't tell me? How did you sleep? How did you eat?" She put a hand to her chest and snapped her eyes shut.

"We don't even know who the father is." Rusty turned, lacing his fingers over his knees.

"I'm sure he's very nice," Judy cooed.

"What's to say he's even involved?" Rusty snorted and looked down between his knees at his feet. They seemed huge to him at that moment, like great boats afloat on the carpet.

"Well" — Judy lifted her hands as if she were supporting a giant bubble around her head — "she can certainly come here. We know a few things about raising a family."

Rusty pushed off from the couch and stood up, bringing a fist down on the TV. "I want no part of this."

"What?" Judy rose slowly to follow her husband into the kitchen. She intercepted him by the fridge, pressing her spine up against the metal handle.

Rusty rolled his eyes and turned around in place. "Come on." He was only half dressed for the day — in a T-shirt and navy sweats with *Poupon U* running down one leg, a souvenir from the Mustard Museum in Mount Horeb.

"We've got a grandchild coming into the world," Judy sang, "who is going to need love and attention. What exactly are you telling me?"

Rusty pressed his palms to his ears for a second and backed up until his thighs touched the set of barstools by the breakfast nook. "All I know is we had three, and look where they are!"

There, he had said it. He waited before raising his eyes to see the blank look on Judy's face. She was a small woman with freckled arms and very narrow feet. Once a year, as a surprise, he brought her home a pair of shoes — designer shoes, that's what she liked. Her father had sold shoes — good shoes, down in Chicago — and if there was one thing that ran in her family, it was a hearty appreciation for Italian leather.

Today she was wearing a pair of mauve pumps. By some stroke of fortune, he had found them in the trunk of a Dodge, brand new, still wrapped in tissue, even in her size. She had shrieked and flung her arms around his neck with delight, promising to wear them on special occasions. He wondered why she had them on now. She had on those mauve shoes and something strange in her hair. When she turned to the side, he caught a glimpse of something white, like a bandage, around her forehead.

"What is that?" He squinted at her across the kitchen.

"What is what?"

"Around your forehead."

"It's nothing." Judy fluffed at her bangs.

"What is it? Have you been hurt? It looks like gauze." He stepped forward a few paces, put a hand on her arm. "A sweatband?"

"Yes, a sweatband." Her voice was curt. She drew her arms in close to her body, pulling away from his touch. "Menopause," she spat. "You know, hot flashes. Don't tell me you haven't noticed."

He dropped his gaze to the floor. "Why are you wearing those shoes? I thought you had a cello lesson."

Judy dropped her hands and went over to the sink. She ran the tap and filled a tall glass, drank it quickly.

"I mean it," Rusty said. "Who is this cello teacher you put on high heels for? High heels to a cello lesson? Plus a sweatband?"

"You can be such a frog brain," Judy said, proffering up just one of the many belittling names she carried with her from gym class.

"Yeah?" Rusty opened the fridge and pulled out a jar of grainy mustard.

"Yes," Judy called over her shoulder as she started for the living room. "You're losing touch, that's what. You've stopped noticing things." She picked her purse up off the couch. Rusty followed her with his jar of mustard and a fork.

In the hall, Judy swung around. "Want an example?"

Rusty opened his arms on his way to his chair. He dropped himself down into its pleather expanse without so much as glancing at her, then fumbled around by the cooler for the remote.

"A few months ago, burglars broke into the house," Judy blurted out.

"What?" Rusty craned his neck around to look at her standing in the doorway, her round white purse dangling from one arm on a thin strap, like a wheel of cheese on some sort of pulley.

"Donald saw them come out of the side door from downstairs and shimmy along the side of the house."

"That sounds like hogwash."

"I swear that's what he said. Two men, one with long dark hair and the other with a buzz cut."

"What?" Rusty's voice rang with exasperation. "Well, why didn't he call the police?"

Judy frowned. "Celeste was on the phone long distance to her niece."

"Did they take anything?"

Judy shook her head. "Not that I could tell. They went through

Gretchen's room. Her bed was all thrown around. On the floor, I found a man's orange glove — the kind people wear hunting."

"Jesus." Rusty sighed.

"I've got to go," Judy called.

"Right."

Judy liked to think of herself as the rational side of the family. She felt things very deeply, but she did not let her emotions direct her. Where Rusty had spanked, she had tried to reason with her children. Where Rusty had highs and lows, she maintained elevation, picturing her mind as a kind of mental butte. She liked to think of things in geographical terms. When her nerves were out of whack, she envisioned a stream of serenity running the length of her arms and legs and forcibly fed it into numerous tributaries throughout her body in order to calm herself.

In the car that Saturday, no such exercise seemed to work, perhaps because the two predominant emotions coursing through her were at odds. She was extremely excited about Gretchen's news, but disappointed that Gretchen hadn't personally contacted her. Instead of starting toward Milwaukee with her cello case, she took the exit toward Chicago, driving exactly four miles over the speed limit.

Judy had never been to Gretchen's apartment. Having grown up in Skokie, she knew well enough how to get around the city, and she had a good idea where Gretchen lived, but it had never occurred to her to actually visit. She'd certainly never been invited to come down, and although she was sometimes curious about her daughter's activities, she tried hard not to be a bother.

By late afternoon, Judy found herself parked in front of Gretchen's apartment on a quiet, oak-lined street flanked with redbrick two-flats. Along the walk, a mother in a long black coat pulled two small children in a red wagon. Two gray-haired men in dark wool sweaters sauntered arm in arm, walking a trio of pugs. They stopped mid-block to look up into some Japanese maple trees that were just beginning to form buds — little sample-size lipsticks, like the ones Judy had once left on people's coffee tables during her stint selling Avon.

Judy took the key out of her Datsun and sat for a moment at the wheel, quietly observing. She was pleasantly surprised by the location, by how familial it seemed. The woman in the long black coat stopped the wagon so that her two children could get out and pet the pugs. From a door down the block, two other children came running out. There was something strange about them, Judy thought, craning her head over the dash to peer out at them through the fogging window, but she couldn't quite put her finger on what seemed different. They scampered about cheerily, squatting along the walk and holding open their palms for the pugs to lick. One child, the smallest of the group, toddled over to the base of a tree and picked up what looked to be a pinecone and tossed it into the street.

Judy rubbed at the window with a glove, squinting. Was it a little girl or a little boy? Whatever it was, it was sweet — rosy cheeks, blond curls poking out from under its black knit hat and over the collar of the matching jacket. And that's when it hit her: all of the children were dressed in black. Were they Amish? she wondered, probing her purse for her lipstick. The mother wasn't wearing a bonnet, though her long coat was dark and tailored simply enough to lend her a stoic look. Yet she appeared modern when she turned around to lift her smallest — pushing aside the gray canvas satchel that rested on her hip, adjusting her squarish glasses. She tucked a strand of reddish hair into a loose bun at the base of her neck.

Judy applied some red lipstick with the aid of the rearview mirror and didn't think anything more about it. She snapped her purse closed and started up the walk toward her daughter's apartment, smiling to herself at the sight of two small feeders suspended from wires over one of the front bay windows. Gretchen had always shared her father's love of birds. Judy remembered the two of them heading out before dawn on the weekends to catch an eagle migration or to attend an Audubon walk. Judy had always used that time to clean, once in a while to practice a little cello in the basement or to stick her nose into an Agatha Christie.

The building where Gretchen lived had a cement stoop with a single set of double doors that led into a spacious foyer. There was no buzzer, and there were no names above the mail slots, which read simply #1 and #2. She wasn't sure what she had hoped to find. It was a Saturday afternoon, after all, and Gretchen might easily be gone — shopping downtown or grading papers at the library. Judy had never been quite clear where Gretchen taught — something to do with a community center, she thought, and wayward teens, teaching them to work out their problems through reading and writing poetry.

Now Judy found herself standing rather nervously on the doormat in her pale blue raincoat, brushing imaginary dirt off of her good shoes and wondering why she hadn't bothered to stop on the way for some flowers. She had been in such a rush that she'd barely remembered to grab a pack of bootees from her basement stash of gifts. What if Gretchen was feeling under the weather and didn't want to see her? She might not like that Judy had come unannounced. After all, Gretchen had called her father — why Rusty? Why not her? What was Gretchen up to these days, anyway?

Judy's mind was suddenly a blur as she tried to conjure the

daughter who might come to the door; she could only picture a young girl, fifteen, maybe sixteen, who used to come padding into the kitchen in her socks with binoculars around her neck. She saw a girl who ate only crustless bread for breakfast, preferably with butter and sugar, and who did not like toast, who liked only water with ice, who couldn't stand the tartness of a tomato or vinaigrette though she would peel and section whole lemons to eat. She saw a girl of contradictions, and at one time, Judy had memorized these idiosyncrasies as mothers are apt to do, but now there was no present recollection of what Gretchen liked or whom she was friends with or even where she worked.

It seemed frightening to her that her own daughter might be carrying a baby, someone whom Judy might somehow be forbidden from visiting. She shivered slightly, standing on the mat before Gretchen's door, purse clutched so tightly that her knuckles had gone white. She cocked her ear, then touched the knob.

"Up the step we go," came a voice from behind. Judy turned and saw the mother from down the block opening the front door for her two children. "Nap time," she was saying as she helped them up the step and into the foyer. "I don't want any fussing."

"Gretchen's at emergent yoga," the woman called down a few moments later from the landing. Her head appeared briefly at the top of the stairs, her face colorless, her glasses still fogged. She seemed not quite human. "Give a knock though. Ray should be home." She flashed a bright grin, then disappeared up the stairs again.

Ray? Judy thought, frowning. She didn't remember Gretchen ever mentioning a Ray. Once she had met a Jeff, a tall, lumbering freckled boy who had bad breath and a Boston accent. She had met a Corey, who was dark-eyed and brainy and wore a wallet on

a thick silver chain. She'd heard about a Seth, who was Jewish —
a fleeting Passover love — and on the day of her graduation,
Gretchen had hung from the neck of a blue-haired comic-book
character named Jackson, whose sketches, she insisted, were brilliant — made of nothing but cigarette ash.

Behind the door to Gretchen's apartment, there was movement. A chair slid against a bare floor. Then came the sound of
the television. Judy scratched a freckle on her wrist and tried not
to appear anxious in case she was secretly being watched. A few
seconds later, the noise from the TV was overlaid with music —
Handel, she recognized, a favorite of hers. She raised her eyebrows. "At least whoever it is has good taste," she murmured.
Then, from behind the door, she heard what she could only guess
was a vacuum cleaner, deep and droning.

What? Judy thought. And after that came a strange, arrhythmic
thumping, as if someone were dancing amid all the ruckus.

She thought to knock, then decided to walk around the back of
the house. Whoever was making such a racket wasn't very con-
siderate of neighbors, especially neighbors with two young children. She certainly didn't want to be in the way if there was a row.

It was twilight now. She skirted some budding shrubs, making
her way to the backyard. There was an overturned wheelbarrow
back there and, in an area of pea gravel, a large air-conditioning
unit. Judy stepped gingerly onto the wheelbarrow, then onto the
air conditioner, which brought her at chin level with the win-
dowsill.

"Oh!" Judy exclaimed, her breath catching. She blinked furiously, covering her mouth. The room was white and furnitureless,
separated from the rest of the apartment by a set of French doors.
A torchère lamp in one corner offered a warm yellow glow, which
illuminated a small color TV propped on a barstool in the middle

of the room. A man in a scoop-neck purple unitard leaped through the air, a great mast of thick dark hair sailing out behind him, his muscular arms flapping. From somewhere out of sight, Handel played on. Judy could see an upright vacuum unattended in the hall. She crouched and focused her eyes on the television. It was some sort of nature program. She thought she could discern the muffled voice of David Attenborough.

"Well, at least we'll have that in common," Rusty grumbled later when Judy, flush with excitement and horror, burst through the front door of her own home and confessed to Rusty all she had seen.

"He was so hairy," she kept saying as she cracked eggs for a quick omelet supper. "I've never seen such a hairy chest, and the way he was leaping around the room in nothing but a unitard, well, it was grotesque."

"Sounds like he's got a chimp complex," Rusty offered flatly.

"That's it exactly," Judy said, stopping to wipe her hands on a dish towel. "He was very animal."

"The chimp," Rusty hooted. "Isn't that just fabulous? Hello, everyone, meet our future son-in-law, the Chimp."

"No," Judy said suddenly, her voice pitching into a squeal. "No, we can't call him that." She paused, looking down into a glass dish of eggs, the raw yolks suspended like individual planets, like great glowing Jupiters. "I'm sure," she said softly, "I'm sure he's very nice."

Chapter 3

THE SHOWER

Throughout the next two months, as the June-blooming perennials began to flower in the yard — great sprays of hardy phlox and spidery clumps of columbine — Judy grew restless whenever she saw new mothers with babies. Since Judy's initial visit to Chicago, there had been a series of phone calls during which Gretchen remained coy about her plans and Judy tried chattering on brightly, until the frayed cord that bound mother to daughter and daughter to mother grew taut, then snapped. Trouble began when Judy suggested a shower. It was against what they stood for, was how Gretchen put it. She accused her mother of contributing to a patriarchal state, of imposing oppressive stereotypes upon something that was yet unborn.

The scene ended in a dial tone, Judy bawling at the little phone table Rusty had built her from old hubcaps, Gretchen standing exhilarated in her kitchen.

"I did it," Gretchen called to Ray, who was in scorpion pose on a sticky mat. "I finally told my mother how I felt."

"I don't know where things went wrong," Judy wailed to Rusty, who was yelling at the TV screen — championship bowling. "I mention bootees, and she's offended." Judy began to sob. "I offer to throw her a shower, and she accuses me of harboring an anti-feminist agenda. I don't even know what that means. Where have I gone wrong?"

The bootees had started it. Gretchen had found them on her doormat one Saturday evening when she returned home from yoga, sweaty but energized, having connected with that deep part of herself that was not Gretchen Glide but a new emerging self — part wild beast, part butterfly. The bootees — pink, blue, and yellow — were lined up in a clear plastic box, and though there was no card, Gretchen had known exactly who they were from. Her mother gave the same gift to everyone who was expecting and had, in fact, a case of them in her basement. She had picked it up one summer on special at Big Lots. The moment an impending fetus made a blot on her horizon, Judy routinely popped a package of bootees in the mail, along with a Hallmark.

"She knows nothing of our lives," Gretchen said, storming around the apartment in her leotard and sweats. Ray, who was busy working on his next show, took her in his arms and kissed her forehead, savoring the taste of her salt.

"Bootees, Ray," she said. "They're like sugar cereal for the uninitiated; they're like saying 'Welcome to the world. Here's your uniform.'" She tore open the box, flinging bootees around the room, creating what looked like a spray of colored marshmallows. Then she stuck her hip out, ran a hand over the prickly terrain on her scalp, and looked as if she might cry.

"We've already decided," Ray said, setting his hands on her shoulders and looking up into her pale gray eyes.

"I know, I know, it's just —"

"I know," Ray said, nodding slowly. "I know."

"You're right," Gretchen said, taking a deep breath. "I'm going to take the bootees and put them out on the compost."

Tired of the drama between his wife and daughter, Rusty finally rose from his chair and said, "Let me call. Time to put an end to this silly business." In his mind, Rusty had removed any notion of a baby from the situation. What bothered him most was that his daughter was living with a stranger who, by all accounts, looked like a monkey and leaped around the house in a unitard. In his thoughts and even in casual conversation with Judy, he referred to Gretchen's partner as "the Chimp."

"This Chimp — what kind of car do you suppose he drives?" Rusty had asked one night, standing in the bathroom doorway as Judy applied her night cream.

"How should I know? He was very muscular."

"But he wasn't masculine? He didn't seem masculine to you?"

"What are you talking about? He was streaking around in leg warmers while the vacuum cleaner was on."

"Leg warmers? You never mentioned leg warmers."

"I just remembered," Judy said to the mirror, pressing her hips against the sink. She had on a long white nightgown with thin blue stripes.

"What? Did they belong to Gretchen or something?" Rusty rubbed his stomach and studied the hall rug with a dyspeptic frown.

"I never saw them before."

"You think they were the Chimp's? You think he's the kinda guy who goes out and buys leg warmers?"

"I don't know. He's some sort of modern dancer. That's what Gretchen made it sound like." Judy dabbed her face with a hand towel and snapped off the bathroom light. Rusty followed her down the hall. Since the children had left, they'd taken separate bedrooms. Judy now slept in what had once been Gretchen's room. Her single bed, which was covered with a bright patchwork afghan, was pressed up against teacup-patterned wallpaper.

"He's a fruit?" Rusty asked, standing with his hands limp at his sides as Judy pulled back the covers on her bed. "Is that what you're telling me?"

"I don't know, okay?" Judy snapped. "It's not exactly our business."

"The Chimp," Rusty had huffed, milling in the hallway for a moment before he headed for his own bed in the room he and Judy had once shared. "No wonder Gretchen never brings him around. Who even knows what his name is?"

"His name is Ray," Judy called after him. "They've been dating for almost two years."

"This is Ray," came a man's voice over the telephone when Rusty finally made the call, Judy sniffling on the couch. Rusty had expected to hear Gretchen on the end of the line and had been prepared to give her something of a lecture, similar to the one he often delivered on courteous driving — a rap he always imposed on his customers, his own small contribution to the betterment of society. Only, he'd planned to revise the speech for his daughter so that the rules of the road applied to families.

Ray's deep voice left him flummoxed, and, caught off guard, he became almost cordial. They would agree to a shower, Ray said, as long as Rusty could abide by a few simple demands.

"Coed," Ray said. "I'd like to be a part of this, and I hope you'll be there, too, Rusty."

Ray's familiar tone gave Rusty pause. "Okay."

"And there's something I'd like to give you."

"Give me? The shower's for you two."

"In a sense," Ray said. "Don't think of it so much as a shower. Think of it as a life-affirming ritual. In Bora Bora, when a couple is pregnant, the whole village meets them with roots, and seedpod necklaces are exchanged among the men."

"Necklaces, huh?"

There was a long pause. Judy flashed Rusty a stern look from the couch.

"One more thing," Ray said. "We prefer black clothing. No pastels, nothing pastel."

"Fair enough." Rusty sighed. Talking to Ray was like reasoning with a kidnapper. Rusty imagined driving a Cadillac to the Illinois line, waiting in a poorly lit parking lot to hand over a suitcase full of dark little onesies — in order to gain what? The Chimp's affection? His daughter's respect?

Ray's voice came softly through the line. There was a little tremor to it. "I mean it when I say this, Rusty," Ray whispered. "It means everything to me that we can talk like civilized people."

At the end of the conversation, Rusty set the phone down and crossed the living room to where Judy was sitting on the sofa. The sofa was velvety, covered with ducks — flying ducks and stolid-looking ducks, their feathers preened. Judy, who had on a long beige bathrobe, looked like a piece of driftwood against it. She turned to him with a disconsolate look in her eyes, searching his face for some tenderness, some reassurance.

Rusty shrugged, hands in the pockets of his gray slacks. "No pastels," he said, rocking on his feet before her. "No big deal, Judy. They've just got their own way of doing things, same as us."

Judy turned her head slowly to the window, focusing her gaze on the bird feeder, where a robin kept stopping with bits of straw in its beak before flying off to the neighbor's shag bark hickory.

"Judy." Rusty put a hand out to touch her wrist but only caught her sleeve as she pulled away.

The shower started out well enough, a breezy afternoon in early July, the last of the Shirley Temple peonies clinging in big, creamy blooms to the side of the house, like blots of Kleenex. Judy and Rusty invited a few friends from the neighborhood, mainly old bridge friends and women from Judy's book club. They came bearing deviled eggs and ambrosia salads, which they set out on the dining room table around a bouquet Judy had made herself from a gathering of rusty foxglove. She'd thrown in some baby's breath and a couple pink- and blue-tipped carnations she hoped might offset the mood.

Six months' pregnant, Gretchen arrived in overalls and a cotton tank that seemed much too light for the unseasonably cool weather — Judy fretted she would catch cold without a sweater, but Gretchen refused to put one on, disappearing into the bathroom for a long period of time while guests arrived. Ray, to his credit, went around introducing himself. He was dressed in baggy linen pants and a loose batik shirt. His hair, Rusty was quick to note, was spun into a tight bun on the top of his head, held in place with a chopstick.

It was all Rusty could do to keep his cool while folks gathered in the living room. He was glad he had plenty of snow handy and took every opportunity to root around in his ice chest, pretending to search for soda brands he knew he did not have.

Judy fluttered around in an effervescent peach dress she'd bought in Sarasota with the idea of wearing it to one of her children's weddings. That morning, she'd unearthed it from her closet and unwrapped it from its plastic sheath, saying she guessed today was as a good a day as any to debut it. To dress it down, she wore a string of amber beads Carson had once left hanging in her bathroom.

A few of Gretchen's old college friends showed up, one of them carrying a baby in some sort of rawhide papoose. The gifts they carried with them were wrapped in newspaper, brown grocery sacks. They were tied up with twine and fraying ribbon, dried flowers instead of bows.

"Look how beautifully these are wrapped," Gretchen said when she and Ray got down to the business of opening gifts so that everyone could finally relax. They took turns opening jars of diaper-rash poultices, hand-sewn bibs, cloth diapers. Judy presented them with a dark patchwork quilt she had tearfully made, all brown and black with — she couldn't help it — some pale pink stitching.

Finally, Donald and his wife, Celeste, exchanged glances and handed Gretchen a large gold bag overflowing with shredded Mylar. "Oh," Gretchen exclaimed, pulling out two hand-stenciled signs, one that read IT'S A GIRL, the other: IT'S A BOY. Donald, who had just retired from Miller, had gotten handy with the woodworking tools in his garage.

Gretchen looked at Ray, then at Donald and Celeste — neighbors she'd grown up with. Rusty could read the dismay on Gretchen's lips. To himself, he said, *Let it be, Let it be,* as he lifted the lid of the cooler to check for a Fanta lime cola.

Gretchen took Ray's hand, and the two of them sat forward on the couch, shoulders touching. Gretchen cleared her throat. "Ray and I," she said with confidence, though a twitch in her eyes belied nervousness, "Ray and I have decided to raise a gender-neutral baby." She turned to Donald and Celeste, holding out the signs. "Thank you, but I'm afraid we won't be needing these."

The room was quiet. The ceiling fan hummed, blowing at the petals of some peonies on the coffee table. Donald leaned forward on a dining room chair and let out a polite laugh, moving a toothpick from one side of his mouth to the other. "Made those signs in my woodshop," he said proudly, rubbing his hands together. "See now, say it's a girl, you put out the 'It's a girl' sign in the yard, and that way you don't have to hassle with people asking. If it's a boy, same thing. It's easier this way. You won't be bothered." Satisfied with his explanation, he sat back, adjusted his ball cap.

Gretchen ran a hand through her hair, which was short and bristly — but at least her natural color, Rusty thought. He let his fingertips linger in the snow, working up a tiny snowball between his thumb and forefinger.

"It was thoughtful of you to make something by hand, Donald," Gretchen began. Rusty closed his eyes as she launched into a speech about how patriarchy began at birth and how she and Ray were part of a new dawn, how they were going to change the world with their new method of parenting.

Rusty leaned back in his recliner and popped the small snowball into his mouth. He let his eyes glaze over and close. What had he ever done to deserve such an absurd scene in his living room? Surrounded by his friends, their neighbors, he could just imagine the tales they would go home and tell their families. "Rusty and Judy," they would say, "they're so nice, but their kids — you wonder how they can all be kin."

Then, just as Rusty was pressing the last of the snowball to the roof of his mouth, concentrating on the coolness spreading through his neck and shoulders, there came a sound from the kitchen — the sound of bells and gongs and what sounded like tribal chanting. When he opened his eyes and craned his neck around the headrest, he saw the Chimp fly through the room in a purple unitard and what looked to be some sort of sarong. The Chimp slid under the coffee table in a single fluid thrust and landed at Gretchen's feet. From the tape deck in the kitchen came the slow beat of drums, which steadily increased in volume and tempo, until the Chimp stood in the middle of the room, his body pulsing.

Rusty did not dare meet anyone's eyes. He looked down at his own hands, which were red and large as lobsters fresh off ice. He fought the urge to lunge forward and clamp them around the Chimp's wrists, to drag him outside, force him back into whatever girly car he drove, and kick the bumper as it backed out of the drive.

A gong sounded, and suddenly the Chimp was on his knees before Rusty's chair. There was a silence; then the Chimp bowed his head and slowly began uncoiling his hair into Rusty's lap. Rusty could feel the Chimp's heart beating wildly against his calf. The Chimp gave off a beasty smell, sweat seeping through the elastic fabric of his unitard, all around his hairy chest.

When the Chimp had draped his long hair across Rusty's knees, a pair of scissors emerged from the folds of the Chimp's skirt. These he slid into Rusty's hands, making a motion that Rusty should cut.

Across the room, Gretchen's old friends looked on almost gleefully. Rusty caught Donald White staring out the window, where the Seville Rusty had sold him sat next door in the drive. The Chimp breathed deeply and seemed to enter a kind of trance as the drums started up again. "Cut," he whispered.

"What?" Rusty spat.

The Chimp pointed to his hair and pressed the scissors firmly into Rusty's hands.

It made a terrible sound, like static, but the Chimp did not flinch. He picked up the coil of hair and carried it around the room like a snake for all to see.

Afterward, when everyone was gathered in the dining room eating cake, Rusty caught the Chimp coming out of the kitchen. "You got me" was all Rusty could think to say.

"I did it for Gretchen," the Chimp said, still breathing heavily. He took the meat out of a little sandwich and ate the mayonnaisey bread.

Rusty felt dizzy from champagne and the smell of perfume. "She's a good girl," he said. "You got yourself the deluxe model." He didn't know then why those words came out of his mouth. They just did. He felt stupid in that moment, stupid and mortified that this was what his life had come to, that a new generation had entered his house and made him feel dumb. What he really wanted to do was beat the Chimp senseless, he thought to himself as he stood in the waning light of the hall, watching the Chimp lick crumbs from the corners of his mouth. In his younger days, he would have done just that.

The Chimp must have sensed this. "Whoa," he said. "Careful there." His eyes flashed, and Rusty could see that behind all that soft fur, there was another side of the Chimp, something a little wild waiting to be let out.

"Listen," Rusty said to the Chimp, leading him down the hall by an elbow, "I know you and Gretchen have been to college and you're full of new ideas. I applaud that, but what you said there about the genderless baby, that seems a little —" He let his voice trail off, hoping the Chimp would fill in the blank, hoping a rational approach might gain him the Chimp's confidence. But the

Chimp stood motionless, breathing deeply through his nose, his eyes opening and closing rapidly — a sign perhaps of pity or exasperation.

"Everyone comes from nothingness," the Chimp said very softly before whirling around on his heels to go. Rusty watched the muscles in the Chimp's back shift through the fabric of his unitard, the way he flipped his head as he rounded the corner of the hall toward the voices in the dining room. He left a gingery smell in his wake, a murky specter in Rusty's mind. Who was this guy? What did he do? Rusty withdrew to his bedroom to hide. Down the hall, he could hear Judy carrying on: "Who cares if it's a boy or a girl, as long as it's healthy! I just want everyone to be happy, happy and healthy!"

From his bedroom window, a while later, Rusty watched his daughter heading down the front walk, her belly hanging off her like an igloo, and he wondered what could possibly be taking shape inside her body. She and the Chimp held hands, his arm dark and tangled-looking, like a vine. Their arms swung a little as they crossed the grass to a red Ford truck.

"A Ford," Rusty said to himself, rocking back on his heels. "Could be worse." But it was the one nice thing he could think to say. A bitter taste rose in the back of his throat, like charred earth, like sour compost. He'd given his daughter no gift that day — no rattle, no car seat, not even a card. She, in turn, had hardly looked his way, gazing, between sips of too-sweet punch, out at the bird feeders that swayed from side to side in the boughs of the old oak, spraying seed into the wind.

Down the hall, Rusty could hear Judy washing the dishes from the baby shower. He thought he could hear her humming, trying to relax. Tomorrow, he knew just how Judy would act. She remembered only the good. She would tell her friends in the teachers' lounge at school that her quilt had made a splash, that everyone had loved the shrimp dip and toast points, and she would call Gretchen "glowing" and deem Ray "unique and interesting" without ever disclosing a hint of her frustration, a twinge of her own grief. She would not mention that most of the baby clothes were black or that Gretchen had given Donald's signs back.

Judy was always one to croon when others brought out their bragging books full of carefully posed grandchildren. But what would she do now? When the baby came, what would she tell people when the first thing they asked was "Boy or girl?" Would her face register the pain, the estrangement she'd carried around since the day she found out that Gretchen had called Rusty with the news? Would Judy remain silent about the birth, hoping people forgot, letting them assume the worst? Or would she hold on to the hope that this was just some fad that Gretchen would eventually abandon?

Rusty hadn't cared to hang around in the dining room later as Gretchen explained that she and Ray were part of an international underground movement of couples who were practicing this new method of child rearing. Ray had stood by Gretchen's side, nodding with his new jagged hairdo, trying — Rusty thought — to look urbane, when really he belonged in a zoo, was cuckoo, was out of his mind if he thought for one minute that Rusty would just play along.

By the time the red Ford had driven away, the shower loot secured under a tarp, Rusty had been seething. It was all he could do to confine himself to the bedroom. And now that they were gone, he made his way back to the living room to look at the ponytail lying on the arm of his chair. It was dark and thick and wavy, held fast by a blue rubber band with gold flecks.

Rusty could not pick it up with his bare hands. He could hardly stand looking at it. It was repugnant. The thought of it having been connected to the Chimp's head, the thought that this hair held the Chimp's history, had slapped against his back as he danced or walked or made love — all that he did — made Rusty's stomach turn.

He went downstairs to dig around in the closet where Judy kept their winter wear. There, among the scarves and earmuffs, he found a single orange glove. How had that gotten there? he wondered. It seemed suitable for the job at hand. He put on the glove and went back upstairs.

Judy, who was still in the kitchen, peered out over the shutters. "What are you doing?"

"What does it look like I'm doing?" Rusty hovered over the hair, frowning. He saw there were a few silver strands. How old was this guy, anyway? Where had he come from? Why had he declined to invite his parents, the neighbors in their community?

"Why are you wearing that glove?" Judy appeared, drying a crystal serving platter.

"What does it matter?"

She shrugged. "That's the one I found downstairs in Gretchen's room after Donald spotted our robbers."

"What robbers?"

Judy sighed and disappeared back into the kitchen.

"I never heard about any robbers." Rusty had on the glove, but he still couldn't pick up the hair. He sniffed at it mistrustingly, then poked at it with a gloved finger as if it might suddenly recoil, then strike. "I'm taking out the hair," he called over his shoulder after he'd managed to pick it up. He held it away from his body,

carrying it gingerly down the hall to the front door, the hair dangling from between his thumb and forefinger like animal remains.

Rusty carried the hair around the side of the house. Outside,
the sky was dusky. There was a light mist in the air, neither rain
nor fog. It left the skin feeling clammy. Rusty went into the
garage, rustled about until he found a cigar box to put the hair in,
then grabbed a shovel.

"Whatcha up to there?" It was Donald calling over the woodpile. Across the way, a streetlight snapped on. Rusty cast a glance
over his shoulder to catch Donald standing under a red umbrella,
puffing on a cigar. Donald pulled a second one out of his shirt
pocket and extended it to Rusty's back.

"Naw," Rusty said gruffly, shaking his head. He hoisted a shov-
elful of earth to the side, making a hole between the drain spout
and a cluster of hollyhocks.

"Sure, go ahead," Donald said. "Meant to give it to you earlier."
Rusty stopped digging, turned his head just slightly to the side,
and, without facing his neighbor, did his best to keep his voice
calm. "No thanks, Donald." Rusty waited, motionless, a pile of
dirt in midair.

A few seconds later, a branch cracked behind him, signaling
Donald's retreat. From the corner of his eye, Rusty watched the
red umbrella fade into the next yard, the smell of cigar smoke still
lingering in Donald's wake.

Rusty sighed through his teeth, tossing dirt at the tops of the
hollyhocks. He finished his work quickly, setting the box into the
shallow hole, then covering it. The sound of earth striking hollow
cardboard made him shiver. Or maybe it was a chill in the air, the
cool mist mixed with his own sweat, making his T-shirt damp.

He left the dirt loosely piled by the drain spout, then hurried
into the garage. After returning the shovel to its nail, he climbed

into his car and sat in the driver's seat, holding the wheel to keep his hands from shaking.

A soft rain started up, thrumming on the roof of the garage, then grew louder. Rusty tilted back against the velour headrest and licked his lips. He could hear his own heart beating so loud it drowned out the rain and seemed to fill the whole sedan. When he rubbed his palms over his knees, he couldn't determine which of his body parts was shaking hardest. He closed his eyes, hoping for respite behind his lids, but all he could see was the hair lying in the box, the box so full it could hardly close, loose strands seeping out around the sides. He saw the hair slithering into the soil, making its way down toward the house, like the roots of hardy vines wheedling their tendrils through the cement foundation.

Why had he buried the hair under the drain spout in a cardboard box that would get soggy? In the morning, there might be hair all over the yard, spread over the tops of the grass, laid out like some sort of dark aftermath from a gruesome battle.

Rusty's eyes flashed open. Before his face, a single yellow orb floated in the darkness. It took him a moment to remember that it was a Ping-Pong ball he'd hung from the ceiling on some old fishing line. The darkness seemed to congeal around him, thick, heavy — it was almost as if he were sitting in dark syrup. On the roof, the sound of the rain was like dozens of small fingers tapping and tapping to be let in.

A light came on overhead, then the door from the house to the garage opened, and Rusty saw Judy's bare legs and feet standing in the doorway. She had on white terrycloth slippers and the turquoise negligee he remembered from the back of her closet. It rippled above her knees, like water.

She descended onto the step covered in Astroturf and leaned

over to peer through the car window, her eyebrows furrowed, her lips together. Around both eyes, he noticed purplish rings, halos of sleeplessness. She cocked her head to the side, wedged her hands between her knees, and stared at him quizzically.

He ran a hand over the plush red velour of the passenger seat, as if it might offer some sort of explanation as to why he was sitting alone. Still, she looked puzzled.

"For heaven's sake," she said, her voice muffled. "I've been waiting."

He shook his head as if he had no idea what this meant.

She crossed her arms. "I'm going in." He watched her feet pause on the step a moment longer. Then she went inside. He knew she would wait on the other side of the door until she heard his movement. She would listen, arms crossed, watching the fluorescents over the kitchen sink flicker.

He had to be quick. He had to go out back and dig up the hair, dispose of it once and for all. "Judy," he called as he stepped out of the car, giving the door a good slam. "I'll just be a minute." His voice echoed through the garage, returning to his ears, confident and commanding.

He grabbed a flashlight and a bucket on his way out the door to the driveway. He turned for a moment, trying to recall where he had left his orange glove, then decided to forget it. The rain had evolved into a steady drizzle. He knelt down by the gutter and plunged his bare hand into the mud, grappling for a hold on the box. He expected it to come loose like a giant tooth, but some force of suction made for an impossible grip. He pulled, and it slipped from his hands, the cardboard slick, almost mushy.

"God," he murmured, securing his weight with one hand on the ground as he used his other to fish around. He finally plunged his hand up under the cardboard flap and yanked the hair free, ripping it up through the ground, straggly and muddy and twisting in his grip as if it were alive.

He let out a shrill cry — unexpected, almost childlike — then thrust the wet clump down into the bucket. He stood up, shaking.

A faint red blur appeared down the block, bouncing under a streetlamp. Rusty squinted and saw that it was Donald's umbrella.

"Donald," he called, shuffling forward, his pants wet, his loafers squishy. He ran his clean hand over his hair as he moved toward the walk, trying to appear impervious to the weather. "Donald." His voice was desperate.

"Hi ho there," Donald called from two houses down. "Need that cigar now, do you?"

"Yeah," Rusty jibed, swinging the bucket behind his back. "You wouldn't want to take a ride now, would you?"

"Kinda late." Donald strolled up and stopped short, producing a cigar in a cellophane wrapper. "Whatcha got there?"

Rusty, who was about a foot shorter than his tall, angular neighbor, looked up into Donald's face. With the streetlight behind him, Donald's skin was free of lines. He looked almost young, except for the thin shell of ice white hair combed back over his ears. For an instant, Rusty flashed back to the day he and Judy had moved in. Henry had been an infant. Donald and Celeste, expecting their first, had come over with some fresh bread, Celeste's belly distended under a checkered sundress. She had sat down on the one kitchen chair they had at that time and rested little Henry against her own full-blown tummy. The world had seemed bursting with possibility.

Donald had helped Rusty move the water bed, and afterward, the two had gone for a drive, gotten high on the hood of Donald's

Chevrolet. Rusty had put his arms behind his head and leaned back against the windshield to look up at the stars, sensing the closeness of other life, as if his own future waited radiantly ahead.

Over the years, he and Donald had gone for numerous drives at night, more often when the kids were young. Sometimes the children had begged to come along, to be allowed to get a cherry ice. But many drives had just been the two of them, carrying on with the windows open, cajoling each other about their wives, confiding in each other. There were things Rusty and Donald had confessed to each other that not even their wives or children knew.

Tonight, Rusty looked up at Donald, then back down at his shoes, and Donald knew. "Come on," Donald said, his voice still carrying the faint drawl of his Texas upbringing. "You won't believe how that Seville handles the open road compared to my V6." He took Rusty by the elbow and led him toward the garage.

Rusty wiped his hands on a towel slung over Donald's workbench, then set the bucket in the trunk of the Seville. The trunk was still immaculate, neatly lined with a child's blanket. Rusty jammed the bucket down next to the wheel well, then climbed in the passenger seat.

"That was quite a day you had," Donald said after they pulled out of the drive and onto Seeley Street, the car gliding into its full-metal dream, noiseless and smooth on the uptake.

Rusty just nodded.

"Can't say that I ever met one quite like — what's his name?"

"I call him the Chimp," Rusty said under his breath.

"Yeah, well, he was an original." Donald gave a little laugh and followed it with a few slow nods. He drove with his arms outstretched, his seat far back and low to accommodate his tall form. Around them, the neighborhoods of Fort Cloud were aglow. A recent initiative had been passed to double the county's street-

lamps as a way to reduce crime, though few could remember anything other than the Dairy Queen's being held up once and, here
and there, a bit of petty theft. Nonetheless, crime was everywhere
in the world, and that seemed to suggest a shady forecast, even for
Fort Cloud. The county supervisor had endorsed the streetlamps
as a preventative measure toward continued bliss. Throughout
downtown, banners had been strung between lampposts and store
awnings, proclaiming FORT CLOUD: CONTINUE THE BLISS. And residents had followed suit with signs on their front lawns, the *L* in
Bliss drawn as a lamppost.

The lamppost initiative had still not quite made it over to Donald and Rusty's street. All spring, work crews had been out, paid
overtime was what people said, to get all the posts in by late summer.

"You got anything else in here to smoke?" Rusty smiled, rap-
ping on the glove compartment. He squinted and raised his eyebrows, trying to appear collected.

"You kidding? With this crackdown on crime?" Donald let out
a whistle. "No sir." He shook his head. "Those days are over."

They drove out onto County A, the bright lights of Fort Cloud
disappearing behind a hill like a sparkler gone out.

"You mind stopping on the bridge up a ways?" Rusty asked.

"All the way up there?" Donald rubbed at his jaw. "It's kinda far."

Rusty was quiet, listening to the engine's purr, watching the
headlights move along the road like a set of ghost eyes, catching
on the occasional dead raccoon or broken tree limb along the
shoulder.

"Donald," he said, "I don't believe I've broken in this car with
a proper confession."

"Yeah?" Donald turned away from the wheel for the first time
toward Rusty.

Something about the way Donald looked at him with his watery eyes, his square jaw set, gave Rusty confidence. He drew in a deep breath. "It's like parts of my life keep unraveling in front of me," Rusty began. "I can't sleep at night, and sometimes even during the day, it's like I'm in a dream, walking past things that have already happened to me in another life."

Rusty looked out the passenger window at the moon, full and gold, following them over the hills. "I've never told anyone this," he said, swallowing. "In fact, I can't remember the last time I thought about it until today — it's like I forgot for a lotta years, and now it's dangling in front of me. Everything I do brings it closer."

A car passed them. Donald flipped on his brights.

"I was in Philly, just out of the service, working second shift on the lines. Came home one day, and there was this kid, this scraggly, bearded, long-haired hippie guy eating at my table. Goddamn breakfast," Rusty said, tossing out a hand as he stared out the window at even rows of corn breaking through the soil. "He'd just let himself in and helped himself to what was in the fridge, used the toaster, fried some eggs. He had a pack of smokes and was reading my paper." Rusty shook his head, then opened his mouth, waiting for the words to come to him.

"I was tired; I'd had a few drinks after work." He passed a hand across his lips. "First thing I did was grab the kid by his hair and drag him off the chair to the floor."

"Well, did he have an explanation?" Donald asked in a low voice.

"Of course," Rusty said matter-of-factly. "He was hungry." Rusty shrugged. "Said his girlfriend had kicked him out and taken up with some guy in a band."

"Did you believe him?"

"What does it matter? I was too angry to believe anything. I pinned him down on my kitchen floor and went at him. But partway through" — Rusty paused — "somehow he got the better of me. He struggled loose and stood bleeding in the corner by the stove, pleading for me to stop. Said he had to pick up his son." Rusty swallowed. "Then he reached around to the back of his jeans — I thought he was going for a knife." Rusty stopped to stare, blinking across the dark car at Donald. "I really did. I thought he was going to pull a knife on me, so I went after him again."

Donald winced. "You finish him off?"

"No, nothing like that. Messed him up badly though." Rusty's voice strained. "Later, I checked his back pocket, and I found what he was trying to show me."

"What was it?" Donald asked, his voice hardly audible over the motor's hum.

Rusty sniffled, tugged his earlobe a few times, then spoke. "A picture of his kid, Donald. He wanted to show me the picture of his little boy. I've still got it somewhere."

Donald slid the car over to the shoulder and reached over to rest a hand on Rusty's arm.

"It was awful," Rusty said. "And what's worse, I'd forgotten about it. I'd clean forgotten." He leaned forward and pressed his cheek against the top of the glove compartment, eyes closed.

"What's in the trunk?" Donald asked quietly. "We're at the bridge."

"The hair," Rusty said, his voice choked. "That's what made me think of this." He let out a loud, short sob, then sat back.

"I'll handle it," Donald said, swinging his car door open and stepping out into the dark air. The car idled. Rusty watched in the side-view mirror as Donald tossed the bucket's contents over the guardrail. He waited for relief to flood over him, but it did not.

"I remember being young," Donald said on the way home. "Celeste and I wanted to buy a farm and have city kids come out in the summers to taste the wild and ride the horses." He let one hand drop a slow arc through the air. "We didn't have a clue what we were talking about."

"That's how it is," Rusty said, starting to peel the cellophane off his cigar. "It's just" — he paused — "you expect to feel less con-fused as you grow older — you keep expecting this to all line up, only to realize you're more confused than ever."

Donald nodded grimly. "We've all been there." He fished in the pocket of his shirt and offered Rusty a light. Soon the car was filled with smoke. They cracked the windows, let the cool, damp air, with its smell of earthworms, fill the car. Rusty looked out the pas-senger window, imagining beyond the guardrail to a place where the Chimp's long ponytail lay among the rocks. He pictured hikers coming across it some afternoon, spotting it from a distance, the hair glinting in the sun. *Is that a body?* they would ask themselves.

And it was. In a way, it was a body — or it led to one, at least in Rusty's mind. Touching the Chimp's hair had cast him back in time to observe, at a distance, his own violent temperament. He could smell that morning in Philly, touch pieces of that kitchen almost. It amazed him, how fresh it had stayed in his mind, though he had called it up from memory so few times. It was like pulling frosty Tupperware up from the bottom of the Deepfreeze, only to find a perfectly preserved meal under the lid.

There had been a few other occasions — when his sons had been young — that he'd flashed back to that day. When he'd dis-ciplined them, for example, when he'd visited the outer limits of his rage. One summer, he had caught Carson lying naked in the backyard, reading on a blanket. The boy had been nine or ten. What exactly had disgusted him? Rusty wondered now. Was it the sight of his bare skin before the neighbors, this skinny blond boy, so hairless and strange-looking, sprawled facedown on one of

Judy's afghans like a feral cat? Rusty had stood at the back door, agog for a few minutes, watching the boy lazily scratch an elbow, then his shoulder blade, legs crossed, toes flicking at the grass.

By a tub of geraniums, the boy's clothes formed a neatly folded pile in the sun, and that's when Rusty had felt the rage at his temples, like a drum. It was the boy's brazenness that got him, the thought of the boy languorously disrobing, then stopping to fold each article of clothing with calculated ease. Who would think to do such a thing — to carry out such an act so completely, down to the ball of socks, the perfectly aligned sneakers with tucked laces?

Rusty, fresh from a church finance meeting, had taken off his blazer and let it drop to the floor. Immediately, he'd removed his belt. He dragged the boy into the house, threw him over one arm of the recliner, and — the memory stopped there. The scene faded, leaving Rusty with a white screen, his mind reeling at the end of memory, a filmstrip spinning the tail of a broken reel. He had no recollection of whether his son had put up a fight or gone down quietly, fearless and tearless below the strap.

What came to mind, filling that void, was his old kitchen in Philly, the way Rusty had watched the sun come through the window over the sink that morning, the way he'd sat at the table, staring at the long dark strands of a man's hair wrapped around his fingers. He had just gotten engaged to Judy, who was still back at home in Skokie living with her parents. She had given him a small gold band with a sapphire, had placed it gently on his pinkie so that he might think of her. At his kitchen table, he sat trying to disengage the hair from the ring's small gold prongs that had held the stone in place. In his fury, the sapphire had popped out, leaving him with a ring that held a clump of hair in place of a birthstone, the sapphire glinting somewhere on his kitchen floor, a watchful eye.

He shuddered to think of it, even now, as Donald's car bounced along the dark road. He shuddered to think of how he hadn't changed.

"It was a different time," Donald was saying. Rusty turned and looked at Donald, the way he spoke with his hands, the way his hands came down on the steering wheel, neatly aligned as if he were holding a loaf of bread, as if all the world's rage might be contained there in the distance between his flat, broad palms.

Rusty looked down at his own fingers. The cigar, which he'd set in the ashtray of the car door, made a smoky trail to them. His hands were large and wide, with squared-off fingers and faint lines — a traceless map, an expanse of yellowish skin with blue veins pulsing beneath it. The veins, which he could only vaguely see when he brought his palms to his face, seemed more plentiful than those of other hands he'd seen — they were serpentine, a muted dark blue, like faded tattoos from another life.

"I should get back. Celeste will be wondering," Donald said.

"Yes." Rusty nodded.

"What's past is in the past," Donald offered, his voice espousing confidence.

"Right."

"You can't look back." Donald rounded a curve.

"No."

"What good does it do?"

Rusty tucked his hands under his thighs, pressing his palms flat against the pleather seat. "Exactly." Through the windshield, all was a dark blur, black beyond black.

* Chapter 4

VISITING HAEL

Toward the end of August, after Judy had recovered from the baby shower, she dialed the operator and asked for a Mrs. Hael Vanhorn of Chicago, Illinois. Judy had carried the name around in her head for weeks, holding it on her tongue like a lozenge. She'd seen the name on a seed catalog lying on a table in the foyer of Gretchen's apartment. *Hael Vanhorn* — it sounded vaguely Jewish, she thought. Was Gretchen part of a religious sect? Judy had scoured lists of cults, even contacted a cult help line she had once made use of when Carson left with the Krishnas, but nobody seemed to know of a group raising gender-free babies. No one had heard of a Hael Vanhorn. Could Judy get them the group's name? a man at the cult help desk had asked her. All the groups were listed alphabetically in files, and there was nothing under *gender-free* or *babies*. He needed more details, a group name. Judy said she would do her best to find out.

There was no *Hael*, the operator informed her, but there was a Leah Vanhorn who lived at the same address. Judy guessed she should try it and was pleasantly surprised when the woman who answered the phone turned out to be Gretchen's upstairs neighbor after all, the woman with the dark coat she had seen toting two small children in a wagon.

"Sure, I remember you," Hael said warmly. "You had on something blue that afternoon. So, you're Gretchen's mother?"

Judy felt a little put off by the last question. Hadn't Gretchen mentioned a mother? Didn't she perhaps keep a picture out? Over the years, Judy had given Gretchen so many. But Judy put her pride aside and explained that relations were strained and that she very much wanted to understand what Gretchen's neighbors were all about. "Do you have any pamphlets?" she inquired brightly. "Is there any literature on your particular group?"

"We're not a cult," Hael said firmly, as if she could intuit the reason behind Judy's call. "What we do is a practice and a growing philosophy. We're breaking the boundaries of gender saturation."

Gender saturation. Judy turned the phrase over in her mind as she made the drive down to Chicago on a windy Thursday she'd taken off from work. The term seemed so technical, almost chemical. It reminded her of her days teaching home ec, when she had stood among clusters of students around stoves, discussing boiling points, explaining the methodology of yeast — what made a loaf light and fluffy as opposed to dense and gummy. She passed out mimeographed sheets on kitchen chemistry, full of charts and definitions and equations.

There were no such equations for raising children, or so it seemed. She had never really thought about it until recently. Having her own brood had seemed so methodical; she had just let things happen. In retrospect, she realized she had not been willful or even active in their conception. She had participated, surely, but it was more like living in a dream, and by watching her belly grow large, first with Henry, then Carson, then Gretchen, she had felt as if she was fulfilling a prophesy, something that was integral to being on Earth.

She had raised her children as she had been raised, creating a wide circumference around them, reeling them in when they hit the outer circle, a sort of invisible force field she sensed on instinct — not from reading child psychologists or being part of a play group. Parenting, she thought, was like driving: focus on the mile markers and swerve around the obstacles. Rusty would like that.

Until recently, Judy hadn't given much thought to her own children's upbringing, though she was keenly aware that all three had built moats around themselves, isolating themselves from one another and their parents. This often left her feeling vaguely despondent, especially when she observed how her friends and neighbors continued to interact with their children. There were tensions, yes, but somehow fewer complications. It seemed funny to her that people concerned themselves with complications during childbirth, when, really, it was much later in life that issues of suffocation or positioning became most critical.

Although she did not like to admit it, she attributed greater family harmony to material success. Donald and Celeste, for example, had four children, all of whom were successful — two of them Realtors, another a lawyer, the eldest a gynecologist. But they had been different children, different almost from birth. These were genetic things. Donald and Celeste's twin daughters, both Realtors now in Fort Cloud, had always expressed a natural curiosity about other people's houses. They had delighted in estate sales and trinkets, had once run an antique booth as a 4-H project. The lawyer had been a sullen type, thorough and logical. He read books during dinner and, at the age of eight, drew up wills for everyone in his family. The gynecologist had been less of a sure thing. A high school quarterback and something of a play-boy, he'd threatened to become a ski bum in Vail, until he got in-volved with a young nurse, surprising everyone when he went premed.

Judy's children had all been surprises. She often felt that they moved through the house like trick-or-treaters, all jokes and cos-tumes. She pushed candy at them and pulled a certain door inside herself closed. She was never quite sure who they were, what words might come out of their mouths. Even when they had crawled in bed with her, though she might put her arm around one, she could not guess with her eyes closed whose breath she felt on her face. They held a kind of interchangeable place within her mind — not three children but a single, multiarmed god. Didn't all chil-dren come from the same place? Weren't they sort of one soul? Didn't they sprout from birth with their own curious goals? Giv-ing them three square meals and plenty of clean bedding was all they really needed to grow. Children, she felt, developed on their own.

Of course, Judy had harbored dreams for all of them — she had hoped Henry would become an inventor; she had imagined that Carson, who was big-eyed from birth, might be an actor. She had tried at length to get Carson, with his golden curls, into commer-cials, but whenever she left his side, he turned whiny and sullen. And Gretchen — she had wished Gretchen might be an explorer, with her natural curiosity about planets and birds. Anything she could touch with her hands amazed her.

That none of her children had followed the dreams she nursed for them did not disappoint Judy, except very slightly. Mostly she was concerned that they did not keep in touch, that they did not hold her dear or need her near them. In part, she blamed Rusty for being too severe, and of course, she blamed herself for needing them too much and for harboring secrets.

She was a private woman, an only child with no remaining family, and she had lived much of her life in quiet observation. She cherished secrets, even little ones — the shoes she kept under the sink in their tissue, for example. These small things, she felt, lent her life mystery, which was, in its own way, a kind of freedom.

A few years back, her book group had taken up archery together after reading *The Last of the Mohicans*. They began meeting across town on their lunch breaks, practicing in secret. More recently, they'd started going to a rifle range — forming a clandestine women's league that none of them told her husband about. The thrill of this was, for Judy, more in keeping the secret than in actually scoring well, though she had excellent aim and was, among her small group (mostly secretaries and teachers aides), referred to as "Bull's-eye." Judy took Rusty's rifle and stored it in her cello case. The rifle range was in Milwaukee.

When Judy arrived at Hael Vanhorn's, she circled the block and parked on a side street. She had arranged to meet Hael during the day, when Gretchen and Ray would be out. It wasn't that she didn't want to see them, she'd explained to Hael, just that she was sure they needed their space. She wasn't one to barge in and make waves. "I'd like to come in secret," she'd said. "Would you mind?"

"Actually," Hael told her, "I'm a licensed therapist. If you'd like to consider this an introductory session, your visit will be in strict confidence."

Still, Judy felt a surge of guilt as she stepped out of her car, and for

a moment she considered turning back around, returning to Fort
Cloud. She could still make the eighth-period health class to which
she had recently been assigned because of a teacher shortage. There,
among the freckled, broken-out faces of her seventh-grade students, she could lose herself in the kids' youthful conversions.
Even amid catcalls and spitballs, she could tune it all out and find
a frequency of solace. She felt a sort of motherliness, too, in telling
them to sit down, to keep quiet, as she stalked between the aisles
of desks in her high-heeled shoes. Watching their heads bowed
over workbooks and homework, it reminded her of the quiet
watch she had taken over her own children.

Upstairs, Judy stood before Hael's door, where a small embossed
notecard read: *We know what we are, but know not what we may be.*
— *Shakespeare*. Judy wondered, as she rapped softly, if it had been
taped there for her benefit. Hael Vanhorn came to the door with
a dish of peas she was wrapping in saran.

"Come on in," she said, her voice welcoming. "The kids just
went down for their naps. I'm just putting away lunch."

Inside, the apartment was spare. A long black leather couch
with chrome feet was anchored at one end, in front of it: a black
lacquer coffee table with an expensive-looking handblown glass
bowl. Near the windows, there was telescope on a tripod.

This does not seem like a home where there are children, Judy
thought. What parents in their right minds would leave out a telescope, a beautiful glass bowl? She ran a hand along the bowl's
smooth lip, where flecks of color made Judy think of a kaleido-
scope.

Judy caught sight of a black-and-white photo on a bookshelf and
crossed the room on tiptoe so that Hael would not think she was
snooping. Judy recognized the faces of the two children squeezed
between Hael and a man she presumed to be Hael's husband, a

balding professorial sort with a gaseous grin and big, woolly caterpillar eyebrows.

"What are the names of your children?" Judy asked when Hael
entered the room on bare feet, carrying a tea tray.

Hael smiled. "I'll get to that in a moment." She set down the
tray and paused with her hands clasped. She wore a long black
caftan and swooshing crushed-velvet pants, similar to the ones
Judy had seen on her school's art teacher, a woman of dramatic
bead necklaces and richly toned head scarves. Judy often admired
her wardrobe from afar.

"Honey? Soy milk?" Hael asked. "I think I might even have
some sugar in the raw." Hael's face was long and smooth as a bar
of soap. Her hands, Judy noticed, were free of any jewelry.

"Honey is fine," Judy said. She studied the spines of the books
lining the shelves. Amid *Our Bodies, Ourselves* and *What to Expect When You're Expecting*, there was the fourth edition of *The
Bright Star Catalogue* and *The First Dictionary of the Nomenclature
of Celestial Objects*, along with titles by H. G. Wells and Robert
Heinlein. Judy had hoped to come across some mysteries so that
she and Hael would have something in common to talk about.

"You're into the stars?" Judy asked when Hael reappeared.

"Oh, yes, you noticed. Glyn, that's my partner, is an astrono-
mer at the U."

"Interesting," Judy said, moving to the couch. She sat back, her
hands clasped around a rugged-looking mug. This was so pleasant,
so normal, she thought to herself. Why had she felt so keyed up
on the way down? She felt the tension drain from her neck into
tributaries along her shoulders.

"Our children" — Hael moved across the room toward some
blurry-looking photographs on the opposite wall — "were named
after these two galaxies."

"Oh," Judy said, standing again. She set down her mug and straightened her skirt.

"Well, actually" — Hael giggled — "this one is technically not a galaxy, but you probably know that. It's an open star cluster." She pointed to a great red blur, which, to Judy's eye, looked like a sort of fluffy pelvis.

"It makes me think of a bird," Judy offered politely.

"Oh, that's so amazing you said that." Hael nodded her head fiercely so that her chin-length reddish hair swung against her long neck in great flaps. "Wow, you can see it then — it's the eagle nebula."

Judy blushed. "It was just a guess."

"No, no, you're very intuitive." Hael waved her hands excitedly. "I've had some people say really creepy stuff about this picture. I mean, it's very exciting to people — all this high-energy radiation from so many massive, hot young stars." Hael made it sound as if she were talking about a rock concert. She leaned into the picture frame, bouncing happily on her toes. "I mean, it's so fabulous, so luminous — I can't look at it for long without feeling almost sucked in." She laughed, stepping back as she pressed a sleeve to her mouth. "Whew," she said, turning to Judy, "it's just like our eldest — all action enmeshed in itself."

"So your eldest is named after this? Eagle?"

"Oh, no, no, no." Hael looked a little disappointed. "Glyn would die if our kid was named something like Eagle. No, the names we've given our children are pretty technical-sounding, especially if you don't hang around star freaks. Our eldest is M16." Hael smiled sweetly, then paused to pick her tea up off the table and blow on it. "Our youngest is M64 — you've probably heard of that because it's a pretty famous galaxy." Hael stepped over to a second photograph mounted on the wall, this one dark black with a single blurry oval off to the side, like a frosted Danish floating in outer space. Judy felt suddenly hungry.

Hael sighed wistfully. "M64 was the first galaxy I ever really felt a passion for. There are so many out there, but you glimpse this one through regular binoculars — it feels almost within reach. I think it's the bright core." She nodded at the photo. "Yeah, I love M64. It's so" — she rubbed her neck, searching for the word — "mythical," she said, turning to Judy. "When I look at it, I'm just transported. It's definitely at the top of my list."

Judy was beginning to feel a little breathless. There was a sour taste rising from the back of her mouth. What did Hael mean when she said a particular galaxy was on the top of her list? Did she actually think she might go there — on a trip? Was she one of those people who dreamed of intergalactic vacations, hanging out on Mars? Maybe she was trying to get a colony started. She seemed a little brainwashed, or maybe she was on drugs.

"So, tell me more about the children here," Judy said slowly, touching her brow with the corner of a tissue. "Are they all named like battleships?"

Hael giggled, then sighed. "You've got a great sense of humor, just like Gretchen." She moved to the couch and sat down, drawing her knees to her chest. A ring glimmered on one of her toes. "Mrs. Glide," she said, her tone suddenly adult-sounding and serious, "I know what you're thinking. I know it sounds like we're a bunch of freaks, but I promise you we all come with the best intentions."

Judy sat stiffly on the edge of a leather cushion, staring at her tea, noticing that bits of leaves and even twigs were floating on the surface. It was as if Hael had boiled a little nest.

"I hope you stay long enough to meet M64," Hael was saying.

"You'll be charmed. He/she is one helluva well-adjusted kid. Everyone says so."

"He/she?" Judy raised her eyebrows.

"We don't say *it* anymore." Hael frowned. "You know, that was just too far out."

Judy nodded. She noticed what looked to be a toy basket in the corner of the room, overflowing with amorphous foam shapes. So that's how these people kept their kids from destroying their nice place. Their kids had no toys, nothing but Nerf.

Hael caught Judy's eye and danced over to the basket. "Aren't these great?" She tossed a gray blob into the air, then a brown pyramid. "There's a new toy manufacturer who is way into us." Hael beamed. "We've contracted with them for all kinds of special games. We'll finally be able to play Candy Land." She threw her arms up with an enthusiastic flourish.

"What's the matter with Candy Land?" Judy asked.

"Well, they're doing an organic fruits version of it." She smiled warmly, tossing a blob at Judy. "But the best part is that we've found a publisher to put out a gender-neutral Mother Goose."

"I don't understand," Judy said, drawing her sweater across her knees. "My children grew up with both Candy Land and Mother Goose. There's nothing" — she shook her head fiercely — "nothing wrong with them that I can see."

"Mrs. Glide" — Hael sank to her knees on the wood floor and tucked her hair behind her ears gingerly — "it's about footing. It's about starting out in the universe with an open signal. Not everyone who lives here is as hard core as I am, but then" — her young face grew earnest, and she drew her neat eyebrows in a line — "I want my children to get a pure start in life — no false impressions, no dogma or pop culture. From the moment they were born, they were people." She paused. "People," she said again. "They aren't complicated by gender or the expectations people string out for them. These are children who have never touched a Barbie, never seen an action figure. They're happy just to play with something as simple as a paper sack."

Judy gathered her things onto her lap. "But it's as if they're cats," she protested.

"Exactly!" Hael's voice was breathy with excitement. "We don't give kittens gender-specific toys. It's like that with the children we're raising here — they *are* more like kittens than little girls and little boys."

Judy stood up, fingers at her temples. "I feel a bit dizzy with all this," she said gently. "It might be best for me to go."

"I've scared you, haven't I?"

"No, no." Judy clutched her purse.

"I think we made some progress, though," Hael said gravely. "Gretchen warned me you were very ingrained."

"What?" Judy shook her head as if she could erase what had just been said. Hael stepped forward and put a hand on Judy's fore-arm. "You're going to do very well. Remember, it's just as hard for Gretchen and Ray to understand you as it is for you to understand them. Think of it that way."

"Is there a name for all of this?" Judy made a last-ditch attempt, her hand on the knob.

Hael sighed. "This is an underground movement. At some point, Judy, sex won't matter. Even names might be moot."

Judy stepped into the brightly lit hall, grateful for the click of the latch. On the doormat, two small sets of shoes — black clogs — were neatly lined up like four little stones.

Chapter 5

MORE BREAKING AND ENTERING

Judy descended the steps from Hael's apartment and gazed around the foyer. Her cheeks felt hot. She set her purse on a thin entryway table, rummaged for her lipstick, and applied it with a shaky grip. What had Gretchen meant that she, Judy, was ingrained? She had half a mind to leave her daughter a note. It seemed time to set things straight, time for Judy to make some demands and to get answers to her questions: Why, for example, had Gretchen called Rusty at work to announce she was pregnant? That was the big one. And there were other things, too. The unacknowledged bootees she had left on Gretchen's welcome mat, Gretchen's cold shoulder at the shower, and a general lack of contact that left Judy feeling empty and alone.

All Judy wanted was connection, a way to be involved in the birth of her first grandchild. All things considered, Judy felt that she had been more than accepting, more than gracious. For goodness' sake, Gretchen and Ray were having a baby, and they weren't even married. Ordinarily, Judy would have had a few things to say about that. But had she ever intimated her disappointment? Had she uttered a single peep? She had taken the news in stride, tried her best to be lighthearted and cheerful on the phone and at the shower, reassuring everyone that she didn't care about the sex of the child as long as it arrived healthy.

Now here was Gretchen's door — closed, and here was Judy standing again before the mat, feeling utterly unwelcome. Other families did not live this way. Other mothers and daughters commiserated over morning sickness, grew close during a pregnancy. She envied Celeste's grandchildren, but more than the children themselves, Judy envied the hours Celeste spent with her pregnant daughters and daughters-in-law, poring over paint swatches for each nursery, tossing around names, knitting tiny white sweaters, swapping stories. Judy could only indulge in these fantasies alone.

One rainy Sunday, she'd taken great relish in slipping off to the mall to stroll through the infant sleepwear, brushing through the racks of soft jumpers as if she were pushing her body through a fleecy car wash, cleansing and readying herself for grandmotherhood. But she had not been able to find a single black item of baby clothing, not even something gray or beige, and so she had ended up in the food court, feeling somber, with nothing to hold but a watery Orange Julius as she watched pairs of young mothers sip sodas together and push strollers piled high with raincoats.

Judy wanted to be asked things. She wanted Gretchen to ask her about her own pregnancies. Now, she wasn't even sure Gretchen would let her come to the hospital for the birth, and oh, how she wanted to be invited. She wanted to be at the birth badly, very badly, but she supposed no one would be allowed in the room, no one but the Chimp. The whole affair, from the black shower to Hael with her Nerf blobs, filled Judy with a sense of gloom. She wondered what she ought to do, and in wondering, she let her hand reach out and touch the doorknob before her.

Without her giving it the slightest twist, the door unlatched and swung back, giving Judy a space of about six inches through which to peer. She could feel her heart pounding. She looked toward the stairs that led to Hael's flat, then carefully put a hand on the door-jamb and let her foot rest on the threshold so that she was partially inside. Before her, she saw a line of shoes on a straw mat — some strappy sandals, a pair of clogs, some striped leg warmers in a wad. The room was spare, the walls white. There was a single cream-colored couch with one black oval pillow. She could see a blond wood table with two plain high-back chairs next to the bay window. The sun glared off the hardwood floors. The room smelled of fresh paint. There was not a single picture or poster on the wall, except for a large square painting placed just to the left of the couch: a gray background with a slightly darker gray orb, floating.

Judy thought she might burst into sobs. Admittedly, she herself was no great decorator, but this — this was downright depressing. She glanced back into the foyer to make sure this wasn't some sort of setup, then slipped noiselessly out of her shoes and closed the door quickly behind her. She was not going to intrude, just peek. She had come this far, and for her daughter's safety, she reasoned, it was her motherly duty to look around.

On stocking feet, Judy tiptoed past the couch to the set of French doors that opened onto the room at the back of the house. It, too, was empty except for a purple mat rolled in a corner and a boom box propped on a milk crate. There was a tape case resting on top, labeled only "Performance X." Judy pursed her lips and put a hand on her chest to suppress a sigh. Was it possible Gretchen really lived here? Nothing suggested a trace of a feminine presence, no wreath, no scented candle, no lace around the windows.

Judy closed the French doors and crept around the corner into a short hall that led to a small bathroom and two square bedrooms. She held her breath before poking her head through each doorway. The first bedroom was empty except for a rocker. The second held a low black dresser and a futon with a cream-colored spread. Maybe, she thought, Gretchen had not yet fully moved in. There was no crib, no changing table. What did Gretchen and Ray think — the baby would sleep with them?

She stopped by the bathroom. Two black towels hanging from silver hooks. Two clear toothbrushes standing in a cup. A long black hair dangled from the side of the claw-foot tub. The medicine cabinet was the only thing Judy left untouched. Now that was their private business.

Judy paused. She thought she heard the stairwell above the bathroom creak. She looked briefly behind the white blind covering the window. Nothing. No movement along the side of the house. The apartment was quiet, except for her heartbeat and somewhere a clock, ticking unseen. Still, her pulse quickened.

She had to get out. It seemed suddenly imperative. She tiptoed back down the hall and was reaching for her shoes when something in front of the stove caught her eye. There was a pool of something on the gray tile. It looked like blood. She crept forward, a hand on her throat, her heart practically in her mouth, like something she could spit out. There, it was only wine, a pool of wine and shards of broken glass. She was careful to step around it. She thought, *Who would run off without cleaning up a broken glass?* Whoever had left before her certainly had been in a hurry.

Overhead, Judy heard someone crossing the floor, a pair of little feet running. She slipped on her shoes and let herself out, heart still pounding, head spinning.

This was their world, as strange as it seemed, she reminded herself. She would have to let them live it, just as she, Judy, had left her parents behind to move to Fort Cloud with Rusty — a marriage her father had cautioned her might cost her her life. Rusty, who had appeared so big and brash and bold — a kind of Marlon Brando — had been so different from her small-boned father, a genteel shoe salesman who had spent all his life holding women's feet and protecting their arches with his hands, always manicured and set off by good dress shirts and cuff links.

"Never marry a man who might crush you in bed," her mother had advised. Rusty, her mother felt, was too much man. She would have preferred that her daughter marry someone more relaxed with a quiet intellect — a teacher, a pastor, the bachelor on the corner who worked for the *Chicago Post*.

But Judy had been smitten with Rusty the first time she met him, on a dead-hot afternoon when she stopped on her way home from her father's store into a bar with a good-size tree growing up through the floor. She had never been in a bar before, other than maybe a restaurant bar, but the door had been open, giving way to a cool, dark space. And there, on a barstool, she saw a man stirring a drink with his pinkie. When she approached, ducking under a tree limb to make her way toward him, he looked up at her, reached into his glass, and held out a single cube of ice for her tongue.

She had taken it gratefully and pulled up a barstool by his side, noting his strong cologne, his big square hands. "A special drink for this one," Rusty had called to the bartender. Then he'd leaned over to ask what her name was, and she — for the first time — had drawn a blank, which was how she knew she was in love.

"You look like a tall glass of water." He'd grinned, letting his gray-green eyes run the length of her. She was happy when her drink arrived, clear and cool with crushed cherries floating among the ice cubes. She'd taken a long sip from the straw, then excused herself to put on some lipstick in the ladies' room — a new bright red tube that she'd been carrying in her purse for weeks in expectation of an occasion when she might need some added flair.

It had started there — her life — in that moment, in that mirror, as she stood in the bar bathroom coloring her lips, her face flushed, her heart pounding almost visibly through her sleeveless blouse. She could feel the rush of the drink at her temples, and she knew almost by instinct that she would marry this man, that they would have at least two children, and that she would wear red lipstick, always, to remind herself that this was the way things were meant to be.

As Judy left Gretchen's building, closing the front door quietly behind her, she could hear the children upstairs giggling through the open windows. They looked down at her, and one waved happily, making Judy wonder if maybe she hadn't been too harsh a judge. Maybe M16 and M64 would turn out all right. Eventually, they would grow up into men or women. The physical transformation would be obvious enough. Why rush the distinction? They were just children, after all, and who knew, maybe the M stood for something — other names, their future identities as Maxes or Maxines, Michaels or Michelles. They would get on just fine in life, even without all the accoutrements of a normal childhood.

And when Gretchen had her baby in October, it would still be a baby — warm and small — and who cared if its name was off the wall or if Gretchen dressed it in dark clothes? The baby wouldn't mind. It would be too young to dream of baseballs or ballet shoes. All those things would come in time. You could never predict what children might fancy. It would be a baby with a secret, and Judy, of all people, knew that secrets held mystery, held freedom.

That same afternoon, while Judy was in Chicago, Rusty began feeling stomach pains at work and drove home for an antacid. He unbuttoned his shirt and yanked at his tie in the bathroom while opening drawers and rifling through cupboards, then finally caught sight of himself in the mirror and was struck dumb. *No wonder I feel sick,* he thought as he studied his profile. His belly looked enormous, like a perfectly domed dinner roll. He turned to the left and to the right, frowning, then absentmindedly ran a hand across his chest and was struck by the rubberiness of his pecs. Once taut, they now drooped — there was definite droopage — they looked like water balloons, like molded custards. He stepped toward the tub, away from the mirror, hoping a few feet of distance would diminish the effect, but it did not. He had the body of a pregnant woman.

This is disgusting, he thought. *How have I let this happen?* He buttoned his shirt back up and trudged next door to see if Celeste could spare him an antacid. Rusty could see Celeste through the front window of her house; she sat at her long walnut table working on a scrapbook. She had six grandchildren now, and that kept her busy, busy, busy, she liked to tell Rusty. That morning she'd waved to him on his way to work, her arms laden with udderlike purses that brimmed with scrapping supplies. "Off to my class at Scrappy-Do!" she'd called cheerfully.

Now she looked up from the table and waved to Rusty through the screen door, beckoning him in. The living room had been redecorated since Rusty had last been to visit. The carpet was now deep blue, the sofas a sandy beige; a large seascape in a gilt frame hung over the mantel. From a boom box on the dining room table came the sounds of seagulls, waves hitting a beach.

"Place looks nice," Rusty said.

"It's my relaxation retreat." Celeste beamed, skirting the table in a pair of yellow culottes, her short, frosted hair neatly curled like rows of shells. "All this scrappin' makes me tense up in the shoulders, but I can't help myself. I just love saving memories. I'm sure Judy will be the same when she has grandkids." She caught herself and flashed Rusty an apologetic smile, nudging a stray curl at her nape into place.

Rusty, still in the doorway, looked down at his stomach. "Celeste," he said, then paused. He wanted to ask Celeste if she had noticed anything different about him, but there was no polite way to phrase it.

She raised her neatly plucked eyebrows, tilting her head slowly on its narrow neck. "Yes?"

"S-sour stomach," he stammered. "You got anything?"

"Sure," she gushed, looking relieved. She darted into the kitchen and returned with a bottle. "Rusty," she said, touching his arm, "I'm sorry about this whole thing with Gretchen. I'm sure it's hard."

Rusty nodded and gave Celeste a two-finger salute on the way out the door. In his gut, a sharp pang made its way through muscle. He took his tablets, then sprawled on the couch to read the *Fort Cloud Independent*, which had recently begun running a series of boxes containing bitesize statistics that usually weren't very uplifting: number of deaths this year due to fumigants, number of mugged joggers from 1980 to 1989, number of robberies resulting in at least one death, percentage of children who die of dehydration. The boxes were intended to keep Fort Clouders up to date on the seriousness of the world, yet inspire them to be tireless in their pursuit of happiness.

After chucking the paper in the trash, Rusty went downstairs to the Deepfreeze to fill his cooler with what was left of the snow. On his way past the old bedrooms — dimly lit, dust motes bobbing in the parts between curtains — he stepped in to study the window casings. It would be so easy for someone to pop out the screens and pry out the glass, slide right on in. He'd read a story once in a magazine about a group of homeless kids who had done just that and set up camp in a couple's basement for several months, moving about the house undetected during the day while the homeowners were at work. The kids had survived by nibbling at the edges of things in the fridge, portioning out tiny bits of peanut butter, a single pickle, a handful of oyster crackers, taking nothing in quantity, disturbing nothing that might be counted, say, a container of yogurt or a can of soda. They skimmed off the couple's toothpaste, used their shampoo, deodorant, toothbrushes.

It all came down to a chocolate chip cookie and a strand of hair. Rusty remembered these two details perfectly — they still sent a shiver up his spine. The wife had baked cookies and allotted herself and her husband two a day while they were dieting. One night, she came home and counted out the cookie jar, only to discover there was an extra one missing, though her husband swore he hadn't taken it. A huge row ensued, and the couple ended up sleeping in separate beds that night. The next morning, the wife stepped into the shower and noticed a longish dark hair by the drain. Both she and her husband were fair-haired. The story ended there.

Rusty was sniffing around the basement, flipping lights on and off, when he heard the footsteps upstairs. The sound stopped him cold; he hovered in the shadow of the water heater.

"Anybody home?" a man's voice called from above. Rusty was almost relieved when he realized the voice belonged to Ray.

"You start reading about all these crazies and you get spooked," he told Ray upstairs in the kitchen. "It's even got Judy all freaked out. She's got this idea that we've had burglars in the house. She keeps bringing it up."

"Hmm," Ray said. "Weird."

"Oh, I don't know." Rusty batted at the air around his head as if there were a swarm of flies following him, then opened the refrigerator and pulled out a six-pack. "Personal safety is such a mirage. We kid ourselves into thinking we're safe, yet every day we cross roads, plug in hair dryers above sinks, you know? You've got to keep your head on straight."

"I can't find Gretchen," Ray blurted out then. "She's taken off. I thought maybe she came here."

"Nawp," Rusty said, leading Ray into the living room, where the midafternoon sun was highlighting dark stains in the rug. He took a moment to survey Ray's baggy shorts and swishy cotton shirt, then handed him a beer. "Noticed your truck" was all he could think to say as he sank into the comfort of his chair. "Nice truck."

"Oh, it's really Gretchen's. She picked it out." Ray popped the tab on his beer can and sipped gingerly from it.

His hair had been professionally cut since the shower. It fell in thick flat feathers along the line of his jaw. Rusty couldn't look at it without getting his hands out of the way, hiding them under his thighs like great manta rays. He felt a sharp twinge below his rib cage.

"I'm surprised you're home," Ray said, casting glances around the living room as if Gretchen might be hiding behind a couch.

"Sour stomach," Rusty said. "Probably stress."

Ray nodded and rubbed his chin. "I could lend you some tapes on Zen," he offered. "I've got one out in the truck."

Rusty ran a thumb back and forth across the upholstery on his armrest. "Maybe," he said between sips of beer. "Maybe."

When she pulled onto Seeley Street, it took Judy several minutes to notice the red Ford pickup parked in front of her house. A pile of dirt by the drain spout caught her eye as she stepped out onto the drive. How long had that been there? Were there moles living under the yard again? Their neighbors, the Epcotts, had gone to such trouble last year to get rid of them.

Judy heard men's voices as she reached the screen door. She checked her watch. It was a quarter to four. Rusty wasn't supposed to be home yet, and the other voice sounded uncannily like that of Gretchen's boyfriend, Ray.

Sure enough, she spotted his truck out front, and when she came into the house, she found the two of them in the living room, Rusty in his recliner with a Miller, Ray squatting by the tape deck. When they saw her, they both stood, Rusty struggling up from his chair, nudging an empty beer can under his seat with his big toe.

"Gretchen's disappeared," he said quickly, hiking up his pants. He was still wearing his work shirt, but it was unbuttoned, swinging open to reveal his ribbed tee and pale chest hair, something Judy despised him for showing in front of company. "Ray's here." The words came out in a strangled-sounding slur. Then he pointed, as if she hadn't noticed.

Judy let her purse slide down her arm. "What do you mean, disappeared? Disappeared where?"

"That's the thing," Ray said, stepping forward, looking shy. He was wearing a collarless white shirt and purple Birkenstocks. "I thought she might have come here. I got home late last night, and the apartment was empty."

"I know," Judy said. "I was just down there. I tried knocking."

Ray looked perplexed. He tugged nervously at his beard with his thumb and forefinger. "You were just in Chicago?"

"Whoa, whoa, wait a second," Rusty bellowed, his body teetering. He steadied himself with a hand to the armrest. "I thought you were at work."

"Likewise," Judy said, shooting him a scowl. She slipped off her shoes and sauntered into the kitchen. "I had a meeting with Hael," she called over the shutters.

"Yikes." Ray emitted a nervous laugh.

"Bring me whatever you're having," Rusty called to Judy. "I don't know what the hell anyone is talking about."

"I'm just having water," Judy said curtly. Her nerves were suddenly on edge. The water felt cool running over her fingers, reinstalling her sense of balance and composure. A glass of water, a glass of pure water, she often thought, was a great equalizer.

"Great. Bring me some," Rusty shouted.

"I'd love a glass," chirped Ray.

Judy came in with three tall glasses, and the three of them stood in the center of the living room, gulping, sullen. Judy studied Ray's feet, their hairy tops — like feet with toilet seat covers, she thought.

"How late?" she asked.

Ray raised an eyebrow, lowered his glass.

"How late did you come home last night?" Her voice came out crisp and stern. She thumbed some dark beads at her throat.

"I'm working on a major performance piece. I only have access to the stage at night," Ray said. "I lost track of time."

"Oh, please." The words slipped from Judy's mouth, fluid, too easy.

"Lighten up, Judy." Rusty set a hand on her shoulder. "Ray's very upset here."

"He doesn't seem upset," she snapped, setting her glass down on an end table. "I come home and you two are drinking beer." She turned her gaze to Rusty. "Am I the only one around here concerned about our daughter's welfare?"

"Actually," said Rusty, "Ray was about to play me a Zen tape."

Judy pursed her lips.

"I'm heading out." Ray raised his palms. "There's really nothing to worry about."

Judy cocked her head to the side. "Your upstairs neighbor has children named after galaxies. They have no toys except for foam blobs, and you tell me not to worry?" She gave an uncharacteristic snort. "What's to say Gretchen wasn't kidnapped? I've seen *Rosemary's Baby*."

"Mrs. Glide" — Ray pressed his hands together and bowed forward slightly — "we're not like that."

"That's what my son tried to tell me about the Hare Krishnas."

"Thank you for the water," Ray said politely, crossing then to shake Rusty's hand. "I'll be in touch."

"Please," Rusty said, seeing him to the door. Judy peeled off her stockings and curled up on the couch in a little ball. "Don't say anything," she said to Rusty. "Don't say anything at all."

All evening Judy and Rusty moved through the house, pacing without pacing. Doors opened, ringing hollowly. Judy jumped any time she heard a noise that sounded remotely like a phone — when a car honked, when Rusty used the electric can opener on the cat food, when he went in and out of the garage. She felt alternately hot and cold. She could not escape the sense that, one by one, her children had disappeared. Leaving no forwarding addresses, they dissipated like mist and left Judy feeling that she had imagined them, that their births had been mere daydreams.

Was this how their cat — Ivy — felt, Judy wondered, when her litter had been distributed among the neighbors? At least in Ivy's case, the kittens still lived nearby. Donald and Celeste had taken one, the Epcotts another, and a young couple who had lived briefly across the street had adopted the third, Judy's favorite. When the windows of all the houses were open during the summer, Ivy could at least hear her kin mewling. It wasn't as if she'd lost track of them.

Ivy scaled the back of the couch and jumped on Judy's chest, kneading with thick gray paws, her low purr like an idling car. Judy wondered if Ivy ever felt depressed, if Ivy ever mourned.

The bird clock in the kitchen let out its digital warble. Rusty was on his third Braunschweiger sandwich. He stood by the toaster, a knife at the ready. The tube of liverwurst looked disturbingly fleshlike — maybe it was just this batch, or maybe he'd just never noticed. It seemed distasteful suddenly, and he put it away. Tomorrow, he vowed, he'd start lifting weights.

The light in Donald's workshop was on next door, and through the kitchen window across the way, Rusty saw Celeste was still working. He could imagine the seagulls, the sound of the waves. He had a flash of what it would be like to be in Celeste's body — mind serene, the world ahead full of happy little grandkids. She and Donald lived a life of easy rhythms, soothing surroundings. He looked over the shutters into his own living room, which had hardly changed since he and Judy had married — same soggy brown couch and paneled walls, same urn-shaped table lamps giving off mustardy glows, same round pleather footstools anchored to the dark carpet. It was like looking at an old forest, Rusty decided, slowly rotting, full of poisonous mushrooms.

He closed his eyes and felt his way down the hall to the bedroom, crawling into the familiar sag of his bed. His belly glurped, audible above the sound of crickets. "Judy," he called faintly, hoping for the sound of her feet in the hall, the smell of her hovering, but the house was still. Rusty rolled onto his side and let his gaze rest on the window, the white sill framing blue-black sky. The moon hung just below the curtain rod, a bleached curve of bone, a broken fragment floating.

In the living room, Judy sat up on the couch, reading, the phone cord stretched across the carpet to the jack so that she wouldn't miss a ring. She started a mystery, then hovered by the bookshelf, looking for something else — avoiding the book of baby names. Eventually, she relented and flipped through the dog-eared pages, now yellow, smiling to herself as she came across names she'd once highlighted. *Myrtle*. Had she really considered Myrtle? There were twenty or so names she'd underlined in red pen — the ink had bled into a smudgy pink over time. Forrest, Casper, Lowell, Dustin, Mariah, Penelope, Jeanette. She had spent hours going through names, trying them out around the house under the noise of other noises. "Casper, Casper, Casper," she'd repeat as she vacuumed. "Lowell, come here, Lowell," she'd mutter under her breath as she washed dishes. "Jeanette, just stop it," she'd say sternly, flipping on the garbage disposal.

For her first pregnancy, Judy presented Rusty with her perfect name at dinner one night. "Forrest Lowell," she had announced. Rusty had looked up, giving her a one-eyed stare. "Who's that?" She presented the name again with all the conviction of a woman in a commercial, selling scouring powder or instant pudding. "Forrest Lowell, that's the name if we have a boy," she'd said brightly, smiling with all her teeth. Forrest Lowell had instantly been shot down by Rusty, who deemed the name too state-parkish. "Henry," he'd said over his pork chop. "Henry is clean-cut, sensible — we'll get a lot of mileage out of a strong American name like that."

And so Henry it was, Henry Buck. All of Judy's rigorous testing and on-site application were for naught. Though the name Henry Buck Glide appeared on the birth certificate, Judy had reserved her own special name for when she was alone with her baby. From time to time, she would whisper, "Hello, little Forrest Lowell."

By the time her second child was due, Judy waited to announce the name she'd been rolling around on her tongue until she and Rusty were in the car on the way to the hospital. "You got to name the last one," she told Rusty gently, "now this one is mine." She'd closed her eyes to let a contraction pass, then said proudly, regally, as she stared straight ahead at the sunshine beating on the dash, "Constantine Wilhelm" — a name so fabulous, so gallant-sounding it made her shudder.

The brakes squealed, and Rusty turned to her and told her she could get out and walk to the hospital if she thought he was going to raise a son with a name that sounded more like a fancy chicken dish than a little boy.

And so their second son, born just after midnight, was named Carson, after the man who had parted the rainbow-lit curtains and brought Rusty back to life after a long day in the waiting room: Carson Jonathan Glide. "Here's Johhhhny," Rusty liked to say when he held Carson as a baby, chuckling to himself. Judy had only frowned.

With her third pregnancy, Judy had been resigned about a name. Her only hope was that if she had a girl Rusty would not name her after his mother, Clematis — an unwieldy pessimist

who had passed away that winter after neglecting to go to the doctor for pneumonia, insisting that she could cure herself with plenty
of hot onion juice. If Rusty pushed the name Clematis, Judy had
decided she would suggest a different kind of creeper: Ivy, Ivy Jane.
But Rusty had solemnly presented the name Gretchen — a ran-
dom and unexpected gift. And Judy had stowed the name Ivy away
for a cat, and when that cat had kittens, she got her Forrest, her
Lowell, and a Constantine Wilhelm, the runt.

At 4 AM, Judy was still awake. Through a slit in the living room
curtains, she could see the old woman across the street waiting for
the paperboy. The drapes were drawn, and the woman sat in her
living room, smoking, a miniature dachshund lying beside her in
the rift of the couch cushions. From time to time, the woman
went to the kitchen to refill her coffee, then came back, sat down,
crossed her legs, checked her watch. Judy had never observed the
routine, but she had heard the story from other neighbors. Early
risers like Donald knew all the neighborhood rhythms.

Two years back — or maybe three — the house across the
street had been for sale. A young couple with a baby had moved
in and sent for the grandmother, who at that time lived in Tucson
or Santa Fe, somewhere south. Judy had watched the old woman
wheel the baby up and down the block, day after day, while the
parents were away at work, and Judy had often smiled to herself at
the arrangement, which seemed harmonious enough, though the
family was never friendly or keen to visit with the neighbors.

Then, as quietly as they had come, the couple moved out, leaving the grandmother in their wake. She never closed her blinds
and rarely left the house. All day she thumbed through the
paper — smoked, drank coffee — and in the evening, by the light

of the TV, she could be observed eating her supper on a little fold-out tray, unraveling a great pile of sweaters in between slow bites. She had a whole box of them, and from time to time, she would take the recycled yarn and knit it into other shapes — little hats, scarves. Her dachshund had a marvelous trove of walking vests.

Judy watched the woman light another cigarette and was swept up in the loneliness of the scene, the loneliness of being up at 4 AM in a dark house, clocks ticking, the moon still a numb drop in the summer sky. And slowly, Judy began to move through the house, running her fingertips along the wallboards as she drifted down the hall, feeling — in her long nightgown — like a ghost in her own house.

From the doorway of the master bedroom, she observed Rusty sleeping, a bump on the bed, the white spread rising and falling with his breath. His leather slippers lay scattered across the carpet. His pajama bottoms were in a heap by the nightstand, like shed skin. Pale light seeped through the sheers.

Even though the room was just as it had always been, it seemed impossible that she had ever slept there. The cherry headboard and the painting of *The Blue Boy* mounted above it seemed both familiar and foreign, in a way that made her uncomfortable. Was it possible, she wondered, entering the room, touching her hand to the corner of the bed, that all three of her children had been conceived here? It had been so long ago, yet the same bud vase had been on the dresser, many of the same clothes in her closet. She ran a hand across the row of sleeves, watched them ripple like water lilies.

The air was heavy with moisture from a humidifier Rusty kept at the foot of the bed. This must be sort of what it's like to be in a womb, Judy thought, curling up for a moment next to Rusty on her old side of the mattress. She fingered the silk cord that ran along the lapels of her robe and imagined it was an umbilicus. She seemed to float above the room. Nothing in here mattered to her anymore; she felt no connection — not even to her trunk in the corner, filled with family treasures (her mother's rings, her good linens, her wedding dress), not even to Rusty, who lay next to her, warm, softly snoring.

From the kitchen, the tufted titmouse chirped five. The paper was probably on the front stoop now if she cared to read it. Mostly she just skimmed obituaries for interesting names and clipped coupons she rarely used, an old habit. Judy raised her head off the pillow and looked at Rusty's sloping form huddled under the blanket, his face just barely peeking out. His forehead twitched; he scrunched up his nose. Judy wondered if he was aware of her, if he was faking sleep. It had been so long since she had watched him this closely, she no longer knew his patterns.

Earlier tonight, she had longed to be close to him. But he was preoccupied, sitting in one of his cars again. She didn't know why he didn't just move out to the garage. Sometimes she envisioned that when he got old, he might just retire in a grand sedan and live like one of those people who have trash crammed up to the back window and spilling into the passenger seat. He could keep a little TV on the dash and open the glove compartment to make a tray table when he wanted to eat. If he backed the car into the garage, he could use the garage door as a front curtain, raise it every morning to watch people all along the street as long as he pleased.

At times like these, Judy fantasized about living in her own apartment, everything around her familiar and in its place, no surprises, all her secrets out in the open. She pictured a quaint one-bedroom like the one Gretchen had taken during college, a place with nice molding and built-in bookshelves and a fireplace with a detailed mantel. There, she might finally have some anonymity, coming and going without the sense of being watched, a feeling that had prevailed ever since Carson disappeared.

Though she had invited just a handful of neighbors to Gretchen's baby shower, a number of others had stopped her over the last few weeks, their voices hushed. "Is it true? You're going to be a grandmother?" Their voices, inflected with exclamation points, still belied a tone of judgment, pity, so that she knew when she turned her back, lips would purse, heads would shake, all would think, *Poor Judy.*

Poor Judy, one of her kids disappears, joins a cult; the next one goes off with a deadbeat rock band and never calls. And now the third, knocked up and living on a commune.

Judy could hear it all, as if her ears were satellite dishes picking up the lone remarks her neighbors made to each other across telephone wires: *You wonder what happened in a family like that. . . . Judy gave those kids everything; they were just rotten eggs, nothing you can do about that. . . . It's sad, isn't it? Some people's lot in life. . . .*

Every holiday, Judy observed how all the other driveways were jammed with cars brimming with car seats and suitcases. If she stood too long at the window, she felt a hollow place open in her chest. Rusty didn't understand. "You want cars, I can get us cars," he'd brag, swaggering through the house. "I can get us cars all up and down the block. I could park this whole place in."

"You know that's not it," she'd say.

"Then don't bring it up."

If she was lucky, she got a postcard from Henry, his sloppy handwriting letting her know he was in L.A. or heading off to a tour of the U.K. The Brother of Carson Glide was still together and had slowly gained some national acclaim, although Henry was the only original member. Last she'd heard, he'd changed his name — he was always metamorphosing for the stage — one time he signed his name "Siggy," another time just "H." The last post-card had been from "Ransom." Over Christmas, he'd written to her that he was working on his sixth album (she'd never heard the first) and that he was riding in the same tour bus as Alice in Chains (Judy hoped she wasn't his girlfriend). "Better keep this card," he'd written. "We've got a radio hit in the works. This'll probably be worth something someday." The card, a shot of the Hudson River, had been ringed with coffee stains, and in one cor-ner there was a dark red smudge that suggested either blood or ketchup.

Once a booking agent had called the house looking for Henry, had left her a number. Judy kept it and had considered calling it to reach Henry about the shower. But there was only so much weirdness she could take. It was bad enough that she'd had to add an addendum to each cute Peter Rabbit invitation, explaining that Gretchen had requested black baby clothes only. Judy had put in parentheses: *They don't show dirt!*

The sad thing was that Judy had always dreamed of attending the birth of a grandchild. She envisioned crocheting in the wait-ing room of the hospital, relished the thought of biting her nails, waiting up all night, eating prepackaged ham sandwiches from the staff fridge. Her own births were such vague but happy mem-ories. There were whole albums downstairs on the bookshelf, each devoted to a pregnancy, dutifully documented by Polaroid snapshots of her belly from month to month. With each birth, her face had grown rounder, her hair shorter — from a flouncy pony-tail with Henry to a cut-and-sprayed shoulder-length shell with Carson, to a tight bulb of screw curls with Gretchen.

With Henry's birth, they had planted a redbud tree on the southwestern edge of the property, and during the next two pregnancies, she had posed in front of it at some point in spring, wearing a Japanese-style maternity dress — red with dark pagodas — while holding a paper umbrella. Both were gifts from her father after a business trip.

She got up from the bed to go to the window, then stood in the first light with her hands clasped, looking out across the square yard at the tree, its leafy plumes like a shot glass full of swizzle sticks, to remind her of things past. But there was something else out in the yard. She saw it now, a dark shadow moving along the woodpile. It came to the redbud tree and scampered up the bark.

"Well, I'll be," Judy said under her breath. She made a grab for the binoculars Rusty kept on the dresser and peered through the pinkish dawn up into the bright arms of the tree. There, perched like an owl on a limb, was the runt of Ivy's litter, Constantine Wilhelm — or, as the couple across the street had called him, Connie. How the cat had made it back was a mystery, unless maybe he had never left. Maybe the couple had driven off with their baby and abandoned its grandmother and their cat.

Through the binoculars, Judy watched his gray eyes, slow to blink. His tail swung from side to side in slow rhythm, like the pendulum of a grandfather clock. Judy could see the whites of his whiskers against his dark face, his one white front paw.

Chapter 6

MISSING CHILDREN

When the phone rang the next morning, Judy — who had fallen asleep next to her husband for the first time in five years — shot up from the bed, only to discover that it was Hael, her voice friendly and ringed with bright energy.

"Judy, hello," she said. "I realized I forgot to ask you if you wanted to schedule a second appointment."

"A second appointment?" Judy rubbed her eyes and stared at the phone cradle as if she didn't quite recognize something about it.

"The first session is always a bit of a shock," Hael continued cheerily but matter-of-factly. "The thing is, Judy, I really like you. I'd like to take you on as a client, free of charge."

What kind of sales pitch was this? Judy scrunched the lapels of her robe together at the base of her neck. A few dark leaves fell out of the creases from when she had tried shaking the redbud tree to draw down Constantine Wilhelm earlier that morning, but he had only stared at her in defiance and lashed his tail.

"I'm afraid you've caught me by surprise," Judy said. "I just woke up."

"Oh, I'm so sorry. I hope everything's okay. You left looking so dismayed. I'm afraid I sometimes forget how jarring it is for people from the outside to come here."

Judy could hear the pleasant voices of children chirping away in the background. "Gretchen's gone," she said, hearing her voice tremble. "She's left Ray."

"I heard," Hael said. "Just a little spat though. Not to worry."

Judy narrowed her eyes at the phone cord. There was something suspicious about Hael's reserve. Rusty appeared in the hall, rubbing his eyes, looking stricken. He gave Judy a quizzical look, then passed her to head for the kitchen.

"Thanks for the offer," Judy said frostily into the phone. "I think I'm doing quite well."

"I'm going down there to look for her," Rusty announced as he waited for an English muffin to toast. He drummed his fingers on the counter and stared out the kitchen window at a hummingbird at the feeder, the slender beak a needle, the wings whirring like an electric razor.

"Don't be silly," Judy said breezily. "I'm sure it was just a spat."

Rusty squinted at her, craning his neck across the counter. "Where is this place? You been there?"

Judy shrugged. "Just some apartment buildings near Logan Square." She filled the kettle with water. *Tributaries*, she thought to herself.

"You don't want me to go down there, do you?" His voice was testy.

She jumped at the sound of the toaster. "What's the point if she's gone?"

"You think something's happened to her?"

"Hael said it was just a spat." Judy faced the window next to him, pressing her hips to the sink and letting the water from the faucet course over her fingers.

"Who is this Hael?"

"Just a neighbor."

"Is she one of those nuts with the phony kids?"

"They're not phony. They're regular kids. There's nothing wrong with them."

Rusty looked at her with disbelief and stuffed half an English muffin between his teeth, chewing hungrily. "You're brainwashed," he said. "You went down there and they brainwashed you."

"No," Judy said. She could see Rusty's face going red.

"Yes, they did." He nodded slowly. "You planning to leave too? Or are they coming for you?"

"Rusty, you're acting crazy. Nobody's coming to get me. I'm sure Gretchen is fine — let's not interfere."

Rusty turned around in place with a snort, then took the other half of his English muffin, covered in peanut butter, and hurled it over the shuttered doors of the kitchen into the living room. "You're a piece of work, Jude, you really are," he stormed. "It's your attitude that's gotten us here — three kids all out there, we don't know where, because you" — he stuck out a finger — "you don't care."

Judy felt her neck go red, heat flash at her temples.

"You coward, Rusty," she hissed. "How convenient for you to blame this on me when the real reason is that you, Rusty Glide, never gave our kids an inch. You are the reason they left, the reason people like Gretchen and Carson turn to cults." Judy set the kettle on the range and cranked up the gas flame.

Rusty stood seething in the kitchen doorway, his knuckles pressed into the countertop. After a moment, he opened the door to the garage, slammed it behind him, and drove off wearing nothing but his robe.

She had said it. She, Judy, had said it. She felt brazen and light — a stone had moved, a chip had toppled. She didn't even care that, after combing the living room, she couldn't find the far-flung English muffin. She went to her closet, dressed quickly in a blouse and skirt, and headed for Fort Cloud Middle School to prep for her one o'clock health class.

Penis and *vagina* were not words that passed easily through Judy's lips. It was hard for her to utter them above a whisper, which is why she had been practicing these words aloud in the car with the windows rolled up. She couldn't very well use *twig and berries* or *china* with her seventh graders, though such trusty synonyms had always served her well around the house. They were safe words that conjured approachable, multipurpose images — never mind that she herself had routinely blushed in front of supper company whenever someone complimented her on her good dishes.

Judy was teaching seventh-grade health, the school synonym for sex ed, because she was the lone female gym assistant now that the county had liquidated 20 percent of its teachers, based on seniority. Her two colleagues, coaches Bud and Bruce Luger (twins), didn't feel qualified to teach the topic since they had never raised daughters. Until Judy came along, the Lugers had always taken a family vacation during the one-week sex ed unit, leaving a substitute with a stack of filmstrips on abstinence and menstruation that had been in use at Fort Cloud Middle School since 1965 and were otherwise stored in the library vault.

Two students in the class had already presented Judy with notes from their parents to excuse them on the grounds of explicit language and adult content, leaving Judy with eighteen wild-eyed, smirk-stricken young girls and boys drumming their fingers on the yellow desktops and looking at Judy with quiet anticipation. In her younger days, Judy had been an expressive and rigorous teacher, well known in the home ec wing for her sharp criticism of piecrusts and keen eye for sloppy stitches. She had inspired fear in the hearts of her pupils during the unit on gelatin and was said to detain students after school if they forgot to sanitize their kitchenette before leaving for the next class. A fashionable young teacher with feminine wiles, she had also cultivated a following. She was the kind of woman that young girls idolized, the kind of woman young boys imagined naked.

But time had caught up with her after she quit school, the year Henry was born. And when she returned two decades later, her children mostly grown, the school had modernized, eliminating the home ec wing to make room for computer labs. Judy had been forced to start over, returning first as a hall monitor. Checking for passes, twirling her whistle, she had become keenly aware that the students had changed, though she had not. Her clothes were the same, her hair, though she'd begun to color it, was the same length, and she still wore the same shade of red lipstick.

From time to time, one of her students turned out to be the son or daughter of someone Judy had taught in one of her first home ec classes. Sometimes these old students came back as parents. They caught Judy in the hall, and shaking their heads, they'd laugh at her. "Mrs. Glide," they'd say, "you haven't changed at all." Judy would try to take this as a compliment, but wandering the halls when classes were in session, she sometimes felt as if she were chasing an old self that kept turning corners ahead of her. Occasionally she would catch up with it, and she would feel through her whole being how she had aged. This feeling had never been more prevalent than when she'd been asked to step in and teach health. "Penis," Judy practiced under her breath. "Va-va-geeeee."

Judy stood at the front of the classroom, digging her fingers into the wood podium as a few stragglers filed into their seats after the bell. She looked over her notes on ovulation and stalled by digging through the pockets of her purse for a piece of hard candy in case her voice broke. A snicker started in the back by the dry-erase board, then threaded itself audibly up and down the aisles. When she looked up, the faces before her seemed theatrical and wild — girls with huge painted eyelids, shimmering like beetles, and boys with stiff, shiny hair, spiked up like barbed wire. A green-haired sprite in the second row twisted around his tongue to reveal a silver ball, then offered Judy a suggestive wink. Next to him, a barrel-chested boy giggled in silence, shocks of laughter convulsing his whole form, until he burst forth with a surge of wheezing guffaws, and the whole room turned to howls.

They sounded like penguins, Judy thought, rocking back on her feet to observe. She offered a fleeting smile, then pursed her lips, but this only seemed to send the students into an even greater swell of laughter, their cackles turning into something more menacing — a roar. They shrieked like monkeys now and pointed to her, and Judy experienced the strange sensation that humans have long only imagined: the notion of sitting in a zoo while the animals line up to gawk at you.

Finally, a quiet girl in the front row flipped her braids back, looked squarely at Judy, and demanded to know what Judy had above her lip.

Judy touched her mouth. "It's probably just lipstick," she intoned, looking at the girl, puzzled. "It's Cherry Fire," she offered, tugging a tissue from the sleeve of her blouse and beginning to dab at the corners of her lips. "Is it smudged?"

New giggles erupted from the back by the dry-erase board, though the rest of the room sat under a hush. "Higher!" called the boy with green hair.

"Yeah," challenged another, this time from the far left corner. "I can see it way back here."

Judy drew her brows together, then reached into her purse for a compact. "I don't see anything," she said after a quick glance in her mirror.

"Look closer," whispered the barrel-chested boy. "Don't you see it? You've got to see it." He wrapped his arms around himself, a preemptive move to hold in a wave of forthcoming laughter. "Do you see it? It's so obvious!" He clapped a hand over his mouth to conceal a grin.

"Mrs. Glide," said the girl with the long braids stoically, "you have a mustache."

The room fell silent. The kids went ashen. No one scratched a scab, no one chewed gum. Judy surveyed the faces, striving for connection — were these human children? Did they really belong to people? Had they really been infants once? Weren't they really monkeys? A different generation, a different species?

"For heaven's sake" was all Judy could think to say, clucking her tongue. She eyed the girl with braids warily. "Do I need to write you a pass to the office?" she said. "And the rest of you?" She looked around, then stepped out from behind the podium in her mauve shoes, her body rigid, her eyes ground into little points of gray light. Still, she could feel her hands trembling, the pear-shaped earrings dangling erratically from her ears.

"Penis," Judy said sternly, spitting out the word like the hull of a seed. "Vagina," she said seconds later, beginning, slowly, to walk up an aisle. The faces rotated on their stems away from her, unable to meet her sharp gaze. Her heels clicked satisfyingly against the tile, resounding against the chalkboard. "Go ahead," Judy called, fighting the wavering tone in her voice. "Say it with me. I want you to feel comfortable in your bodies."

Slowly, a few voices joined her, dissonant and squeaky. She passed through an aisle of scraggly sideburns, halfhearted goatees, hands on knees, knees that were jumpy, shoes that were unlaced. Ears glinted, full of silver specks; wrists rustled, hooped and wound with string. "Say it with me," Judy commanded. "Don't be afraid."

She stopped at the back of the room and rapped her knuckles on the board by a red-haired boy who was feigning sleep. "Robert," she said, leaning down, grinding her palms into his desk. She mustered her energy. "I can't hear you." She waited for his answer and was determined to stare his eyes open, even if it demanded the rest of the period. But he shifted, and something on his shirt caught her eye. She looked down to read, in dark red script: *The Brother of Carson Glide U.S. Tour.*

Judy felt herself go hot, begin to perspire. "Where did you get that shirt?" she asked quietly, careful to keep her voice steady. The boy opened his eyes, looked down at his chest, then sat upright in his chair, breaking into a wide smile. "They were in Milwaukee last night," he said grinning. "Think you could get me an autograph?"

Judy felt her lip twitch. She stood up, hands limp at her sides. "Let's watch a filmstrip," she said, her voice barely above a whisper. Then she walked toward the door, flipped off the lights, and started the film she had picked up at the library as an emergency backup. She sat apart from the rest of the class, her face obscured by the camera and the reel of film. She kept her eyes on the screen, fighting the lump in her throat, running a finger carelessly back and forth over the top of her lip, where a cluster of downy hairs brought her a strange sense of momentary relief.

On the pull-down screen in front of the chalkboard, small children danced delightedly around a new mother and her baby. A sperm, shot in close-up through a microscope, appeared briefly, its tail waving like the string of a balloon sent up on a windy day. An egg appeared, clear and round against a gray background, like a contact lens floating on water. Then a happy couple came into focus, seated on a couch. The camera panned their wedding rings. They kissed, smiling bright, overwhite smiles, and squeezed their hands together to imply excitement.

By the time the pink diagram of the birth canal appeared on the screen, Judy's cheeks were wet, her makeup smeared. It all came back to her now — the joy, the anticipation, the fear. Had she been able to imagine then the life she led now, she wondered how she might have acted differently. She peered over the projector at the room full of heads, boredly propped up by palms and elbows. If only they knew, she thought. But there was no way to tell them.

Trembling, she stood, excused herself to use the restroom and did not come back. She stopped by the front office to let the secretary know she was inexplicably ill and went straight to the parking lot. All the way home, she held her hand to her breast.

During this time, Rusty had spent the morning circling Fort Cloud in his Pontiac, observing work crews around the city as they installed new lampposts, men in hard hats digging holes along curbs and planting huge posts, silver and slender with fat round bases, each one like the leg of a supermodel with elephantiasis. The lamp at the top was bulbous with a flat sort of lid — a combination, Rusty thought, of something otherworldly and ultramodern. At the bank a few days before, he'd heard someone in line whispering about how some of the lights were rigged with cameras. A teller confided to a client that the new streetlight in front of her house made her feel as if there were a man outside her bathroom window.

Later, Rusty stopped at a drive-through for a bag of fries and drove out on the highway toward the old rifle range he'd once haunted in his youth. The sign for the range was gone, the roof of the shelter sloped with rot, and the range itself was full of tall grasses and saplings. But off to the side, in what had once been a well-used parking lot, the old Sunbird Rusty had bought for Gretchen's graduation was still there — the white paint now yellowish from pollen, the hood splattered with impressions of dead maple leaves, like faint handprints all over the body.

Three tires were flat, the front lights were smashed, but the door to the backseat swung open, easy as pulling back a bird's wing. And Rusty, impervious to bits of straw and chunks of yellow foam flecking the backseat, climbed in with his bag of French fries and drew the door closed with his feet.

Inside, it smelled dank and beasty, of rain and mildew and body odor. There was a white nylon stocking on the floor mat, a neat pile of bobby pins arranged like a haystack on the back dash. Rusty reclined in his bathrobe, lying on his side, knees bent, eyes closed. Lips smacking, he reached into the greasy paper sack by his chest, savoring each salty bite. So much for lifting weights today.

Despite the odor of decay, there was something comforting about the backseat. It reminded him of the time he'd taken his boys camping when they were young, how they'd set out with the station wagon full of tents and mats and sleeping bags — the boys so enamored with the idea of sleeping out under the stars — only to find them both curled up in the car come morning, all the doors locked for fear of bears. He had peered through the windows at them, feeling a sweetness wash over him, as if he were looking at small animals behind glass. He watched their shoulders rise and fall with each sleeping breath; he studied the hair pasted to their cheeks, and the way the piping along the backseat left long marks across their faces when they rolled over, so that his boys looked like newborns again — red and dew-soft looking — except for their long arms and big feet.

For a long time, he'd watched them, sunlight catching in their hair as morning emerged from the pines. Finally, he'd opened the trunk, which they'd neglected to lock, and climbed in with them. Curling around them, he'd closed his eyes and listened to the sounds of their shallow breathing until a soft rain overtook them with quicker rhythms. Then, he too had lapsed into peaceful sleep.

Now Rusty closed his eyes and let his body relax against the mildewed seat. He so rarely clambered into the back of any car these days, had done so maybe only a handful of times since that morning with his two sons. And here, in this quiet, lost place, he felt happy again, well hidden and between worlds.

He licked his fingers, rolled onto his back with his knees up, and rested a hand on his belly for a nap. But instead of sleeping, he felt his stomach turn, his insides swirling and gurgling audibly. It sparked a memory of the dream he'd had the night before, a disturbing dream: He had been onstage before television cameras, sitting comfortably in a gray studio chair, the way he usually might, but when he caught sight of himself in the monitors, his own body shocked him. In his dream, he appeared on national TV, pregnant. What amazed audiences was that he was not part of a scientific experiment; he was simply, miraculously, with child.

That's why his stomach rumbled. That's why he'd had to borrow an antacid from Celeste. There was a baby growing inside of him, and television audiences around the world were waiting, day by day, they were waiting, for Rusty to give birth. The question was simply, To what?

Rusty crumpled the French fry bag and tossed it onto the back dash. Though Rusty was not the superstitious sort, the dream made him feel uneasy. More than uneasy — downright concerned, frightened that somehow it might hold some truth. When he looked down at his own stomach, bursting through the ties of his bathrobe, it startled him, not only in its size, but in the fact that he could feel something shifting around inside. Something or someone was trying to get out.

Instead of taking a nap in the Sunbird, Rusty found himself clawing at the door handle. He purged himself at the base of a locust tree, holding onto the car's bumper for stability, then stumbled, in a daze, back to his Pontiac to drive home.

He came careening down Seeley Street just as Judy was turning onto the block ahead of him. He flashed his brights at her, but she did not raise her hand to wave as he expected. Instead, she slammed on her brakes, nearly causing their cars to collide. He rolled down his window to shout at her, his head still swimming, then noticed something ahead parked in the drive: a huge black bus — shiny, with dark, tinted windows and airbrushed stallions along the side.

Chapter 7

STRANGERS

"Oh my gosh, oh my God," Judy cried as she clambered out of her Datsun and started toward the drive. Rusty was behind her, slamming a car door, his slippers scuffing on the walk. She tossed a glance over her shoulder at him, rubbing smeared makeup away from her eyes so he wouldn't know she'd been crying. He had one hand on his stomach, the other raised in the air. "What the hell is this? Someone tell me what's going on!"

Judy circled the front of the bus and cupped her face to peer in through the door, then rapped on the glass. No answer. She stepped back to study the airbrushed seascape, horses on a beach, their manes tossed back, their eyes full of red fire. "I don't believe it," she said, breathless. "Pinch me."

Rusty stood with his hands at his sides. "Who is it?"

"What?" Judy turned to him.

"A Volvo bus?" he hissed at her. "Who do we know that drives a Volvo bus with Texas plates?"

"You're a fool," she said.

Rusty was silent, his eyes cloudy. He rubbed his stomach, then followed her toward the front steps.

They approached the house cautiously, as if it were no longer their house. The front door was open. The screen door, which did not quite fit the frame, was ajar, blowing open slightly, like a flap of skin. As she stood on the stoop, feet sinking into her own welcome mat, Judy paused. No noise came from within.

In the kitchen, there was a bag of Corn Nuts on the counter and a large, thawing turkey. In the living room, a skinny stranger with neon yellow running tights was asleep in Rusty's chair, eyes obscured by large, mirrored shades. Creeping down the hall, her shoes in her hands, Judy found a second sleeper, slack-jawed and snoring in her bed, the face half obstructed by a matted-looking teddy bear. Farther down the hall, in Rusty's bed, a set of callused feet stuck out from the foot of the mattress, the head covered by a sheet.

Judy turned, moved back down the hall in slow motion, and stood near Rusty, who gaped in astonishment from the foyer.

Behind the bathroom door, the toilet flushed, and when the door opened, Henry appeared bare-chested and bleary-eyed before them, barefoot in black vinyl pants. His dark hair, combed forward, fell in oily splinters across his forehead and along his sunken cheekbones. Around his neck, on a black leather cord, a single eyeball dangled in the crook of his sternum. He rubbed his eyes and regarded his parents with indifference.

Judy stood frozen, staring at the figure a few feet from her with a combination of horror and pity. He was too skinny and tired-looking to be her son. His skin seemed almost yellow with fatigue. His eyes were much too far back, crouching in their sockets, pinkish and swollen-looking like the eyes of a sick rabbit. She was overwhelmed by the urge to feed him, to take her big, bony boy in her lap and nourish him back to health with a small eyedropper.

Yet there was something disarming about him, the way he stood blinking at them, shifting his gaze from her to Rusty, the edges of his full lips turning slightly down. He regarded them with a steely look and scratched one of his nipples. Under his piercing gaze, Judy felt that her heels were sinking deeper and deeper into the carpet, and she remembered that when he left — now some nine years back — he had sworn to her that he would never return.

"This is it, you'll never see me again," he'd cried over his shoulder as he crossed the lawn that summer evening, a duffel bag dangling from one arm, a guitar strapped to his back. In the driveway, friends waited for him in a rattling Nova. He had been nineteen then, and still Rusty would not let him drive the family car. Henry's anger over this had filled the house with so many squealing guitar riffs and shrieking vocals that Judy had felt relief to see him go.

She had stood on the stoop with her arms crossed, watching him storm away. Heat lightning had flashed in the distance. The air carried that pre–rain shower tension, all silence and unshaken ether. Partway across the front lawn, Henry turned suddenly, as if she'd called his name. For a moment, something passed between them. Empathy? Brief comfort? His friends called for him to hurry. She gave a little nod, a sort of last-resort gesture for the moment, a moment in which she felt too paralyzed to do otherwise. It was as if her arms would remain permanently folded, as if she might never leave the stoop. Henry had flashed her a quizzical look, raising his palms as if he might come toward her, return to her — at least for a hug, a kiss, if only she'd reciprocate in some way, urge him to stay. And yet she couldn't. She couldn't feel her feet. She couldn't move her fingers. Her tongue felt as if it had dropped through her body and into her shoe. Henry had shaken his head at her, a resigned expression on his face, then lunged toward the idling car, tossing his things in the backseat ahead of him. She'd closed her eyes, waiting for the scrape of the front bumper on the drive and, soon, the sound of the rain. It was an hour or more before she was able to reenter the house.

In the years following, she'd often remembered that day and yearned for him in a quiet way, roaming the house by herself, thinking of his voice, imagining she saw her tall boy in the door frame, both her tall boys, Carson too. She imagined how she would hold them if they ever returned. She would find herself, some mornings, with tired arms from clinging to her pillows at night, dreaming of their bodies. Her hunger for them would come in cycles, a week at a time, a day, when she seemed to see them everywhere, in crowds, a few seats ahead of her at a movie, a few doors down at a neighboring house, during a sports event on TV. She felt her heart race in those moments, bursting with joy and recognition, every one of her cells rising up to go meet them.

Now she felt a shrinking, a quivering. Where do you start when you've spent so many years apart, in doubt, in frustration, full of anxiety and remorse? She faced a grown man now whom she knew she should recognize, embrace — yet nothing about his body seemed familiar. None of his gestures suggested kinship, affection. She was struck by the urge to turn away from him toward the wall, to wait for him to leave of his own accord. Yet she burned for something.

She realized what it was. She burned to have birthed something different, someone she understood. This one did not fit the vision. There must have been some cosmic mix-up. Somewhere, she felt sure, a man who should have been her son was walking through a door toward an ill-matched mother, and that man would be grinning and tan and well heeled. She saw it play across her mind like a commercial. She yearned for that other son, like a shopper who, too late, realizes she has grabbed the wrong brand. Then immediately, thinking these thoughts, Judy felt her stomach turn.

From the living room chair there came a cough, and that's what set Rusty off. "Who do you think you are?" he demanded, stepping forward in his robe, his hair uncombed, his voice husky, as if he still were not quite part of the day.

Henry ignored him, shifting his stance. He thrust a hip out and leaned his body against the bathroom doorjamb. To Judy he said, "I'm tired."

"You should eat something." As she spoke, she felt a sudden surge of happiness at the thought of rustling about in the kitchen for him. She would prepare a huge meal for everyone, could instantly see the table laid out with her good dishes, steaming bowls of potatoes and carrots and gravy.

"Naw." Henry yawned, running a hand over his hair. "Got to keep my figure for the fans."

"You look famished." Judy pursed her lips. "When was the last time you ate a home-cooked meal?"

Henry dug in one ear with his pinkie nail. He squinted. "I found an English muffin with some peanut butter by the record player," he said flatly. "It hit the spot."

Judy suppressed a sigh. "Let me make a big dinner. I could invite some neighbors."

"Oh, God." Henry turned, revealing a great eagle tattoo on his back, the wings open across his shoulder blades. A blonde hung from its beak, wearing a torn red dress that exposed one of her breasts. Her legs ran the length of Henry's spine, cutting off her feet just below the line of his pants.

"Oh!" Judy gasped, reaching to touch it. "Is that real?"

Henry didn't turn to answer. "Doesn't it look real?" Then, starting toward the living room, he sent a sidelong glance over his shoulder. "We head out in the morning."

Judy tried to muster her enthusiasm. There would be time to do a big family supper. She would call Celeste, get her to come help. She would call down to Ray, see if there were any new leads on Gretchen. Warmth began rising up through her chest. She had her Henry back. After dinner, there would be time to catch up, maybe break out a game of Monopoly — no, cards! Henry had always liked cards, had been an expert shuffler as a boy. Memories shot through her mind like stars.

Rusty, who had maintained his silence and composure near the entryway, now began to grumble as Henry lumbered past him, pulling a pack of cigarettes from his back pocket. "Wait a second." Rusty lunged forward, sputtering, "Now wait just one second. No one said you could stay."

Henry stopped, tapped the pack of cigarettes on his palm, and, towering over his father, said, "Can you keep it down? People are sleeping." Henry produced a lighter, flipped his hair back with great fanfare, and lit himself a cigarette in Rusty's face.

"I'll call the police," Rusty said, hands moving to his hips. "This is breaking and entering. Judy!" His voice was advancing to a roar. "I think we've found our burglars."

Judy closed her eyes, shook her head. She had no energy left for this.

"Everybody out," Rusty bellowed, pushing past her now down the hall. His arms flapped wildly. He shook the house with his stomping feet, his voice echoing off the bare walls, caustic-sounding. *Deranged*, Judy thought. *He's deranged.*

Bodies staggered into doorways. Long-haired heads turned, thin arms clutching small piles of clothing. There were more of them than Judy had realized, five, six — scraggly and disheveled. *These are rock stars,* Judy thought. They pressed past her, groggy, cursing, scratching themselves.

"What's happening?" asked a bearded man in nothing but underwear and boots. He groped toward the living room, cradling a bottle of whiskey. "So much for the zzz's," he said, brushing past Judy.

Henry had on motorcycle boots now, spurs that rattled as he rounded up his crew. He gave Judy a pained look and tossed her a T-shirt. She could feel herself beginning to deflate. She caught the shirt and started after Rusty, who was knocking around the living room. "They just need a place to sleep, Russ," she said.

But Rusty was on a crusade. "How'd you get in?" he was demanding to know. "Crawl through a window in the basement? Pop the lock off the sliding door?" He stood shaking by the kitchen, shooing them out with his hands, the belt on his robe coming loose, revealing a fat man in frayed boxers. The slumped figures filed out, some flashing Judy a sad smile, a peace sign.

They left nothing behind but the smell of smoke. They took their Corn Nuts, even the turkey, leaving a wet pool on the counter, bodily imprints in the beds. Judy roamed between the rooms in a daze, touching where they had slept, running her hands across the dents their heads had left in her feather pillows.

The house felt different. She couldn't put her finger on what had changed. She wanted to touch everything, things she hadn't touched in years. She opened closets, let her index finger trace down the old linens, the *Sesame Street* bedsheets she still kept there, board games, boxes of Easter ornaments, and old summer hats.

All of these things seemed infused with life again, or maybe it was just that new memories rose from each of them. When she looked at the silk ribbon on an old hat she could remember Henry holding her hand. She could hear Carson singing in the basement when she pulled out the old bathroom scale and saw the bag of yarn with his old latch-hook tool at the bottom of the closet. She sniffed at some floral soaps under the bathroom sink that had never been used — too pretty — and remembered the scent of Gretchen's hair when she let it air-dry on Sundays. Before Judy left the bathroom, she set the soaps out in the soap dish.

Rusty was out in the front yard, flapping his arms. Judy paused to watch him through the picture window, then headed for the basement. She wanted to look at the children's rooms, see if anything had been moved. It had been years since she'd really examined them — the books on the shelves, the knickknacks on the desks, the old shoes in the closet.

But there, in her old bed, Judy found Gretchen, lying on top of her old pink spread, toes curled, one arm draped across her big belly. And Judy felt not just elated, but that she had another chance. Maybe this would be the baby she herself had always wanted to have, a little Forrest Lowell or Constantine Wilhelm.

She stooped over to look at Gretchen's sleeping form. Her face was serene, her brow free of creases. She smiled in her sleep, letting out a whispery snore. She had on a brown linen dress with little wood beads along the hem. Except for her short hair, which was shaved fine as carpet, the girl could have been Judy. It was like looking in a mirror, twenty-four years younger, unblemished, with a whole life ahead of her and a new life growing within.

For a moment, Judy could remember the taste of such a beginning. She could remember what it was like to hold something inside, how very private it was, how profound to feel it kicking, to own it and be part of it at the same time. It made her feel womanly and strong, a feeling she had almost forgotten. What she realized, sitting there in the fading light, imagining Gretchen's child, was that she herself had been robbed — yes, robbed — of bearing and naming her own children, of keeping her children, of protecting them in the ways she knew how. Forces much stronger than her had taken over, forces no one had taught her about.

"Never marry a man who can crush you in bed," her mother had said. Judy ran her finger over her lip and felt it then — yes, it was true. She was growing something of a mustache. It felt downy to her touch, like the first hair on a baby's head, yet a little manly. Something was sprouting from within, something new, something quite new. She started for the stairs, rushing up the steps into the kitchen. Rusty's house keys were on the table. She slipped over to the sliding glass door, clicked the lock in place, then went around to the front door, pushed in the button, drew the chain across, then gave a final thrust to the garage door and locked that, too.

Rusty was still out in the yard, swearing at the sun as the great bus pulled away. Next door, the sprinklers kicked on, and Judy watched from behind a curtain as Rusty sputtered and cursed. She folded her arms across her chest and stood quietly with her eyes closed, feet together, feeling the house become submerged in the warm glow of evening.

Chapter 8

GRETCHEN'S SONG

Gretchen woke up, raising her head off the pillow, disoriented for a moment by the sight of her old pink dresser across the room. She rubbed her eyes, let her vision go starry for a minute. A faded streak of sunlight spread across her thighs like a loosely woven scarf, and she recalled how, almost eight months ago, she had been in this bed with Ray beside her. A child had been conceived — two cells colliding in the dark, the sperm with its mission, the egg with its grounded sensibility. It was hard to believe that in a fraction of a second an identity had been created, so quickly, so quietly. Her parents upstairs had gone about their business and not heard a thing.

It was amazing to think such a thing was possible — one expected fireworks, at least some timpani, something to announce that a being had been conceived, a little XX or a little XY that would inhabit its mother's middle passage, cells splitting in secret. But no. For weeks, invisible! Just a double stripe on a pregnancy test, a yes from a nurse who administered the blood test. And even then, still a mystery, a tremor of light, a face forming out of sky, shielding itself from attention. And that, Gretchen thought, was what was so beautiful — like in the liquid it lived in, all decisions had to be suspended. It was Occupant X and no more.

Gretchen put a hand on her belly. It was a true presence now, with arms and legs and a tiny secret between its thighs that no one — not even Gretchen — knew about yet. And it would be a long time — maybe three or four years at least — before anyone would know, anyone other than Ray or herself, that was. It wasn't anyone's business, she had decided. It didn't do anyone good to know, other than to establish stereotypes and develop silly monikers, false expectations. She loathed the ultrasound hounds who demanded to know the sex of their unborn fetuses in order to prepare the nursery accordingly. To go around discussing the sex of a child before anyone had even viewed the little face — it seemed so presumptuous, so peculiarly obsessive.

What a lot of baggage for something yet unborn. Little He or She enters the world in one of two categories, based not on the color of its eyes or the shape of its navel but according to the color of a onesie that corresponds to its genitals. Before the infant knows what is happening, its tiny body is pushed into a largely defined role, and on it rolls, into adulthood, surrounded in the trappings of its sex, rarely stopping to question, unless it comes across something quite out of context that gives it pause and cause to wonder: Why am I what I am?

For Gretchen Glide, that moment still stood out rather distinctly in her mind, as distinct as the little slides she used to study under her microscope as a child, bringing cells from her tongue under scrutiny, looking at gnats, clippings from her father's toenails, hair from the cats under the light. How she had loved to scrutinize the minutiae of ordinary life, long before she suspected something in their house was not quite right and that the greatest secrets could not be magnified.

She remembered the time perfectly. She had been nine or ten, and in the quest for new things to look at under her scope, she had planned to sneak into her parents' room, where she had designs on their closet — going through their pockets in search of interesting specimen. She wasn't sure what she hoped to find, but she was sure that within the lining of her father's suit coats and her mother's dress pockets she would find choice specks of dirt and grub to rub onto her glass slides. And she was sure these things would reveal truisms about her family — creepy-crawly things, maybe even lice. It was simply a matter of waiting until her parents were gone some night and Carson was babysitting. From time to time, her parents slipped next door to visit Donald and Celeste for a nightcap — "a little drinky-poo" was what her mother always said.

On one such occasion, Gretchen had crept into her parents' bedroom. From the windows the voices next door rose and fell, her mother's tinkling laugh, her father's one-note harrumph. Their bedroom was dark, their bedspread still taut. She ran a swab over her mother's dressing table, tucked it in a Ziploc, then made a move toward the closet. As she pulled back the door, it stuck to the track. Then from behind it came the faint sound of something scuffling around amid her mother's shoes. She'd paused. Was that breathing she heard? Surely not.

She'd hesitated, then yanked the door open and jumped back, expecting a mouse, a monster — she was not past such fantasies — but the closet was quiet, the clothes on the rack swinging slightly to and fro and sending up the faintest smell of her mother's perfume. She surveyed them in the dark, her mother's A-line skirts and puffy blouses, then decided to start at the far end, where her mother kept a satin robe and a few night things, including a turquoise negligee Gretchen had often eyed, though she'd never seen it off the hanger.

Gauging the giddy laughter from next door, she decided she better make the most of her time by yanking the negligee from the rack and giving its lacy trim and gathered satin pockets a thorough scouring. But the turquoise negligee did not want to part with its hanger. In fact, the turquoise negligee seemed to have a mind of its own. Something inside it kicked at her when she tugged the lacy hem, and moments later she found herself flat on her back, looking up at a strange specter that hissed, "Why aren't you in bed?"

She had been too surprised to struggle, staring up into the eyes of her brother — or was it? The figure had Carson's narrow shoulders, his delicate hands and hairless wrists, even his long face, but the lips were painted like a bold red carnation, and the eyelids shimmered with mothy powder. Its mouth twitched, its eyes grew glassy, on the verge of tears. For a moment, in the half-light, she could read something there, detect something more intricate than anything she had studied under a mirrored lens. The creature was half man and half woman.

A notion fluttered up and through her mind, a notion that would recur from time to time throughout her life, like the beginning of a question she could not quite phrase — it brushed her insides like a different kind of butterfly, reminding her that the surface of things was not necessarily as strange as what might lay beneath.

She'd fled her parents' room and gone hurtling into her own bed, where, staring out the window, she had quietly imagined a race of people that were neither male nor female. Somewhere out there, maybe on Pluto or Mars, there had to be other life forms that were unlike anything anyone had ever seen in Fort Cloud, unlike anything anyone had even dreamed of in Fort Cloud — somewhere out there on one of those lost-looking dots of white light.

Not long after that night, Carson had disappeared, and though she had understood her mother's despair, Gretchen had felt secretly glad for him. Some part of her had understood that he could not be Carson Glide, not the way he was expected to be. Even at a tender age, she understood this, and she cherished the glimpse of him she had been able to see that night in the closet, a side no one in her family knew existed and one she knew she dared not reveal. It was simply something she could feel, like a subtle vibration or a high-pitched tone that only animals with pointy ears might intercept. Beyond the green welcome signs of Fort Cloud, there were other planes of being.

And so she did not feel the desertion that weighed heavily on her parents and even her eldest brother, Henry, the three of them sulking collectively without any discussion of it, except for her mother, who asked at least once a day, "What will people think? What will they think we have done?" to which her father answered, "For God's sake, Judy. It has nothing to do with us."

The decision seeded itself then — long before she herself experimented with her own identity (the pink hair, the nose rings, the Vampire Lesbian T-shirts) — she decided that she would never force a child to serve an identity. She would not have one if she could not forge some in-between route to gender, an idea that formed in her mind during college and finally made its way to the page in the form of a poem titled "Avant Baby," which she'd written for a women's studies class during her senior year.

I will not make you a girl or boy.
Will not put you through pink or blue.
Rather than watch the lopsided crawl,
I'll refrain from having you at all.

The poem won first place in the campus feminist literary journal, the *Speculum*, and later, by some chance, garnered a response from a university alum who wanted to include the poem in a book she was writing entitled *Man Child, Woman Child, Future Child*. She invited Gretchen out for coffee at a nearby bookstore to discuss the matter, telling Gretchen over the phone, "I have long dark hair, and I'll be wearing a loden-colored cape."

Gretchen, who was just coming out of her hot-pink-trihawk-and-muscle-shirt stage, had almost skipped out on the date. She wasn't particularly intrigued by dark-haired cape-wearers, and she had no idea what "loden" looked like. Sure enough, the woman was easy to spot, with her horsey tresses and her greenish velvety awning.

"I'm pregnant," she had said the moment Gretchen sat down. "That's why I'm wearing the dumb cape." She made a face and rested an arm on her belly, letting her hand dangle boredly.

"Here" — she'd thrust her card across the table — "I've got to use the john."

Leah Vanhorn, the card read. *Intergender Counselor.*

Coffee led to dinner, dinner to part-time work editing Leah's doctoral thesis, and before she knew it, Gretchen was using skills she never dreamed she would rely on again, namely sewing black onesies for Leah's first child, M16. Something good had come of meeting a cape-wearer, and when the cape-wearer gave birth to her first child and inverted her name to add sexual complexity to her person, Gretchen had been there at the renaming ceremony to pull the vegan potpies from the oven, each one encrusted with a salty smile. And when Leah, aka Hael, and her husband, Glyn, had confided in Gretchen that they were looking to start an intentional community of neofuture parents, Gretchen had said, "Count me in." Two years later, at the shower for Hael's second child, Ray had swept into the room with a performance troupe that called themselves "The Birth Liberation Dancers."

"Ohhh-la-la," Ray had said, pressing a stethoscope to her chest during the show and miming a lovestruck swoon. Two winks later she had a dinner date. That was spring for you. By summer, they were sharing a futon and a minifridge, saving up for a down payment on what they teasingly called an "Avant Baby Village" condo.

Their membership in the community had been unanimous. With Ray's performance art degree and Gretchen's black-onesie cottage industry, they were the picture of post-sixties neodomestic bliss. With no standard gender roles (he washed and waxed, she sewed and maintained the truck), they presented a unified front of vigorous crunchiness and intellectual rigor. Until recently.

Gretchen could smell meat cooking upstairs. She listened for the sound of footsteps, wondering if Henry and his band were still asleep or if they had left for Chicago. She had enjoyed playing the part of the roadie temporarily and had been amazed — even startled — at the extent of her brother's fandom, but she had also been very glad when the bus pulled into Fort Cloud, even if it meant an encounter with her parents.

The phone rang. She heard someone shuffle across linoleum. She guessed it would be Ray calling. She wondered if anyone would remember she was down here. She rolled onto her back and drew her knees up to her belly, felt the baby inside her jostle, its foot jab up under her rib, its head push against her spine.

When she rolled over, she could smell the smoke from her hair in the pillow. The night before she had stood amid a throng of darkly clad teenagers in dog collars, trying to blend in, and she had felt a sense of distance from them already, as they raised their fists, punching beats into the air in time with her brother's howling vocals. She had been partial to the laser light show and dry ice, even though some kids behind her grumbled that it was not as good as at other shows they had seen. She had enjoyed listening in on their conversations as they shared cigarettes, shuffling from foot to foot between sets.

"So who is Carson Glide, anyway?" a boy with red hair and a lip ring had asked his girlfriend, behind Gretchen.

"It's probably just a name, kinda like when you go to Wendy's or Arby's," the girl said.

"Wendy was a real person — she was that old dude's kid," Lip Ring insisted. "The dude on the commercial, the old guy."

"Please." The girl flipped back her braids. She had black branches painted around her eyes and gripped a shiny black vinyl wallet in the shape of a cat face. "They just want suckers like you to believe in a Wendy. There's no Wendy. Wendy's dead."

"Yeah," said Lip Ring. "You're probably right. I was duped. Who would name their kid Carson Glide? It sounds like a deodorant."

"Names are stupid," Kitty Wallet declared. She picked at her lip and stared at the crowd. "Carson Glide is dead. I'm going to start writing that in bathrooms."

Gretchen hadn't been able to contain herself. Did all kids sound so moronic? Had she been one of them? "Carson Glide is my brother," she snapped, turning around and facing the two teens. "Really." She'd raised her eyebrows and held up the VIP pass around her neck, foolishly.

They'd turned away, snickering. "Freak. She's probably a plant," Kitty Wallet said, pushing her boyfriend through the crowd ahead of her.

Gretchen had looked down at the faded Flaming Lips T-shirt that strained around her belly and wondered, *What am I doing?* No matter how you raised a kid, it could turn on you. It came through your legs, screaming, and would probably always scream at you in some way or another. Look at her and her brothers.

She crossed her arms and went out into the hall in search of a soft pretzel. Instead, to avoid the crowds, she shouldered her way into a phone booth and called Ray. "I'm in Milwaukee. I'm safe," she said to the answering machine. "But I'm still angry."

After the show, she'd gone backstage to the greenroom, where people were doing ecstasy. Someone was snapping pictures. A woman with a little Chihuahua in her cleavage had offered Gretchen a hit.

"I'm done with that," Gretchen said.

"Are a lot of people straightedge in the Midwest?"

Gretchen lifted her shirt and pointed to her belly.

"Oh, wow," the woman gushed as the Chihuahua licked her neck. "Girl or boy, do you think?"

"Both," Gretchen practiced.

The woman gave her a confused look, then flicked a wrist of shimmering bangles that encased her arm like a Slinky. "I get it," she'd nodded coyly. "I get it. Cool."

* * *

In her old bedroom, the light was waning as evening deepened to dusk, and above her the stars were beginning to emit a low-level phosphorescence. A chill ran through her. She rolled onto her side, pulled the bedspread around her for warmth as she stood up, then mounted the stairs. She could hear her mother humming from above.

There were no lights on in the house, except for in the kitchen. Her mother, dressed uncustomarily in all black, was pulling a roast from the oven. On the breakfast bar, next to steaming bowls of potatoes and carrots and hot rolls, there was a single place setting.

"Where is everybody?" Gretchen looked around, peering through the gloom of the living room toward the empty recliner, the dark TV.

"Oh my God, you scared me." Judy stood up from the oven, holding a baster in one oven-mitted hand.

She looked terrible, Gretchen thought. Her eyes were blood-shot; her red lipstick was drawn haphazardly around her lips, as if by a child. From her ears, two huge Halloween spider earrings dangled, caught in her hair. "Gretchy!" Judy sent up a shattering laugh, kneeing the oven door closed and lurching forward, her hands jammed into oven mitts that looked like reindeer. Little bells jangled from her thumbs as she crossed the floor to meet Gretchen in the kitchen doorway.

"Are you for real?" Judy crowed, poking at Gretchen's chest with the baster. Gretchen looked down and watched as a blob of meat juice spread into a little brown oval across the front of her dress. "Here she is in the actual flesh, folks," Judy drawled, "just one of my phantom children, appearing for a limited time only."

"You're drunk," Gretchen said, smelling butterscotch.

"I'm having dinner," Judy said. "No one was available tonight but me."

"Why are you wearing all black?" Gretchen asked.

Judy licked the tip of the baster and smiled agreeably. "Why do you think? I'm in mourning."

"For what?"

Judy turned and sauntered shakily toward the silverware drawer. "Everything. My children. Your children. Nothing is right."

The fluorescent light over the sink flickered. Gretchen scanned the kitchen; all the appliances were wearing crocheted hats — the toaster in pale yellow, the blender in mint green. "Well, I had to put them on something." Judy hiccupped, catching Gretchen's glance. She strained a dish of peas.

"Where's Dad?" Gretchen asked, pulling the bedspread more tightly around her shoulders. "Where's the band? Did you see Henry?"

"I've never been really drunk before," Judy was saying. "Do you realize that?"

"Where's Dad?" Gretchen asked again.

"Questions, questions," Judy slurred. "What about me? When am I going to get some answers?" She turned, holding the strainer. Water from the peas drizzled all over the floor.

"Mom!" Gretchen started forward, clenching a reindeer.

"I drive down to Chicago and you're not there. You've disappeared!" Judy's voice lilted into its highest register. "Next thing I know Ray's here, then Henry shows up, then they all fly away."

"Mom." Gretchen heard her voice come out with an unexpected note of reproach.

"No one informs me of anything. Are you or aren't you inviting me to this birth?"

"What?" Gretchen jumped.

"If Ray's not there, someone has to be."

"Mom" — Gretchen coaxed her mother toward the sink — "Ray and I are just having a disagreement."

"Oh, one of those." Judy nodded mockingly. "Well, get used to it. I've never been in a happy marriage, and I probably never will be. In fact, when I sober up —"

"Mom." Gretchen made a grab for the peas. "That's not it. Ray and I have just been arguing. I haven't been myself lately, and his mother is behaving badly."

"What's this?" shrilled Judy, relinquishing the strainer and teetering toward a barstool. "The ape has family!"

"I'll choose to ignore that," Gretchen said, dumping the peas into a shallow bowl.

"Not that bowl!" Judy cried out. "That's for the Jell-O!"

"How was I supposed to know?" Gretchen jumped back.

Judy lumbered forward and made a grab for the oven handle, narrowly missing it. "Oh," she managed, her head lolling forward. "I feel sick."

"Mom, let me do that." Gretchen pulled Judy away from the oven. "I'll make sure the roast is done."

"You're a vegetarian," Judy whimpered.

"Well, I can read a meat thermometer," Gretchen said, resituating her mother on the barstool with her head between her knees. On the back of Judy's neck was a faint smudge, a birthmark Gretchen had never known existed.

"Would you like a glass of wine?" Judy's voice was muffled. "There's some chilling."

"I'm almost eight months' pregnant!" Gretchen gave a snort.

"So you are." Judy sat up, leaned her elbows on the counter, and cracked her neck. Her eyes swirled lazily in their sockets. She looked like someone else's mother, Gretchen thought, someone's mother on a miniseries.

"Judy," Gretchen said, then paused — it seemed so much easier to address her mother with a name rather than a title; maybe she would do this always — "I don't want any family at the birth, and that's not meant to make you feel bad. I don't know what Ray told you, but it's my birth, my body. I don't want anyone at the hospital pressuring me."

"I'd like to get pregnant again," Judy mused, crossing her legs deliberately and swiveling around on the stool. "I think I deserve another chance."

"Whoa," Gretchen said, hoisting the roast.

"Don't worry." Judy hiccupped. "There's no chance of it." She hiccupped again. "Menopause," she added sullenly.

"This is still way pink," Gretchen said, jabbing the roast, crinkling her nose at the smell of it. She added, "Mom, it's grotesque to cook this much meat. There's no one here to eat it."

"Rub it in," muttered Judy. She stared into space and joined her hands on the counter so that it looked like the reindeer were biting each other, or kissing.

"Where's Dad? Where's Henry?" Gretchen maneuvered the roast back into the oven.

"Banished," Judy said quietly, looking down. "Everyone's been banished."

Gretchen sighed and put a hand on the small of her back to balance her weight. The faucet dripped. A plane passed overhead, scraping against the sky — a deep purring sound. Gretchen looked hard at her mother, at the golden cast to her hair, at the spider earrings swinging along her jaw, at the red smear of lipstick around her mouth. How was it possible that this was her mother?

"Here" — Gretchen went around Judy's side with a paper

towel — "you've got lipstick everywhere," she said. "I don't know why you put so much on."

"Do you see it?" Judy frowned, keeping her body still as Gretchen dunked the tip of the towel into a water glass before proceeding to wipe further. "Do you see it above my lip?"

"See what?" Gretchen stepped back.

"You don't have to pretend," Judy said. "You can tell me."

"What are you talking about?" Gretchen screwed up her face and leaned in closer. Her mother's breath smelled sweet. Her eyes were glossy.

"Enough," Judy said with a wave of the reindeer. Her eyes welled up. She patted at her mouth, then stood up. "I'm too tired for this. Wake me up when the meat is done."

In the doorway to the hall, Judy paused and made a final attempt at maintaining balance. She turned in place and touched a hand to her chin. "You know what name I've always loved?" she asked, emitting a sad titter. She swayed in the doorway, her head tipped slightly back, her stained lips poised to whisper. "Virgil." She nodded, looking up as if in thought. "I can't say why. I just do." And with that, Judy disappeared down the dark hall toward her room. Gretchen heard her door close; then the house was silent.

She stood for a moment at the back window, watching the empty feeder, waiting for a bird to alight, for a pair of dark wings to break open the motionless setting of the backyard, where nothing — not even a lawn chair — cut across the clean sweep of dry grass. Just below the window, the bushes rustled. A cat crossed the lawn languidly, then slid through the fence.

Gretchen remembered the night she and Ray had broken into the house, jimmying the back latch with a hairpin just as she had done as a kid. They had moved through the rooms in the dusky light, touching nothing, looking at everything. How unfamiliar ordinary objects seemed without her parents moving among them. And to look through their rooms — to see her mother's comb on the edge of the sink, her father's heart pills laid out on the dresser — it was as if they had died. They seemed to be people she hardly knew. Was her mother reading mysteries? There had been a neat stack of paperbacks in a corner behind her bed. Gretchen had studied the magazines in the rack, squinting at the spines, wishing she had a flashlight, feeling like a burglar. *McCalls, Family Circle, Redbook* — and what was that? — a manual on gun safety. She'd frowned, stooping lower to make sure she'd read it correctly, then shrugged. Must have gotten mixed up with the magazines somehow, she'd thought.

The cat entered the yard again with something flapping between its jaws.

"Well," Gretchen said, looking down at her belly. She gave it a loving rub, then entered the kitchen, took a plate off a shelf, and spooned up some peas, some lukewarm mashed potatoes. In the oven, the roast was still sputtering.

Out on the stoop of her parents' house, Gretchen set the plate on her knees, taking in the evening sounds of her old neighborhood. She felt a combination of love and hate for the houses around her, for their cheap-looking pastel siding, their clumpy hedges and blocky lawns with American Turf & Beauty signs stabbed into the earth by each driveway. From down the block came the all-American thrump of a basketball resounding on concrete, behind it the distant revving of a scooter, and closer — the sound of men laughing.

That was the problem with small towns; they had such singular sounds. They were so different from the assemblage of noise one heard in the city, where ringing phones, unwinding sirens, people screaming at all hours in all languages, and car alarms wailing through the night made up a kind of bearable scramble, an unpredictable yet comforting white noise. Towns were like pop songs — they were so dated; you tired of them too quickly. And yet their breezy cadences allowed you to pause for two seconds of nostalgia, to observe a moment of reverie.

Something about the air tonight reminded Gretchen of the evenings her father had taken her out driving, back when she was thirteen or fourteen. He let her choose any car off his lot, then handed her the keys. It was all done in silence. Out on the back roads, the car would list dangerously close to the shoulders. She'd swerve back and forth over the center line as if it were a game. There would be no word from her father in the passenger seat, no admonishments, no barking orders. He sat perfectly erect, looking dead straight ahead, no seat belt on.

There was only one time she made him cling to the door by slamming on her brakes — a deer had appeared suddenly in their path. He turned to her, face frozen with fear. "You drive now," she whispered, preparing to relinquish the keys. No, he shook his head ferociously. Then he said a strange thing: "This is good for me."

How different her life had been then — those tests of her wits, those quasi suicide missions. From day to day, things had always seemed in limbo, the family always in flux. She'd sworn she'd never live like that again, yet here she was, nearing the brink of birth, sitting on the stoop of Seeley Street where the Chem-Lawn and the vinyl siding presented a perfect facade to a crumbling interior. Her mother drunk and cooking a roast. Her father off somewhere. How did one incorporate all of these things into a new life? How were children supposed to evolve if one had to keep introducing the past to the future? She wondered now, as she often had as of late, if she should follow her brothers' course and sever all ties completely.

"You have to," Henry had advised, sitting her down for a pep talk in his tour bus. "They're like anthrax."

"But a baby, it needs family," she'd pressed. "It deserves that much, doesn't it?"

"You want a welcome wagon, I'll give it a concert. Fans, man, that's all you need. Fans." Henry had run a hand across his mouth, then pointed his finger at her, making a cocking sound with the back of his teeth.

The other couples in her neighborhood hadn't offered much more in the way of guidance. Glyn and Hael had split off from their parents entirely, demanding to raise their children in a sphere of unbiased smiles and unremitting equality. They pursued their ideals like elk, more like hunters than parents of two small beings. Like the concepts of maleness and femaleness, the term "grandparent" simply did not exist as part of the household lexicon — not that it was forbidden, exactly, but as Hael had described in her second book, *Parenting Without Sex: New Hope for Gender Equality and Children*, certain false boundaries had to be erected in order to create space for exploring authenticity.

"In their first years of life," Hael had written, "it's imperative that children be protected, not just from dangers in their environment like, say, hail and bathtubs, but also psychological elements: scorn, animosity" and something Hael termed Prefab Gender Pollutants, or PGPs. A PGP could be something as simple and amorphous as a stereotype, e.g., a mother taking it upon herself to bake all of the family's birthday cakes ("fathers bake great birthday cakes, too!" Hael had written in parentheses) or something as obvious and concrete as a Barbie doll.

Hael's chapter "No More Sex in the Kitchen" provided a list of tips on how to declutter one's home of gender-based cultural indicators, from canceling magazines to removing packaging that depicted, say, a woman washing windows. "Even yogurt containers in pastel cartons are subtly encoded to attract the female eye with supple, low-cal slogans," Hael pointed out. "Of course, you have to decide where to draw the line. Just remember: Your child's world is only as solid as the one you create. Whom do you want to run their life? You or Yoplait?" The last item on Hael's list had suggested decluttering of a different kind: "Limit time with un-like-minded entities, including extended family."

Hael explained that raising a child in a gender-neutral home required diligence and a commitment from the surrounding community. Insulating oneself, at least for the first few years of a child's life, was no different from the actions of a pair of birds building a nest in a high tree. If either parent abandoned the nest and gave in to the pressures of society, it would become more of a struggle for all in the community to sustain their promise. And having aunts and uncles around who looked on with scorn made everyone uncomfortable, especially the children.

For Gretchen, this had hardly been an issue during the first few months of her pregnancy. She was only occasionally in touch with Henry when he sent her a new CD, and Carson had long ago stopped sending her birthday cards, so what little contact she had with her family rested on her parents, both of whom had been withdrawn for so long that they seemed hardly to exist in their physical bodies. Keeping them at a distance had never been the issue; in fact, they seemed more comfortable that way, to live free of confrontations with their children.

But Ray was different. He saw confrontation as a must. How else could there be evolution? Since they joined the community of gender-neutral parents just over a year ago, he took it upon himself to incorporate their core philosophies into his every movement, from his art to his weekly talks with his mother who lived in Florida. And therein was the problem. Whereas Gretchen was hell-bent on laboring in private, Ray was all for extending a family invitation to the birth. At the very least, they should be invited to the hospital, where special doctors and nurses were familiar with the ground rules of this new way of parenting — one obstetrician had even considered joining the group as a full-time member.

After a few glasses of wine one evening, Ray confided in Gretchen that his mother insisted on coming, and that he'd finally agreed on the grounds that it was part of her continuing education and that the birth itself was a live performance. Ah, the fury. "I'm not going to let this birth turn into some sort of night class." Gretchen glowered at him across the kitchen. "If you want to make this into some sort of arty statement, then take it to the stage for your own show. As for me, I'm hoping for as few lights as possible and an audience of two or three — the doctor, me, and this baby. If you can't accept that, then you shouldn't come at all."

"Don't be ridiculous," Ray said, his eyes warm with wine and laughter. He'd moved across the counter to put his arm around her. She'd ducked and stood crossly in the center of the floor, tapping a clog.

"Call her," she demanded. "Tell her."

"Gretchen, she's my mother."

"You are a wimp," Gretchen said, pronouncing the words slowly. Ray flinched.

"Wimp," Gretchen said again.

"We're in this together," Ray said firmly. "We're pregnant."

"*Wimmmmp.*" Gretchen let it out slowly, like a low call.

"Please don't say that again." Ray set his teeth.

"Really?" Gretchen had raised her eyebrows. "You don't think that caving in to your mother's demands is wimpy? You don't think it's a form of faltering on our values?"

She locked eyes with him. He adjusted his head scarf, took another sip of wine.

"I've had a full day of practice; I'd like to discuss this tomorrow," he said curtly, folding his arms.

"I don't think I'll be here tomorrow." With that, Gretchen plucked her car keys from the hook, stuffed a change of clothes in her shoulder bag, and left the house. "Wimp," she called before closing the front door on her way out. On her way down the sidewalk, she heard the sound of breaking glass through the open window.

She had been glad for the concert ticket from her brother. She had been even happier still to pull up to his tour bus in the parking lot behind the club and find him alone inside, leaning against the plush red seats, his boot propped on a chrome rail as he studied his face in a mirror. He applied ash and black lipstick.

"This Ray guy, he sounds a little wacky," Henry said when Gretchen told him about their fight. "Listen, you can ride with us as long as you want." Henry's eyes, usually bloodshot and sullen, lit up. "We could start a spin-off," he gibed. "The Niece/Nephew of Carson Glide."

Gretchen poked at some peas with her fork, then set a single green orb before a dung beetle on the walk, hoping it would stand up on its back legs and push it along down the street. She imagined a neighbor — Donald, maybe — coming out of his house and seeing a single green pea going down the walk. That would give him pause. The beetle stopped, seemed to frown, then moved on toward the dirt under the front stoop.

Off to her right, the garage door went up unexpectedly. Gretchen stood and smoothed her dress down over her belly. She carried her plate out onto the lawn and peered into the garage, surprised by what she saw: her father sitting in the passenger seat of a new Pontiac, wearing what looked to be his bathrobe. He seemed equally as surprised to see her, raising his eyebrows as she strode around to the driver's side. "Dad," she said, putting a hand on her back as she stooped to peer in his window. "How long have you been sitting here?"

"In here?" He drew his eyebrows together and looked as if he were formulating an estimate.

"Yes. Mom's been in there preparing a huge dinner."

"Well." He rubbed his chin. Then he asked in a low voice, "Are the doors still locked?"

"The doors?" she puzzled.

"Yes, there was that bus in the drive, and your mother got so freaked out that she locked all the doors."

"That was Henry, Dad. That was Henry's band."

"I don't care who it was," Rusty fired back. "They took up the whole goddamn driveway."

"Why are you in your bathrobe?" Gretchen reached in through the window and fingered a fraying lapel.

Rusty looked down and drew the robe closed, tightening the sash along the side of his stomach. She saw him eye her belly. "How's everything going in there?" His voice sounded sheepish.

"Okay." She nodded. "You?"

He shrugged. "A little hungry."

"Here." Gretchen speared two peas and ran them through her remaining mashed potatoes. Later she would think, *Did I really feed my father half my dinner through the window of his car?* Rusty smacked his lips appreciatively and opened his mouth for more, craning his neck up like a little bird.

"How was that for a role reversal?" Gretchen giggled, leaving the clean plate on the garage steps and clambering into the driver's seat. "Shall we go for a drive?"

"Sure," Rusty said. "You okay to drive?" She could feel him watching her as she squeezed behind the wheel, fumbling madly for the lever that would push the seat back.

"It's all automated, buttons along the door," he said proudly. "You have to start the car first. Then you can tip it back, raise it up, do a million different things."

"Fancy," Gretchen said, turning the key and fumbling with the buttons. The windows in the back slid down. The side-view mirrors craned this way and that.

"Here." Rusty leaned across her lap. She felt the weight of him against her belly, a hot heap of a person. The baby kicked.

"Whoa!" Rusty sprang back.

"It's just kicking." Gretchen said.

"Feels like a strong little guy, a soccer player." Rusty's eyes lit up.

"Dad, girls play soccer, too."

"Tennis, more like." Rusty shrugged. He sat up in his seat and reached for his seat belt. Gretchen clucked her tongue and nosed the car out onto the street. In front of them, a streetlamp that she hadn't remembered seeing before came on. It lit the yard like daylight. "Ach," Rusty said, swatting his visor into position. Down the walk, other lights, taller than the trees, winked and flickered until dusk felt strangely like dawn. "Good Lord," huffed Gretchen. "What is this? A tanning salon?"

"It's to cure depression," Rusty snickered. "The mayor's new initiative to make everyone happy — longer days."

"But it's almost fall!" Gretchen cried. "The days aren't supposed to be longer."

"Maybe they're just trying it out."

"This is bizarre," Gretchen said. "This is very bizarre."

"Cuts down on crime, too. Double bonus," Rusty murmured.

"Crime? In Fort Cloud?"

Rusty spun his head around to face Gretchen as she eased the car around a corner. "We've had break-ins, your mother and I." Rusty's nostrils flared.

"When?"

"Last winter." Rusty's voice hit a sharp note. Now he was excited.

"Nooo." Gretchen rolled her eyes.

"I swear!" Rusty undid his belt and reached his arm back behind his seat. "Look," he demanded, "your mother found this downstairs."

On the seat between them was an orange glove. Rusty poked at it with his finger as if it were a crab. "In your room," he said quietly. "Lying right next to the bed. Someone" — he shook his head — "was in there."

Gretchen swerved, nearly hitting a parked RV as she squinted down at the mitten on the seat. It was Ray's old winter glove, of course. She smiled to herself, remembering how she and Ray had stepped into the dark, snowy yard after lovemaking, how Ray had fumbled for this glove, patting at all the pockets of his snowmobile suit. "I've got to go back in," he'd said. But before he could turn around, the sliding door had opened and Rusty had stumbled out with his cooler. He'd lugged it out into the middle of the yard and passed out then and there. Ray had been the one to run over, to make sure her father was okay. She could remember watching from the bushes how tenderly Ray touched this stranger, pulling up her father's T-shirt and listening to his heart. The thought of it now made tears well up in her eyes.

"Once I get things squared away with your mother, I'm going to put bars on the windows," Rusty was saying. "We need new locks, an alarm system." He waved his arms.

Gretchen checked her watch. Ray would be getting home from practice right about now. She could almost hear the flap of his thongs in the entryway, his footsteps leading up to the door. He'd be in one of his leotards — the new gray one she'd made him, maybe — and it would be damp, as musky as moist earth under her nose when he leaned down to nuzzle her and stretch his hand out to touch the baby, crooning, "Hey, little one, hey little john-nycake or jillcake, how's it going in there?"

"Dad." Gretchen's voice was soft. "Gotta quarter?"

"What?" Rusty turned to her, lowering his arms midgesture.

"I'm going to pull over up there at the phone booth, okay?" Her voice wavered. "I'm going to call Ray."

Chapter 9

CHALKINGS

That night, as Rusty slept in the back of the Pontiac in the garage, he dreamed he was carrying a being that was half man and half woman. Its tiny body had both miniature breasts and a very small branch of flesh between its legs. It was, he thought, grotesque. But because it was part of his body, he could not ignore it and had to, therefore, pretend to adore it.

As the face came into view, he saw that it was familiar to him, though he could not remember where he'd seen it before, and as the world around him watched his stomach expand in his dream, he began to grow his hair out in the hopes that it would grow down past his waist and hide his burgeoning belly. Your hair grows faster, he'd heard Judy say, when you're pregnant.

In the morning, he awoke early, unrested and aching. His stomach growled. He unfurled, rubbed his eyes, and sat up in his robe. He squinted at the Ping-Pong ball hanging above the windshield, caught sight of the orange glove on the front seat, and turned it over in his hand. What had Gretchen said? That the glove belonged to Ray? That made no sense. Either he was losing his mind — and this seemed more and more likely — or she had been thinking of something else. He sat forward, let himself out of the car, and opened the side door to the outside.

It was still partially dark. The light was gray, a thin layer of fog all over everything. Or maybe he was just squinting. He stretched in the drive, observing the dark houses around him, the maple trees already tipped with color, and then realized something was funny. There were chalk drawings all over the drive — stick figures in dresses with red lips and mustaches.

Rusty rubbed his eyes to make sure he was seeing them correctly. Then he looked down at his belly and, trying to hold it in, turned his gaze to the left and to the right. In a whisper, he said, "Surely not."

By the early light the drawings on the damp drive seemed to dance — all of them alike, like strange hieroglyphs. He looked across the street and down the street. There were CONTINUE THE BLISS signs on most all the lawns, but no one else had strange figures drawn in chalk.

Rusty went over to one of the drawings and rubbed at its face with his big toe. The red lips smeared. The childishly drawn squiggles of hair smeared slightly but appeared to be stuck rather stubbornly to the concrete. He bent down to watch a dark caterpillar inch across a messy black mustache. Unnerved and hoping to catch a report on the forecast, he headed back to the car. There was only soft music at that hour. Rusty laid his head against the wheel and fell asleep.

Hours later, Donald appeared on his stoop, took a brief look around the neighborhood, and noticed what looked like alien etchings next door. He took an extra CONTINUE THE BLISS sign from his garage and put it on his property line closest to the Glides' as a sort of protective shield. Then he went back inside.

Ray drove up later that morning in the truck to pick Gretchen up, and the two stood in the drive with brows raised. "The whole town must have known I was here last night." She frowned.

"This is great," Ray commented, wandering around slowly, hands in his pockets. "It's gorgeous." He smiled. "I want to incorporate them into my new show somehow."

"Not that again." Gretchen sighed.

"It's a collage about our lives," he said, holding open his palms. "I see this reaction as very integral. Plus" — he bent down on one knee to study a stick figure closely — "there's something so primitive about them, yet they portray such *joie de vivre*. I wish I knew the artist. It's really fantastic." He scratched his chin and stood up again. "It's like a symbol of so many things — male/female, man/ wife. I see it as a very progressive step for Fort Cloud." He nodded, then pointed, newly excited again. "Look!"

Next to a stick, someone had written the word *penis*. They had chalked *vagina* next to a sidewalk crack.

"Brilliant," Ray marveled. "So abstract."

Only Judy did not wake in time to catch a glimpse of what her pranksters had left on the drive. She had gone to bed drunk and slept until noon, by which time a rain shower had washed all the chalk away so that even Rusty, when he drove off later to his lot, wondered what he had dreamed and what he had seen. Reality had never seemed more slippery.

Chapter 10

SUNNY AND KLAUS

Three weeks shy of her due date — after multiple talks with Ray and consultation with Hael — Gretchen called her mother and said, "You may come to the birth — not into the birthing room, you understand. But into the hospital." She added, "Ray and I would like you and Dad there."

Ray, who was sitting on the couch, shook his head. As someone who had peered into this family through windows, he had a pretty good sense that having the Glides at the birth would spell disaster. But he was feeling guilty himself, guilty for succumbing to the pressures of his own mother, who had announced that she not only would come for the birth but had subleased a condo for three months along Lake Shore Drive. She was coming, she said, and there was no stopping her.

"We'll do anything, anything," Judy was gushing into Gretchen's ear. "Tell us how we can help!"

"Well" — Gretchen paused, trying to gain strength from Hael's suggestions — "I have a bit of an assignment for you."

She could hear Judy's breath catch.

"Nothing big," Gretchen said. "You just have to remember that this is a really private affair for us, and we don't want a lot of commotion."

"Sure, sure," Judy said.

"Just you and Dad and Ray's parents, no one else," Gretchen continued.

"It's not as if we'd invite the neighbors." Judy laughed at her own joke.

Gretchen was silent. "Okay then."

"Just tell us whatever you need, hon." Judy was on a roll. "We can run last-minute errands, stock the fridge, paint a bedroom, I could make some of those little —"

"Mom." The word came out like a dart.

"Fine, fine," Judy said. "You'll call us, then?"

"Just remember what I said. No commotion. I don't want you even to ring up friends. Just come and make sure things stay calm, quiet. Can I trust you to do that? That's your assignment."

"Absolutely," Judy said. "One hundred percent."

"Good." Gretchen breathed a sigh of relief.

The next week, Ray's mother and boyfriend flew in from Florida and called from the airport. Though Gretchen had never met her, she had talked to Ray's mother, Sunny, on the phone. Sunny had a showboat voice, loud and spunky, with just a hint of her Brooklyn past, so that "Ray" sounded like "Way" when it came out of her mouth. Sunny, who had never married, had gone from hopping around communes in her younger years to living in a grotesquely overdone beach house on an island off the coast of Florida with Klaus, a retired ophthalmologist and her partner of fifteen years. Ray had been down to visit them once and came back appalled by his mother's abuse of shell wall hangings and gauche peach-tone furniture. After her wild youth, she told Ray, she ached for normalcy, and surrounding herself with mass-produced date palm prints and copious seafoam throw pillows seemed to play into this fantasy.

To Gretchen she said things on the phone like "I bet your flat is too adorable" and "It sounds like you and Way are having a lot of fun with this neutral baby fad." Then she'd add, "Have you tried those vitamins I sent you — the shark cartilage? The raspberry leaf capsules?"

The other thing about Sunny was that she was a distributor for everything — always scheming, always mailing Ray pamphlets and catalogs with things circled in red pen, a note in her bubbly scrawl alongside: "What a good deal on this humidifier!" or "Aren't these wind chimes nifty?" Anything you mentioned — a vacuum cleaner, sunscreen, kitchen scissors — Sunny seemed to be an independent contractor for some company that sold it.

It didn't sound like a very profitable career choice for someone living on an island with few inhabitants and no real commercial businesses, but Ray intimated that this situation was the key. Sunny could strike up a conversation with anyone, and she had a pool pass to the resort on the island's eastern tip. It was just a five-minute ride by golf cart. She'd saunter through the gate with her straw hat and a beach bag full of product leaflets, plop herself in a lounger next to some sucker lazing poolside with a giant rum drink, and, well, Sunny knew how to spot an opportunity.

"They're tired from their flight. They want us to come over for takeout," Ray told Gretchen when he got off the phone with Sunny.

Gretchen flashed him a pained look. She was reading on the couch in a black sports bra and underwear. "You've got to be kidding. I thought they were going to entertain themselves until the birth."

"They want to meet you." Ray looked sheepish. He sniffed his armpits. "It's my mother." He shrugged.

"They could come here. You should have told them to come here." Gretchen put down her book on the Bradley Method and rested it on top of her stomach.

"Don't be grumpy." Ray stood with a hand on his hip in the hall and ran a washcloth over his chest. His eyes followed the motion of the rag, like a cat fixated on a toy. "Believe me," he added, "it's better this way. She comes here, she'll want to sell us stuff for the kitchen."

Gretchen sighed and hoisted herself off the couch. "You owe me," she called over a shoulder as she padded into the bedroom. She poked her feet into flip-flops. "I have half a mind to show up in my underwear."

"Go in your underwear," Ray said.

Gretchen pulled a black elastic skirt and a thin sweater over her belly, then waited out on the front steps for Ray. The air felt heavy, full of the damp smells of early October. M16 came toward her across the yard, kicking up leaves, a Nerf bat in one hand and what looked like a Barbie in the other.

"M16, does your mother know you've got that?" Gretchen asked. She pushed her sunglasses back on her head and leaned forward over her belly.

M16 hid the Barbie under one arm and stood before Gretchen, looking down at where one small clog was covered in mud.

"I found it in the dog park," the little voice said.

"I don't think your mother would be very happy about that." Gretchen tried to use her most reproachful tone, but already she felt herself caving. She remembered her own collection of Bar-

bies, and despite all the implications of Barbie's blazing feminin-
ity and unattainable body, she had turned out all right.

M16 held out the doll by its feet. "You take it," the little voice
said sullenly. Barbie's blond hair swung across Gretchen's kneecap.
She took it reluctantly and put it in her carryall. She watched M16
squat down and scratch at a patch of bald grass with a stick. As
much as she believed in following through on the community's
mission, there were times when she found herself feeling ambiva-
lent about some of the policies. She was all for gender neutrality,
but even she thought foam blobs in lieu of actual toys were a bit
harsh. The rule at Hael's house, though, was "no gender-centric
toys on the premises." It was unrealistic to think that kids might
not come into contact with them at someone else's house, although most of the group's children were young and didn't circu-
late much. But once they hit six or seven? M16, the group's eldest
child, was just now five.

"Listen," Gretchen waffled. "How about you come with us? We're
going to meet Ray's parents downtown. If you come along —"
Gretchen tapped her shoulder bag — "you can play with it there."

M16's deep blue eyes brightened.

"Run up and ask your parents," Gretchen said. "We'll wait right
here."

Ray emerged in a fresh T-shirt and rainbow sarong. "You put on
aftershave," Gretchen observed.

"For my mother." He shrugged, then said, "It was a present from
her."

M16 bounded down the stairs and out the front door onto the
stoop, ringlets of shoulder-length blond hair bouncing. "It's okay,
I can go. But I'd like to be home to watch a documentary on rock-
ets with Glyn later."

"Great," said Gretchen, taking M16's hand. "Did you hear that,

Ray?" Gretchen called to Ray, who was sauntering ahead of them, snapping off the heads of some dead marigolds along the walk.

"Yes." Ray nodded. "I heard. We won't stay too long."

In the car, Gretchen changed her mind about the Barbie. What had she been thinking? It was against every bylaw she herself had helped draft. She and Hael sat on the policy committee, which meant distributing copies of policy changes to all six families and keeping a master copy, which was bound and stored in a supply closet. Every Sunday, the policy committee met in the gazebo out back and hashed out conflicts, ironed out policies that were too strict or too vague, mulled over terms. Several meetings ago, for example, it had become clear that some residents were uncomfortable with the term "gender neutral."

"It's not like we can be neutral, not after living in a society that has pushed us to believe in the adherence to two and only two codes of behavior," said Kenn, the group's newest member.

"How about 'gender open'?" offered his partner, Colima.

"How about 'belated genderists'?" called out Glyn.

"But isn't our ideal really gender neutrality?" asked Kenn.

"Good point." Colima was there to back him up.

"Well, we're really questioning what gender means, whether it needs significance," Kenn went on. "It's such a guarded belief system — I like to think of myself as a 'gender warrior.'"

Gretchen had rolled her third eye, a practice she'd learned from Hael. "How about 'gender lax'?" she suggested offhandedly.

"Hmm," said Colima.

"Hmm," said Kenn.

"I'd like to suggest the community work with 'gender lax' on a trial basis," Glyn volunteered.

"Do we have consensus?" Hael asked.

All heads nodded. Other issues proved much harder — like at what point a child's true sex could be revealed to the greater community. Some argued for a strict age — say, five. A school-age child is fully aware of his/her genitals and even when home-schooled within the community will want to share and exchange information, sometimes information of a personal nature, with his/her peers. To shun this and commit children to secrecy seemed false. That was one opinion. Then there was the question of how to tell the greater community — some argued for a ceremony, a rite of passage. Others felt that gave a child's sex too much of a spotlight.

At present, there were only four children in the community, though others were imminent. Besides M16 and M46, there was a set of twins that lived two doors down: Trust and Chance Figgis. Their parents, two outgoing nudists who taught anthropology at Loyola, raised issue with trying to foist too much gender-lax dogma on children who, accustomed to the community vibe, would nat-urally express their sexual potential in ways that did not necessi-tate administrative oversight. The Figgises, who had once been accused rather vehemently at a community picnic of joining the group as an anthropological prank, took great pride in running against dominant paradigms. Though they appeared uninterested in community events after the picnic incident, they continued to hover about the sidelines, jotting things in notebooks when they thought no one was looking. Lately, their termination from the group was under discussion since four-year-old Chance had taken up the practice of flashing passing cars — something the Figgises refused to address for fear of impinging on Chance's freedom of expression.

"Now everyone will know Chance's sex," Gretchen had fumed

at Eve Figgis one morning in the yard when she'd caught Chance in front of the oak tree, pants down. "That's not exactly helping our cause."

"Cause!" Eve snapped, slamming her little notebook down on the front steps. "Just what is our cause? To suppress our children's naturally forming identities or to encourage them to develop at their own rate?"

When Gretchen tried to interrupt, Eve hedged. "Maybe the problem, Gretchen Glide, is that people like you haven't learned to wean themselves of their own maladjusted extremism."

Gretchen was stunned. She'd stood dumbstruck on the walk, feeling impervious to the lawn mower across the street or the children tossing gray blobs at the pigeons. Her, an extremist? That seemed ridiculous. She was about to say so when Eve promptly stood up and went back into her apartment. Gretchen spun around and sauntered breezily off to the corner grocery as if nothing had happened. But Eve's words had haunted her. Even after Eve stopped by a few days later with a basket of wheat-free muffins and apologized, explaining that she and her husband, Stu, were having problems, that her parents were applying pressure to send the twins to a mainstream private school, Gretchen went on feeling mortified and sheepish.

Maybe she *was* an extremist. She had never thought of herself in those terms. She always considered herself a rather quiet, shy person who survived the mainstream by secretly ducking off the road for private diversions. Her women's studies major was one such detour — one that she never had the guts to face her parents about in case they threatened to freeze her tuition. Ray was another such secret detour. She'd spoken to very few people about him during their two-year courtship and probably wouldn't have if she weren't pregnant. The baby, in fact, seemed like her first public statement, the first real admission of who she was and what she believed. She wasn't like some of the others in the community who had grown up in unusual circumstances: Ray had been raised moving from commune to commune, Hael came from a peculiar background of Quaker Trekkies, and even Eve Figgis had run away from home at a young age and foraged in the woods for nuts and berries until nudist Stu swooped her up.

Gretchen was doing her best to break out, and that meant trying to forge a new order, to create a new community, to reinvent the rules. So she was in favor of the strictest gender neutrality — did that make her an extremist? She saw good sense in cutting out television, dressing babies in black onesies, keeping a spare house, limiting contact with the outer world, and forbidding public removal of clothing or any talk about a child's sex. Until the child is at least five, she felt, pretend it isn't there, pretend the only thing between a child's legs is air. Together she and Ray had spent hours role-playing with the other couples and chatting over the Internet with several like-minded families who were trying to develop communities elsewhere. Hael's book had inspired underground "maladjusted extremists" in New York and even Shanghai to work on raising children with less gender specificity. True, no other group was as absolutist or as organized as theirs, but all of them made use of Hael's guidelines in one way or another, even if they didn't have the courage to practice them in public. Many progressive expecting couples practiced her exercises, something Hael recommended even for those who didn't have children.

Q: Isn't that a cute baby. Boy or girl?
A: Either way.

Q: Is _____ a boy's name or a girl's name?

A: It's both.

Q: Is your child male or female?

A: Our child's gender is a private matter. How would you like it if I made inquiries into your sex?

Over the winter, Gretchen and Ray had attended several conferences with Hael on raising gender-free babies. They weren't publicized or even very organized — just people who met on the Internet and offered up their farmhouses or their flats to work through this new notion of parenting. Some were middle-aged, frustrated with their teens who for some reason had ADD or no self-esteem. They were curious about whether this new method of child rearing offered a solution. Most couples were young, in their twenties and thirties, looking for a new vision. Some were lesbians or gays seeking the company of a supportive network.

And, somehow, the term that stuck was "Future Parents" — FPs. "My friend so-and-so is interested in becoming an FP," someone would write. "Does she need a license?" Letters and e-mails had begun to flood Hael's house over the summer: "How can I find out more? Are you teaching a seminar?" Part of Hael's mission was to raise awareness about gender in the community through subtle means, but people from all over the country, a little pocket of maladjusted extremists here or there, seemed to demand it.

Hael, who never expected a surge of interest about her book, published by an obscure little press out of Maine, never took calls from the press and begged everyone to keep things under wraps. "This is not the sort of thing we want to make public until we've really got a strong base." In a recent step to address these issues, she had banded together with Ray on his latest performance piece. Set up as a pastiche loosely based on the experiences within the community, it was scheduled to debut in late fall and would be followed by a spring tour.

"Hello, gorgeous!" cried Sunny from the balcony of her rental condo when Gretchen and Ray stepped from the car with little M16 in tow. She was four floors up and wearing a loud turquoise muumuu with what looked like peach jellyfish all over it. She waved frantically and raised a glass. "Room four-fourteen," she called over the railing. "Just tell the door guy you're with me."

Ray took Gretchen's hand and smiled sheepishly. His head, recently shaved to mirror hers, now looked like a foreign bulb, a strange thistle she did not quite know whether to touch. She had loved his long hair so much, its deep shade and soft girlishness. It was the first thing she'd noticed about him, seeing him across the room, his back turned. She'd been almost surprised when he whirled around to reveal a face with a beard.

M16 hung by Gretchen's leg, one hand on her shoulder bag. "Now can I play with it?" the little mouth asked as they crossed the parking lot.

"Just a minute," said Gretchen. "We're going to meet Ray's mother." Then she added, "Our baby's granny."

"What's a granny?" asked M16 as they passed the doorman in the lobby. Gretchen furrowed her brow. She'd forgotten that M16 had no contact with the parents of Glyn and Hael, and now she felt guilty for bringing it up. "It's nothing, sweetie," she said as she nudged M16 into the elevator.

Ray gave Gretchen a tight smile, then leaned down and wiped his brow with the flap of his sarong. "I have to pee" was all he said.

"Why are you acting so nervous?"

Ray shrugged.

"Look, if your mother's a pill, we'll just leave," Gretchen whispered, her voice matter-of-fact.

"She won't be a pill, I promise," Ray said. He shifted nervously from one foot to the other. "It's just that there's a lot happening, and I'm tired."

Gretchen put her arm around him. He'd been practicing his new show with Hael sometimes late into the night, trying to get as much done as possible before the birth. Despite her own discomfort, she tried to be sensitive.

The elevator doors parted, and down the hall a door flew open to reveal Ray's mother in all her glory — a tall, angular woman, whippet thin, with red spiky hair and freckled arms glittering with bangles.

"Granny!" cried M16 joyously. Sunny looked from Ray to Gretchen to M16 as if she didn't know whom to hug first, then commenced weeping. "Oh, oh, this is too much," she cried. "And this must be Gretchen, and, Ray, you look so handsome, darling — come here and let me kiss you. And now who is this little wonderbug?"

M16 stepped forward proudly. "I'm M16. Don't ask me what that means!"

Sunny bent over to shake the small pink hand, then scooped the whole bundle up in her arms and carried M16 through the doorway and into the living room. It was then that Gretchen noticed Sunny's muumuu — it wasn't covered in jellyfish at all; it was printed with little fetuses, jumbo-headed, snail-shaped fetuses. It was both too awful and too good to be true.

The condo was airy and empty except for two curvaceous hot pink couches in front of a white tile fireplace. On the mantel there was a row of fertility dolls. "Magnificent, isn't it?" crowed Sunny over her shoulder. "We're renting from two lesbian obstetricians."

Sunny deposited a giggling M16 on one of the couches and scuttled off to the kitchen, beckoning wildly with one of her gilded arms. "You like smoothies? Klaus makes the most fabulous smoothies."

In the kitchen, which was lilac with scrumptious pewter cabinet knobs, a lean hairless man with a Florida tan worked the blender.

"And this is Klaus, of course," cried Sunny, swooping down to pick two tall glasses off the marble counter and press them into Gretchen and Ray's hands. "You're going to love these," she said with a titter, "and if you don't, well, we can just toss them over the balcony or something." She stepped back to watch their faces as Gretchen and Ray stood in the middle of the kitchen, gulping. "Oh, my." Sunny clapped her hands together. "Isn't this wonderful? I've been so excited about coming here I even had this special outfit made." She curtsied.

"I love it," Gretchen gushed. She felt suddenly overcome with emotion. "I wish my mother would come up with stuff like that."

"I'm touched." Sunny chuckled, her bright eyes twinkling. She was darkly complected with a warm, weathered face and long manicured fingers she kept rubbing together. "This baby is going to have one wacky granny!" she roared, forcing a coffee-colored nail into the air. "But that's only because this granny is so overwhelmed with happiness." She fanned her face and dabbed at the corners of her eyes, using the edge of her wide sleeve.

"I want a granny," called M16, jumping up and down on the couch. "Please, please."

Gretchen reached into her bag and passed M16 the Barbie.

"Oooo," cooed M16. "I love this granny."

*   *   *

Out on the balcony, Sunny ushered Gretchen to a patio chair and pushed a footstool under her legs, giggling to herself and snapping her fingers as things occurred to her. "You need anything" — she snapped — "you just tell me, and it's done." She gave a quick little shrug and sat down, crossing her legs. "Any worries" — she snapped again — "you just ask Klaus. He's a doctor — was a doctor. He gives a great massage." She winked and took a sip of her smoothie.

Klaus, who was bronze and boyish, even in his seventies, gave a monkish nod as he came out onto the patio. His chest and thighs glistened as if from health. He wore satiny blue running shorts with the waist pulled up high. *These two will be good for Judy and Rusty*, Gretchen thought.

"Listen" — Sunny leaned forward and, as if she had channeled Gretchen's thoughts, said, "I'd like to propose a little dinner party. All of us and your parents — what do you think? A sort of prepartum party, a mixer. I'm thinking kabobs, I'm thinking strawberry daiquiris, a prebirthday cake." She leaned back in her chair and folded her hands in her lap. "Or not — you know, we can go with the flow."

"Actually —" Ray said from the doorway, a note of protest in his voice.

"I think it sounds wonderful," said Gretchen. "And I hope you'll wear that muumuu again."

"I loved the baby lady," said M16 on the way home.

It was dusk and the sun coming through the leaves struck Gretchen as golden and magical. "Your mother is wonderful," she said, reaching her hand out to cover Ray's, which was clamped over the truck's gearshift.

"Maybe," said Ray. "We'll see."

Later that evening, Judy called. "Ray's mother is such a dear," she said to Gretchen. "She invited us to a party. I'm supposed to bring deviled eggs. It's a prepartum party — isn't that cute? Everything is going to be birth-oriented, even the food." Judy giggled.

"I thought we were having kebabs," Gretchen said.

"Oooh, I doubt that, not at a party for a baby. Those sticks are choking hazards."

"Mom." Gretchen paused. "How are you and Dad doing?" She added "with things" when she sensed a long pause coming. Gretchen was lying in bed with a pillow under her knees. Next to her, Ray snoozed naked, the breeze from the rotating fan ruffling his chest hair.

"Oh, it'll be fine," Judy said. "How are you feeling?"

"Easy breezy," Gretchen said. "I'm feeling more relaxed by the day." She was sewing a seam on a little black onesie. The fan made it flutter like a bat. "I never got to ask you about Henry's visit," Gretchen said. "I thought he and the band were going to spend the night."

"Oh, you know," Judy babbled brightly. "They had to push off sooner than they realized. I'm just glad that he even thought to stop by and see us."

"He's wanted to come home for a while," Gretchen ventured, licking her finger as she rethreaded her needle. "Especially now that things are happening for him. He's got a new song that's making the charts. He finally feels like he's worth something."

Judy was quiet.

"If you showed some interest, Mom," Gretchen went on. "He feels a lot of remorse about how he left."

More silence.

"I think both he and Carson would come visit if Dad wouldn't act like such an ogre." Gretchen sewed drowsily, aware suddenly of the clock and the dark night behind the window screens. From somewhere outside, she heard a little voice cry, "I want a granny."

In her dimly lit kitchen, Judy stared down into the pot on the stove, where she was boiling eggs. Bubbles gathered at the water's surface, rising from the shells. The eggs knocked together like something tapping to be let out. Judy lowered the flame and stood over the stove in her robe, letting the steam dampen her face. "If you showed some interest," she heard Gretchen say, replaying the conversation in her mind. "If Dad wouldn't act like such an ogre."

Beyond the kitchen door, in the dark of the garage, Rusty was sitting in his car, Judy knew. All day he'd sat out there, smoking cigars, listening to talk radio. She wondered if Henry's song ever came on, what his voice would sound like through the speakers — a voice that had come out of her, now rippling through static, playing back to her that first primal cry in the birthing room.

Judy sighed. Why hadn't she taken an interest? From the first moment Henry announced that he was saving for a guitar with the money from his paper route, she'd bristled. And when he began practicing in the basement, his voice wailing through the vents, she'd always found a reason to leave the house. Before that, there had been Carson's crooning falsetto, a sound she loved, the mornings she awoke to him practicing his warm-ups, like an angel calling her from sleep. Those had been sweeter days, she reasoned, the whole family together.

Then the angel he was disappeared, her dear blond boy. One

morning, the house silent, no voice in the vents, just Rusty breathing beside her. She'd crept to the top of the basement stairs, waited, her breath already tightening in her chest. Step by step, she'd descended, feeling a heaviness enter her feet, a heaviness that had still not left.

The air in the basement was still, both bedroom doors closed. *Please let him be sleeping*, she thought as she gripped the knob to Carson's room, pressing her forehead to the door. But his room was empty, the bed made, the walls padded with neat rows of bright, square rugs — a patchwork of hearts and stars, flowers and birds, forest scenes and still lifes of fruit. And there, on the floor by his twin bed, was a new rug, his final yarn opus. From a cream background, two faces stared up at her. The face on the right was an image of Rusty, his narrow eyes woven in angry yellow; his mouth, bent into a frown at the corners, was open with a snake slithering out. Judy shuddered. To the left was a woman in profile, red lips pursed, eyes closed. Above the heads, black yarn formed the words *Who are these people?*

Over and over, Judy read the words, studied the faces, her head shaking. An ache started at the back of her throat and moved, like vines, down through her knees and ankles. While the rest of the house slept, Judy crept out the back door and stuffed the rug into one of the trash cans behind the house, struggling to close the lid, fighting back tears.

Back inside, she'd pulled Carson's door closed and swore never to think of the rug again, to void it from her mind. Only then did she realize she was standing by his door, eyes closed, lips pursed.

The steam from the eggs was becoming more than Judy could stand. Her face and neck were wet, her cheeks burning. Below her, six eggs sat perfectly still in the water. One by one, she lifted them out with a slotted spoon and placed them gingerly in the deep pockets of her robe — three in one pocket, three in the other — then opened the door to the garage and stood in the doorway.

The air was thick with smoke, the windows to the car all open. No sound. "If you showed some interest," she heard Gretchen say.

"Rusty?" Judy called into the cloudy dark. In a far corner, she could just make out last year's Christmas tree, its glinting ornaments still stuck to the plastic needles. "Rusty," she said again, her voice just above a whisper. "There's something I have to tell you."

Rusty sat in the driver's seat, eyes closed. His hands were folded over his stomach, his head bent low, but Judy could tell he was not asleep. His cigar, resting in an old metal soap dish on the dash, was still aglow.

Judy rounded the front of the car and opened the passenger-side door, frowning distastefully at the smell. She slid into the seat carefully, the eggs jostling in her pockets, then pulled the door closed.

"I'm done talking," Rusty said thinly.

Judy leaned forward and turned the knob to the radio. "Then it's time we listen."

Chapter 11

THE PARTY

In the morning, Gretchen awoke from an intense kick. She touched her belly and drew her knees inward to pacify the being inside. No luck. It thumped like something caught in a trap. Gretchen sat up on her elbow and put her hand on Ray's sleeping chest, letting her fingers wander through the dark forest that had seeded itself across his sternum and down his midriff. *What if,* she thought, *this baby comes out like a little hairy Ray?* She laughed to herself, then realized it was the first time she had ever pictured the child as a particular sex. Until now, it had always been just that: an itty-bitty it-child. As she had sewed up the black onesies and even readied the second bedroom with a fresh coat of muted loden and a changing table from Hael made of pickled birch with a gray changing pad, she had never given any thought to the fact that this child really would be a male or female, even if its identity would be shielded from others during its early childhood years.

That seemed weird, newly and oddly. For a fleeting moment, she wondered if she could hold on to such a big secret for such a long time. What if she let it slip? Then what? Hael had assured her that once she got into the rhythm of it, she'd forget — change the diapers, pat the back, with no real consideration of it one way or another. Of course, there would be inherent challenges. You couldn't really ask someone to babysit for long periods of time or depend on someone outside the community to change a diaper, not without swearing them to secrecy. And even then you put all of your trust in their hands. Outside of the community, it was a no-man's-land. You were an anomaly, you and your mystery child.

And later on — what then? How might this child adapt to society? When it realized it had been raised differently from other kids, would it rebel? Would it develop some bizarre scar, a repressed sensibility? Would it function normally?

The ceiling above Gretchen seemed too bright, the thin bedsheet too heavy. She pushed it back and closed her eyes — this was just anxiety. Hael had warned her of this. Hael's own parents had been relentless with their questions until she simply cut them off, leaving their phone calls unreturned, their letters unopened. Glyn's parents were so horrified that they asked him not to speak to them until he was ready to act like a normal human being. Gretchen drew strength from these stories. It was possible to start anew, possible to divorce yourself from such scrutiny with the help of an accepting community. She felt lucky, so lucky now to be living here in this place, according to her will. She felt sure she was doing the right thing and secure that no one and nothing could undermine it.

Even Henry had said, "Wow, you're — wow — you're my hero."

There was a knock at the front door. Ray stirred but did not open his eyes. Gretchen grabbed on to the edge of the bedside table and hoisted herself up off the futon. She lumbered through the living room, where the shades were still drawn, and opened the door.

Hael stood there in a black bathrobe, her eyes pink-rimmed and puffy. "I had to come see you." She hiccupped. "We were up half the night with M16 crying out for a granny."

Gretchen pressed her lips together and stepped back. Hael shuffled into the kitchen and sank down into a chair, plunking her elbows on the table. "So you know what I did this morning?" She looked up at Gretchen, who ran a hand over her belly as she moved toward the stove. "I got on the phone and I called Glyn's parents and I called my parents." She paused. "I told them the kids want to meet their grandparents."

"Wow." Gretchen spooned some loose tea into cups from a mason jar and put on her teakettle.

"Glyn is furious with me, but I had to do it. I mean, M16 wants grandparents, and I just feel terrible for depriving the kids of a relationship with them."

"Wow," Gretchen said again, sitting down at the other end of the table. She bit her lip.

"I mean, what were we thinking? What were we thinking we'd tell the kids — that we came from outer space? That we had no parents, no siblings? They would have figured it out sooner or later and then resented us for not telling them the truth. I mean, isn't that just the saddest thing you've ever heard — a kid crying out in bed for a grandmother? It really crushes me. I feel like I've gone about this all wrong." Hael withdrew a Kleenex from the pocket of her robe and pressed it to her eyes. "I've been so obsessed with my own ways of parenting that I've completely deprived them of an extended family."

"Listen." Gretchen extended her hand to Hael, then drew it suddenly back to her tummy. "Ow. It's really active in the mornings."

Hael smiled weakly. "I really admire you and Ray . . ." — she sobbed a little — "for not giving up on your families. At some point we've got to acknowledge what we're doing here, that it's pretty far out." She sniffed. "We can't expect everyone to embrace it."

Gretchen nodded and continued to rub her belly. She had one hope just then, and one hope only — that her water wouldn't break that night at Sunny's birth party.

That evening, Gretchen tried on different balloonish black and brown dresses, then dug through the bag she'd prepared for the hospital and pulled out an oversize black T-shirt and Ray's rainbow sarong. *Go bright,* she thought. *Why not?* When Ray came out of the bathroom in jeans and a light sweater, she swatted him with a towel. "Be more fun," she teased.

"I don't feel like fun," he said. "Mind if I do a few stretches before we leave?"

Gretchen followed him into the living room and over to his mat. "What's the matter?" She swayed over him, adjusting the sarong around her belly. "You've acted strange ever since your mother arrived."

"Too much family," he said. "Makes me edgy." He rolled onto his stomach and went into a camel pose.

"Well, I think it's great." Gretchen crossed her arms. "I think you've just got stage fright."

Ray breathed.

"You're spending too much time working. You need to relax, have fun with this." She nudged him with a toe.

"You're so carefree?" Ray unfurled. "A month ago you stormed out of the house because I invited Sunny to the birth."

"It was an enlightened decision on your part."

Ray gripped her ankle. "Get down on the floor with me."

"You'll be responsible for pulling me back up," she warned, grimacing.

"Done and done," he said.

This time when they pulled up to Sunny's condo, Judy was on the balcony to wave at them. "Hello down there," she called, one hand cupped around her mouth. "You're not going to believe your eyes when you get to the top of the stairs," she bellowed.

"Is she drunk?" Gretchen murmured, shielding her face to look up at Judy, who leaned precariously over the railing.

"It looks like she's got on my mother's muumuu," said Ray. He gave Gretchen a wink and took her hand.

"What do you think they've got planned up there?" Gretchen waddled along with her hand on the knot of her sarong, conscious that at any moment it might come loose.

"If it's like any of my mother's parties," Ray said, "it will be a little over the top."

Gretchen shrugged.

"It might even be *very* over the top."

The doorman greeted them with a teasing grin. "I know just where you're headed. Have a beautiful night." He tipped his cap. Gretchen felt him watching them all the way to the elevator.

Up four floors and *ka-ching,* the metal doors parted. Gretchen stepped out, looked down the hall toward 414 and stopped short. "Oh, my God," she said, "is that what I think it is?"

The doorway to 414 was surrounded with a ring of black faux fur, and the door itself was painted to look like a very abstract pink flower. From the other side of the door a voice sang out, "Come into the living womb!"

Ray shook his head and reached forward to take the knob.

"Wait," Gretchen said. "I just want to stand in this moment. This . . ." — she paused — "is so great."

"Surprise!" Sunny cried out when they opened the door a moment later. She and Judy bounded forward in identical muumuus, tossing up handfuls of red confetti. Gretchen stepped back, startled and giggling. "You guys are wild," she said.

"This is a little weird, frankly, Mother," Ray said, his voice dour.

"Come here, baby," Sunny said, grabbing her son by the shoulders and maneuvering him into the kitchen as if she were pushing a shopping cart. "Let's get a drink into you." She pressed a smoothie into his hands and plunged a straw into it. A tiny plastic baby was glued near the top.

After a moment, Judy drew up to Gretchen's side, her face flushed. "I'm having the best time," she gushed. Then she whispered, "I've been here all day. It was my idea to decorate the door like a vagina." Judy wrung her hands and went from flushed in the cheeks to a full-on blush from the neck up.

Gretchen caught herself on a sleek iron bookshelf to keep from toppling over in shock. "You?"

Judy nodded to one side, then the other, as if to a small crowd around her feet. "Well" — she waved a hand — "Sunny did most of it." She hiccupped, then broke into a full round of nervous giggles.

Gretchen caught sight of Rusty standing alone in the far corner of the room with a beer. He was facing a row of long windows that overlooked the lake. Without seeing his face, Gretchen read his scowl.

"What's with Dad?" she asked her mother.

Judy shook her head and batted at the air with both hands as if she were dispersing flies. "Oh, I don't know. Probably just grouchy. He just got here and has hardly said hello to anyone."

"You drove down here separately?"

Judy shrugged but offered no explanation.

"Well, I hope he doesn't try to drive home by himself too late. He can barely see." She furrowed her brow, rubbing one arm absentmindedly.

"Listen," Judy said casually, leaning in close. "Let's both just have a good time, shall we?"

"Dad." Gretchen reached around her belly to give Rusty a hug and was surprised when she met his eyes by how sunken his face looked. His hair looked strangely straggly — not that he had much up there but a patchy gray nest, but he had always been extremely fastidious about cutting it; now it wisped out over his ears. It was only a matter of weeks since she'd seen him, and already he seemed to have changed, or maybe it was just more obvious here by the window with the clean light coming off the lake.

"Hey," he said. His voice sounded forcibly cheerful as he patted Gretchen's back.

"Have you lost weight, Dad?" Gretchen asked.

"Aww, it's nothing," he said. It was his old firm tone. "Looks like you're gaining for me."

"Tell me." She swayed in place. "I feel like I could pop and drop it any minute." Then she took his hand. "Come on in the kitchen. Have you met everyone?"

"I'm good here." Rusty stood firm, raised his beer. "Just enjoying the view of the water."

"So you've met Klaus?" Gretchen asked, looking up to see Judy spinning out of the kitchen with a plate of what looked like deviled eggs. There was music playing, and Judy seemed to know the words.

"Is this Cat Stevens?" Gretchen asked Rusty.

"Hell if I know," Rusty said under his breath. "Maybe."

"I'm surprised Mom knows the words. I don't think I've ever seen her sing along to music."

Rusty sat back against one of the couches and slung his arm over a pink cushion. "It's her new thing," he said. "Last night she forced me to listen to the radio with her in the car."

Gretchen put a finger to her lips, then bent over to speak in his ear. "Promise not to be a crank tonight. Sunny and Klaus are really nice."

Rusty just raised his eyebrows and gave Gretchen a quick two-fingered salute.

Out on the balcony, Gretchen was surprised to find Klaus manning the grill in khaki shorts and what looked like plastic breasts under his apron.

"*Hej,*" he said to Gretchen, offering a too-bright smile that revealed two lines of long, thin teeth. "That's 'hello' in Swedish."

"Ahhh." Gretchen leaned against the balcony and set her feet together. "What about that getup there? A little Nordic fetish?"

Klaus pulled aside his chef's apron to reveal a jumbo rubber breast with a garishly painted nipple. "Just for parties," he said, bobbing his head happily.

Judy swung out in her muumuu, holding what Gretchen was glad to see looked like a glass of water. "Have you checked out the hors d'oeuvres?" Judy asked, pointing to the patio table behind Klaus. The tablecloth was fashioned out of the same material as the muumuus and tied at the corners with pacifiers. There was a platter of raw veggies with dip served in baby-food jars, a tray of Judy's deviled eggs with tiny cutouts of baby faces stuck to tooth-picks, and to top it all, some sort of molded shrimp dip in the shape of an infant sucking its thumb.

"Sunny really knows how to throw a party," Judy said, stabbing at the molded infant's foot with a knife and smearing it onto an oval cracker.

"Okay, everybody!" Sunny's cry came from the kitchen, and the next minute she poked her head out onto the balcony, her mouth wide open to reveal all her bottom teeth carpeted in gold fillings. "Is everyone ready for their baby bib?" She closed her jaws and bestowed her best coral smile on Gretchen. "I'm just kidding, honey, but I do have champagne" — and here she thrust an arm out from behind her — "in a bottle!"

Sunny hooted at her own joke and clapped a hand to her chest. "You first," she said, extending a big white baby bottle to Gretchen. "Just a sip."

"I'm still nursing my smoothie."

"Ha! Great pun. She's one of us!" Sunny spun around, carrying the bottle high up in the air, and marched to the table as if she were leading millions.

Gretchen exchanged glances with her mother and smiled, pleased by the general spirit of gaiety, even if Sunny was begin-ning to get just a teensy-weensy bit on her nerves. When she en-tered the living room, she was glad to see Ray and her father sitting together on the couch by the window.

At dinner Gretchen sat across from her mother, remarking to her-self on Judy's easygoing yet chatty edge. When had she become so bearable, even a little spunky? she wondered. She couldn't re-member the last time she'd been around her parents someplace other than their sobering living room with the odious pheasant couch and the TV going full volume. Get them out of that clam-shell, and they acted almost like human beings. It was amazing.

To complete her party theme, Sunny served skewers of grilled baby vegetables, mixed baby greens, and baby loaves of corn bread. "Everything's darling," Judy cooed. "I've never had such delicious vegetarian food."

"Actually, it's all vegan," Sunny said, beaming. "Klaus can't di-gest dairy. It makes his stomach bloat."

Rusty's ears perked up. "Is that right?" It was the first time he had spoken.

"Good Lord, when I met Klaus he ate any old thing he pleased and weighed about sixty pounds more, all gut. The first thing I did was get him on some Pro-Shape vitamins and a weight-loss plan."

"I feel great." Klaus thrust his fork in the air and flashed his crocodile smile.

Rusty leaned in on his forearms, listening intently. He cleared his throat. "Pro-Shape vitamins? You just pick those up at the store?"

"Nope." Sunny popped a tiny carrot between her lips and smiled coyly. She chewed slowly and deliberately, her eyes locked with Rusty's. After a dramatic swallow, she said, in a voice that was stunningly casual, "Can I tell you something that will change your life?"

"Mom." Ray let his fork drop to his plate and put both hands squarely on the edge of the table. "If you start in with the sales shtick, I won't forgive you."

Sunny looked hurt for a brief moment, then emitted a low

laugh. "Don't be silly. We're having a nice dinner." She leaned toward him. "Relax."

Ray flared his nostrils, something he was famously good at, and picked up his fork to stab a fingerling potato. Gretchen put a hand on his leg under the table.

"I'm an independent contractor for Pro-Shape," Sunny offered sweetly to Rusty. "I can tell you about it at a more convenient time." She raised her glass and offered everyone around the table a festive smile.

"That'd be great," Rusty said, spearing a mini-ear of corn and giving it serious consideration.

"I can honestly say that Pro-Shape saved my life," Klaus offered.

"He's right," Sunny couldn't help but interject. "Before taking Pro-Shape, Klaus was lethargic and sedentary. But now" — she looked lovingly at Klaus — "he's got so much stamina, and it's all because of Pro-Shape smoothies. All you do is mix a little Pro-Shape with some ice and fruit juice, and, well, it's even had an effect on our sex life."

Here Judy burst into seismic giggles. Ray stood up, throwing his napkin toward a centerpiece of miniature roses.

"Oh, come on, Ray," Gretchen whispered, tugging at his arm.

"I've said all I'm going to say." Sunny held up both her palms. "Honest, really."

Ray watched her carefully, then slowly sank back to his chair and resumed eating. He wasn't seated for a minute, though, before Klaus, who had gotten up to pour another round of wine, bent down between Rusty and Judy with some Chablis and said, "I've even tried Viagra, and I tell you, this stuff whips the pants off it — plus you lose weight."

"Imagine, it's like an aphrodisiac and a PowerBar all rolled into one," Sunny whispered across the table, using the back of her hand.

Ray was gone. He made no noise in leaving, no sound as he drew the screen door to the balcony across its track. Gretchen turned in her chair to watch him at the railing. The city was dark. She could barely make out his shape against the sky.

"Ohhh," Sunny moaned. "I've ruined everything."

"I'll talk to him." Gretchen pushed her chair back and prepared to hoist herself up.

"It's my fault." Rusty stood and started for the balcony before anyone could protest.

There was silence at the table. The black candles around the centerpiece flickered. Sunny just smiled apologetically. Judy twirled some beads around her neck and sipped from her wineglass thoughtfully. For the first time, Gretchen noticed, her mother wasn't wearing bright red lipstick. Her lips looked mysteriously pale and supple, a little purplish in places from the wine, as if she had dabbed on a little black lipstick.

Judy caught Gretchen's eye and fingered her upper lip self-consciously.

"Is he always this touchy?" Sunny pushed her plate away and leaned her elbows on the table.

Gretchen frowned. "He's been rehearsing a lot," she said. "The show he's putting on in a few weeks has him feeling really pressed for time, especially with the baby."

"I think he's gestating his own little pet peeve," said Sunny, reaching for the champagne bottle. She lifted it over the mini-roses and sipped delicately but noisily from the nipple.

Gretchen looked over at her father's plate and noticed he had hardly eaten a thing. She stabbed at his baby greens and ate them hungrily.

"Dammit!" Sunny's hand crashed to the table suddenly. "I knew I forgot something."

Gretchen jumped. "Jeez, Sunny," she said, rubbing her belly.

Only Judy seemed not to notice. She rested her chin in her hand. "I like wine," she said to nobody. "I didn't used to."

"I meant to pack Ray's baby pictures," Sunny said, offering a melt-away smile. She put a hand over her mouth and said to Gretchen, "He was *soooo* cute, *soooo* hairy. Like a little gorilla, really. I mean, it was unbelievable, the hair." She clapped a hand to her chest. "Of course, it all fell out later, but I couldn't give him the name I'd picked out. Not with all that hair — no way."

Gretchen tried not to appear shaken. "I didn't know babies could be covered in hair."

"Most aren't," hooted Sunny, "but your Ray there, he looked like a little baboon." Sunny broke into a fit of giggles. Rusty stepped up to the screen from the balcony and looked in at the table to see what was going on, then turned away. Klaus just sat and smiled, working a toothpick over his teeth.

"Well, my goodness," Sunny went on, "I was all set to call him Abe, you know, but of course I couldn't, I was afraid, you know, that people would take one look at him and call him 'Ape.'"

"Oh, goodness," murmured Judy absentmindedly, pressing at her upper lip with the tips of her fingers.

Gretchen closed her eyes briefly, wincing as the baby kicked.

"The nurses, well, they'd never seen anything like it. I mean, it was like he came out in a little costume, hair from head to toe." Sunny gestured with her hands, gushing giggles, then, sensing Gretchen's discomfort, changed the subject. "Do you and Ray have names picked out, or shouldn't I ask?"

"We have a name in mind," Gretchen said.

"Alex or Chris would work," offered Judy, cocking her head

across the table, suddenly alert. "But I suppose you've thought of those since they work both ways. I had a Jamie in one of my classes — she was a girl. And there was a boy once named Kelly."

"Mother, I didn't know you were giving this so much consideration."

Judy blushed. "I have a pretty good baby book."

"How about we clear these plates and have some cake," Sunny chirped, standing up. She rolled her eyes at Gretchen as if to commiserate about Judy's names, then started loading her arm with dishes.

"Don't forget, Judy," Sunny called over her shoulder. "We're going to share birth stories over dessert."

Between courses, Gretchen took the opportunity to rejoin Ray while Rusty used the bathroom. She sidled up to him by the railing and looked out over the city. "Feel," she said, putting a hand on her belly. "It's really at it in there."

"It's probably trying to stomach the present company." Ray rolled his eyes and tossed a glance over his shoulder toward the kitchen.

"They're trying," Gretchen said. "This is a really nice party."

"I don't want any of them at the birth," Ray said, looking out. "I think we should go with your original plan."

"Lighten up." Gretchen rubbed his shoulder. "It's going to be fine."

"Those dresses, the food — my mother makes a mockery out of everything." Ray pressed his fingertips into his temples and exhaled deeply. "And her stupid sales pitches. She's got to act out an infomercial anytime she's got company."

"Ray, everyone's got their thing," Gretchen urged him softly. "Look at us, we've got ours, too. I'd say everyone's doing pretty well, considering what we've asked them to be a part of."

"You watch," Ray said, fuming. "My mother will show up while you're in labor and recruit for Amway in the waiting room."

"Ray." Gretchen cocked her head to the side. "Was it true you were born looking like a little baboon?" She giggled and tugged his ear. "I wish you'd grow your hair out again. I liked it all over me in bed."

Ray sighed and gave her forehead a kiss. Gretchen closed her eyes and felt a surge of love — not just for Ray but for all of them. Tipsy Judy. Sulky Rusty. Nutty Sunny. Even Crocodile Klaus. She felt grateful for all of them, for their idiosyncratic affection, for their disparate moods and their unpredictable natures that, in some unspoken way, allowed her to explore her newfangled identity as partner to Ray, as mother to the yet unborn Baby X.

Who would it be, this little masterpiece conceived in that dark winter room below her parents' footsteps nine months earlier, there in that pink-ruffled setting that had once been her pod, her shell, a sort of ongoing womb?

Now she was an igloo. Now she contained all of it, was its house, its rind, its reigning mind. But very shortly — indeed, any second — it would free itself and become someone else, a separate venture, its own capsule of stars, a legion of cells grafted to the core of the universe. It would be so small and yet so staggeringly large. It would be, Gretchen thought, perfect.

And in that moment, under the portentous glint of Pluto and above the lapping shore of Lake Michigan bathed in city lights, Gretchen's water broke.

Chapter 12

IN THE WAITING ROOM

In the hospital waiting room, two sets of future grandparents sat watching the nightly news, Judy and Sunny, in their muumuus, listlessly flipping through magazines, Rusty and Klaus sitting stiffly with their hands on their knees. Gretchen and Ray had been admitted to a birthing room, and Ray had given explicit instructions that no one should come near.

At eleven, she was four centimeters dilated, and the heads of the late-night talk show hosts appeared — giant faces that filled the screen with their own self-important laughter. Rusty shifted his weight in the utilitarian chair, trying to find a comfortable way to lean on the wooden armrests. "Still can't beat Carson," he offered to no one in particular.

Judy looked over at him and drew her brows into a line. Rusty saw the flicker in her eye, not of the TV's reflection but of the name he had uttered for the first time in fifteen years. Something in his belly sent a searing pain down into his groin. He shifted his weight to the other side of his chair and closed his eyes.

"Johnny Carson?" barked Sunny. "I don't think I ever missed a Carson show, except when I was meditating."

Rusty kept his eyes closed. He was both remembering and trying not to remember. In his mind, he traveled back to the night Carson was born. How enthralled he'd been at the sight of his second son, the bright eyes, the small fists. The birth of his first son had been something of a blur; he'd been all nerves. But Carson's birth had elicited an immediate, visceral reaction. He wept on and off for hours, then went home and slept alone, feeling so lucky, so endowed with life. Two sons — who could ask for more? An only child himself, he was touched deeply about bringing a second child into the world.

It made him love Judy more, even like himself more. To be part of such creation struck him as staggering, and for a while there, he wanted nothing more. He worked extra hard to insure the future of his family, sold more cars, spruced up the lot that once belonged to his father, and donated a Pinto to a raffle for the hospital on Carson's first birthday.

As his young sons became boys, he seemed unable to take his eyes off them. They were a part of him and they were growing, and through them he saw himself coming into the world for a second time. It was a bold thing, a heavy thing, to regard your sons in this way and then to observe as they turned into people so unlike you. If they had been female, it would have been different, he supposed, but with his boys, he expected to see a mirror image. He expected them to take an interest in all the things he loved — fixing cars, hunting, rejoicing in the hot curve of a baseball in summer.

But of course, it wasn't so. Henry cried out for a baby guitar from the first instant he could talk, and Carson stared enthralled from his crib when Judy would sit in his room at night and sew, singing softly to him from her neat red lips. It was Judy that Carson admired. Rusty had looked on and known a kind of jealousy — the way Carson curled up in Judy's lap, the way he sucked his thumb and twisted a lock of her hair around his finger at night, the way he studied her earrings, fascinated by anything sparkly. But when he'd wanted to dress up in Judy's shoes, try on her lipstick, Rusty had insisted it stop there. It was too much like watching himself do those things, like seeing his own feet jammed into Judy's small shoes, and for no other reason than pride, those things offended him deeply.

As his boys grew bigger, Rusty felt himself grow smaller, pulling away. He retreated from Judy, though it wasn't her fault the children didn't take after him. There were nights when he felt like an outsider when he moved through the house, hearing the music behind Henry's door, watching Carson bent over his latch hook on the floor. Rusty would leave the house, sit in his car, sometimes even start it up on the pretense of leaving for good. Instead he usually stopped over to see if Donald wanted to take a drive, and as the car careened out of town, he would confess, "I feel like an alien. There are days I do not, cannot, love my children anymore."

"Bah," Donald would always say. "It's just the age."

Rusty had nodded, had waited for the phase to pass as the moon phased in and out of wholeness and slivers, but, give or take a day here and there, he felt only disappointment. Sometimes when he drank a few beers, he thought back to that early morning in Philadelphia when he found the stranger at his table eating breakfast. Rusty would hear him apologize, see him reach for the picture of his little son. "Someday, you could be in my shoes, man," the stranger had said, "with no idea why your life has slipped away from you."

"Impossible," Rusty had fired back, insulted.

It had cursed him, Rusty decided. He still carried the little boy's picture in his wallet, folded twice and tucked deep in a leathery corner — once a memento, now a reminder.

"I'm heading out," Rusty said now, addressing the other faces in the flickering light of the waiting room.

"Now?" Judy asked. It was the first time in two weeks that she had spoken to him directly with any gentleness in her voice.

Rusty turned and paused to try to think of something clever to say, but after a few moments passed, all he said was "I need some rest."

It wasn't true — he wasn't the least bit tired, but sitting in the waiting room, chewing on his thoughts was only making him sink deeper into a place where he knew he did not want to touch bottom. He started for the door and, beyond it, the dull glow of the hallway.

"Wait!" It was Sunny who caught his arm. She dug down into her purse and thrust a small white bottle into his fist. "Here are some of those vitamins."

Rusty nodded in thanks. In the hall the lights were dim. Women in various shades of blue scrubs passed him like fast-moving weather patterns. He thought he could hear Gretchen cry out from behind a heavy wooden door marked 1224, and he felt gripped for a moment, but then lumbered on.

He had no feelings about the baby on the way, not that he didn't want to feel something. He simply couldn't. Other than the weird rumblings in his stomach, he felt as dead as a bird. His heart felt as cold as the Deepfreeze in the basement. He hoped Judy would stay on for a few days in Chicago so that he could have the house to himself. He'd had visions of secretly moving out, of packing up his things and disappearing, maybe even selling his car lot — one of Donald's sons-in-law had expressed interest. It was time, and Judy would be glad to see him go. He only wished there was something he could offer her, some small gesture to compensate for the brute he'd been, and still was.

"I'm too wired to sleep," Judy confided to Sunny in the waiting room. In a dark corner, Klaus had shoved two chairs together and was snoring softly. The TV was mute. The one torchère lamp emitted an unrelenting buzz and a moonish halo. A nurse popped her head in to let them know there was fresh coffee in the kitchenette.

"Is there any word on Gretchen and Ray in twelve twenty-four?" demanded Sunny. "We're the future grandmothers."

"Afraid not. They've still got a ways to go." The nurse flashed them a gap-toothed smile and left.

Sunny crossed her legs and leaned over the armrest. She whispered, "Klaus thinks he may know their doctor from a conference. He thinks we can probably find out the sex."

Judy flinched. It had never occurred to her to attempt anything so sneaky. All these months she had been trying to prepare herself mentally to handle the great question of this child's mystery organs — the things she would say to the neighbors, the subtle machinations that would be required to hide not just the matter of the sex from them but the fact that there was any issue at all. It had caused her months of consternation. She had even considered telling everyone it was a girl, just to make it easier, and of course there was a fifty-fifty chance it would be. The only problem was that if down the road it were revealed that the child was a boy, she'd have some explaining to do.

But now Klaus and Sunny offered a clever plan. Would it be so bad if they knew, just for practical purposes? She could still play along with Gretchen and Ray. She would just have to be very careful in front of Gretchen not to let the actual pronoun slip. But she could hold her tongue easily enough. Rusty couldn't be trusted, that much she knew, but Judy felt she could incubate this secret for however long it was required of her, and she felt that just knowing, just being sure, would ease all her apprehension.

"That would be such a breach of confidence," she said slowly to Sunny. "I mean, I am dying to find out, but . . ." She tried to sound casual in case this was a trap.

"I already have my suspicions," Sunny said, crossing her freckled arms and scratching at a nonexistent fleck on the front of her dress. Then she turned and put one coffee-colored nail to her temple. She said, "I've been known to be psychic."

Judy licked her lips, newly aware that she'd forgotten to put on lipstick. "So I guess you've known all along, then. Why bother with the doctor?"

"Well, psychics can be wrong," Sunny said, her tone belying a hint of sarcasm.

Judy lowered her chin to her chest and looked straight ahead. Out of the corner of her mouth, she whispered, "So, which is it?"

"It's best if I don't say." Sunny shook her head. "Not until Klaus confirms."

Judy examined her hands, feigning interest in a cuticle. "Whatever you think," she said under her breath. "But we've got a long night ahead of us."

"I really shouldn't." Sunny gave Judy a pained look, then reached over to pat her hand. "Don't take it personal."

Judy gripped at the armrests and gave a few slow nods. The

blood was rushing at her temples. A hot flash was coming on. She said, "I think I'll change out of this dress."

"I'll go get us some coffee." Sunny launched herself forward from the chair. "Cream or sugar?"

"Just black," Judy said.

Judy gathered up her purse and tote bag and started down the hall. The bathroom was a sickening pink, the tiles old and grimy along the cracks. There was something about a hospital bathroom that kept her from having much confidence in all the hoopla about new medical discoveries. Screw the discoveries — didn't anyone who worked in health care know how to keep a bathroom?

She soaped her hands and avoided herself in the mirror. She had enough to think about. When her fingers touched the unmistakable round sheath of plastic she knew to be a tube of lipstick in the bottom of her purse, she took off the lid, scrolled up the nub, and applied color, eyes closed. Since the incident at school with the mustache, she had sworn off her reflection.

When she had changed out of her muumuu, Judy switched off the light and stood for a moment in the dark bathroom, glad for a moment to collect herself. Rusty had taken off, as was to be expected. And Sunny had proven to be more perplexing by the minute. Judy breathed deeply and tried not to imagine anything beyond the bathroom, not the next hour, not the next day or week. She was here, where she wanted to be.

A tentative voice from behind stopped Judy in the hall on her way back to the waiting room. "Mrs. Glide? I thought I might find you here." It was Hael. She had on black sweatpants and flip-flops. "I came as fast as I could. Have you heard how things are going?"

"No, no one's been allowed in the delivery room." Judy heard her words come out with a harsh ring she hadn't intended; something about seeing Hael made the hairs on her neck bristle.

"Still, it's nice to be here, I'm sure." Hael rested a cool hand on Judy's arm. "I'm really impressed that you and Gretchen were able to work out an arrangement. No one else where we live really has."

Judy flashed her a brief, faint smile. "And where are you headed? To the delivery room?" She tipped her head to the side and watched Hael twist a commemorative *Star Trek* key ring around a middle finger.

"I don't even want to go near the delivery room," Hael said, giggling. "Believe me, I spent plenty of time there. Actually, I came to check on you."

Judy wasn't sure whether she should feel grateful or offended. She stepped back, frowning.

"It's okay to feel uneasy." Hael swept a loose strand of hair behind her ear. "It's a really exciting time, and I'm sure you're going to feel the same curiosity all of us do and the same pressure to explain why we do what we do. But, Mrs. Glide" — Hael paused to press her lips together and look into Judy's eyes — "once you get used to seeing that baby without any sense of its sex, you're going to be surprised. You're going to realize that it doesn't matter, and that it's actually easier to express your true feelings without all that baggage, all those expectations."

Hael sighed and pressed her palms to her cheeks as if she could feel herself flushing. She was starting to get a little choked up. "I mean, have you ever tried that? Loving something for what it is, without judgment?" She stepped back, moved her fingertips to her lips, and whispered almost inaudibly, "It's awesome."

Judy licked her lips and blinked quickly. She had her tote in one hand, her purse in the other, and when Hael sprang forward and gave her a hug, Judy only lifted her arms awkwardly, afraid to let both bags go clattering to the ground.

"I'm sorry. I'm a bit of a mess," Hael said into Judy's ear. "I just got in touch with my parents. I haven't seen them in five years." She stepped back, sniffling, her dark hair shiny under the hall lights, her face washed out and blotchy. Then she asked, "Do you know how to get chocolate out of wool carpet? I've been on a ridiculous cleaning spree."

"Now there I can help you," Judy said, brightening. She motioned Hael into the waiting room. "Did you know I taught home ec for thirteen years?"

"Well, well, who is this?" Sunny appeared with two coffee mugs and set them down on the waiting room coffee table. "Hold on, I'm nuking a Danish."

When Sunny returned for a second time, Judy attempted an introduction. "This is Hael," she said. "Ray and Gretchen's upstairs neighbor."

"Oh, sure, you're one of them." Sunny's voice was clipped. She took her seat without giving Hael another look and busied herself with some napkins.

Hael just smiled. "It's nice of you to camp out," she said warmly, still standing. From the corner came a low snore from Klaus. "I'm sure your presence means a lot to Gretchen and Ray," she continued, nodding at Sunny.

"I'm here for my son," Sunny flared up. "And for Gretchen. But I'm not sure I like what the rest of you are all about."

"And what are we about?" Hael asked, quietly, calmly, firmly.

"I've followed gurus, been a part of what some people would

call cults. I see what's going on here." Sunny raised her coffee mug to her lips, her eyes set on Hael across the rim.

"There's no reason to get upset," Hael said. "You can ask me anything."

Sunny blew at her coffee and blinked furiously. She took a sip, then set her mug clumsily down on the table. Judy leaned forward to wipe up the spill.

"You're raising hermaphrodites," Sunny hissed. "That's why you're so secret about what the sex is. You're trying to start a new race."

"What?!" Judy cried.

"Oh, please." Hael put a hand on her hip, her car keys dangling from a single finger. "This isn't worth discussing."

"What's happening?" Klaus sat up in a daze from his makeshift bed in the corner. "Who's here?"

A nurse ducked in. "Shhh," she said. "This is a quiet floor after nine PM."

"It's true," Sunny spat. "I've read your books. Why don't you come clean?"

"What's the time?" asked Klaus. "Is the baby here?"

"I mean it," the nurse ducked in again. "You'll be asked to leave if I have to say another word."

Hael was already out the door, her flip-flops resounding softly all the way down the birthing wing.

Sunny was flustered. She grabbed her purse. "I need a Xanax," she said. "I don't know how else I'll get through this." She pawed at the contents of her big gold purse, then bustled over to the muted TV for some extra light.

Judy sat dumbfounded, mopping around the coffee cups though there were no more spills. What, she wondered, was a hermaphrodite?

"Oh my God!" Sunny shrilled. She turned to Judy in horror. "I gave your husband the wrong bottle! I gave him my Xanax instead of the vitamins."

Judy felt the blood go from her face. "What should I do?"

"He shouldn't be driving." Sunny waved her arms emphatically. "He shouldn't be going anywhere."

"Oh my God," Judy stood up. "He's a terrible driver as it is. He can hardly see."

She stood up, fumbled for her keys, and started down the hall. "Help," she called meekly, to no one in particular. A custodian pushed a mop and bucket at the end of the hallway. A cry rang out from behind closed doors, the unmistakable sound of something just born. Judy didn't have time to check if it was coming from room 1224.

It was two hours back to Fort Cloud. All along the highway, Judy kept her gaze darting between the shoulders. She looked in vain for Rusty's car, trying to remember the car's make, hoping he would have pulled over. It was red, that was all she knew — a Pontiac? A Chevrolet? For a car salesman's wife, she knew surprisingly little about automobiles, all those years of tuning it out.

And now he was out there somewhere, on the road or swerving off it, and she couldn't even phone the police to tell them whether he was in a Camero or a Chevelle. He hadn't looked well lately. She shouldn't have let him go. She should have insisted on driving down together, but they had spoken so seldom in the last several weeks. After Henry had come and gone, after she'd locked the door to the garage, Rusty had stayed out there every night, sleeping in the car, carrying half his clothes in the trunk, eating who knows what.

Now she scanned the shoulder for some sight of him. How cruel she had been. It would do her right if she found him by the side of the road bleeding from his nose and mouth. Maybe she deserved to live alone. The thought frightened her. She had never seriously considered what it would be like to live by herself, the house quiet except for her footsteps, the basement freezer devoid of snow, the sun rising and setting over Rusty's brown recliner, motionless. Granted, they slept in separate rooms, ate their meals alone, but at least they checked in on each other.

Even if he had taken to the garage, at least he was out there. He hadn't up and gone. She'd give him that. Had she ever loved him? Yes, she thought she had. He wasn't perfect, but she hadn't expected him to be. She just never imagined that being married could be so lonely. She'd expected it to change once children came, but it hadn't. It hadn't changed much at all. And with the kids grown, she'd gone on being lonely, feeling it stretch far beyond her, feeling its endlessness unravel as the house became quieter, one child then another abruptly gone. Who was there to confide in? Who was there to pull her through? Certainly not Rusty: she'd done it all alone — grieved alone, lived alone, loneliness dangling from everything around her.

But there were moments, specks, really, when he surprised her with something tender and unlikely. The shoes she was wearing, for example. Her favorite mauve pumps. He knew she liked good shoes. He knew she liked Italian leather. He'd brought her these once, and every time she put them on — whether just around the house or for a special occasion — she remembered that night, how pleased he'd been with himself as he came through the door with the box. It hadn't been wrapped — she wouldn't have expected him to do that. But he'd picked them out for her, and they were even the right size.

She thought back to the night before, Rusty sitting there patiently with her in the car, wading through radio songs for some sound of Henry, neither of them saying a word when it finally came on, the deejay sending out a dedication from someone named Tiffany to someone named Brad. "Floating World," the song was called, and through the whine of guitars Judy had made out Henry's purring vocals, low and gravelly. An egg in each hand, she'd listened quietly, trying to understand the words, bracing herself against the seat during the drum solo. Rusty hadn't stirred, was maybe asleep, or perhaps, Judy wanted to believe, he was just listening deeply.

Now, for the first time in years, Judy physically crossed her fingers as she kept her hands positioned at ten and two on the wheel, just as Rusty had instructed her back when he'd taught her how to drive. She slowed for the false carcass of a jeep hunkered in the ditch, her eyes wide, scoping, sleuthing. When flashing lights appeared in her rearview mirror and passed her, she accelerated, her whole body shaking.

Picture a cool river, she told herself, *a rushing stream of calm.* Her geographical relaxation techniques did no good. She rolled down the windows and cranked up the air, and for the first time she didn't even care that the wind was blowing her hair to hell.

"Rusty," she called, just to hear his name go out the window. "Rusty, are you out there?" She passed a raccoon slumped along the shoulder. Rusty would be dead and she would be holding — what had Sunny called it? A hermaphrodite?

Up ahead there was a slow-moving vehicle with Wisconsin plates. Without thinking, Judy flashed her brights and then pulled up alongside, only to meet the eyes of a kid — probably not old enough to drive — who at first looked stricken, then stuck his tongue out, wagging a silver piercing.

Was it one of the kids she'd had on that horrible day in health class? she wondered, revving past. She'd never gone back. As usual, a sub was hired to teach in place of Bruce and Bud Luger while they camped in the Grand Tetons with their kids. Judy had turned in her resignation and spent her days at the shooting range instead. And she'd done something else: She started going through the rooms in the basement and slowly throwing things out. Packing up Gretchen's old pink comforter, stacking her old Barbies in a brown bag for Goodwill, putting twist ties around sacks full of Carson's last latch-hook rugs. How long did she need to keep those things around?

An ambulance flew past, lights sweeping across the road like the gaze of Cyclops's eye. She was just miles from home now, and still no Rusty. She imagined his body being wheeled into the hospital and pronounced dead at the same moment that Gretchen's baby was declared alive. A lump rose in Judy's throat.

The ambulance veered off at an exit to another town, a different tragedy. What were the chances he'd make it home? What were the chances that she'd find him asleep in the garage or maybe back in his old bed, their old bed? There was a rest stop ahead. She swung into it and circled the lot. There were a few abandoned cars, none of them red, all of them seemingly empty.

At the far end, she spotted a pay phone under a light and pulled over to it, craning out the window to dial her home number. She let it ring, then called back again and held the phone to her ear for a very long time, imagining that he would be just walking through the door and reaching for the phone as she hung up.

She rolled up the window, put the car in park, and let it idle for a moment while she thought. Should she go all the way home if he wasn't even there? By now, perhaps the baby had arrived — maybe that had even been the cry she'd heard in the hall as she ran out.

"Hey," she called to a young man coming out of the rest-stop bathroom and crossing to his car. "What's a hermaphrodite?"

The man stopped, fixed his eyes on her through the dark, and said, "Fuck off."

Judy sat awhile longer, then reached down, lifted her right foot off the brake, and took off her shoe — her mauve heel. Once new, it was now creased and in need of a good polish. She studied it without expression, remembering the first time she had tried it on and danced around the living room. Then she lifted up the insert. On the back of it, written neatly in black marker oh so long ago, was a phone number.

She rolled down her window again and pressed the buttons solemnly. The phone rang three times, then came the answering machine. A voice she did not recognize spoke the words: *Please leave a message, we'll call you back.*

Before she spoke, she'd already begun to cry. It was the first time she had cried in so long, and there was so much to cry for that she just let it all out, knowing no one was there on the other end except for a machine. "Carson," she finally managed to say, her voice cracking. "I think Rusty's dead, and your sister is having a hermaphrodite."

Just as she was about to hang up, there was a click on the end of the line and someone said her name. "Mrs. Glide, hello, Mrs. Glide? Are you still there?"

Judy stared at the phone for a moment before putting it to her ear again.

"It's Ben," the voice said. "Carson's already left for the hospital. He should be there within the hour."

"Oh," Judy felt confusion, a rush of blood to her head. It was 3:00 AM by the dull glow of the clock on the dash. "Who is this?" Her head felt light. She cradled her shoe.

"It's Ben — Carson's partner. I thought . . ." His voice trailed off.

"Right," Judy said. "I think he mentioned you once in a letter. It's been so long now. I'm afraid my mind's reeling."

"Sure," Ben said. "It's okay. It's been a crazy night here, too."

"How did you know? Did Gretchen call?"

"No," Ben said. "Rusty did. About an hour ago."

Judy scratched her forehead. "Who? Who did you say called? Do you mean Ray?"

"No," said Ben. "Believe it or not, it was Rusty."

"Then you're sure?" Judy asked.

"Yes. I'm quite sure."

"Very well. Sorry to bother you, then." Judy's voice was barely above a whisper.

"No bother, Mrs. Glide. No bother."

Judy hung up the phone. She put her shoe back on, flipped on the radio, and made up her mind to stop at the first sign she saw for a restaurant where there might be coffee. It was going to take all her energy to make it back to the hospital without falling asleep on the way there. She could not go home, not now, not after all she had been through. Besides, she had promised Gretchen that all would remain calm and cool, and she aimed to see that promise through.

Chapter 13

A CHILD IS BORN

When Judy arrived back at the hospital, the sun was just beginning to rise, a hot pink glow at the base of the horizon. She parked her car in the ramp, searching blindly for Rusty's Wisconsin plates as she spiraled down to the lobby level, her heels clacking against the cement, a light sweater swinging over her arm. The lobby was quiet, though someone stood at the vending machine of flowers, pressing the button to make the vases of roses turn, shivering alongside the gears.

"Mom?" It was Carson's voice. "You got a quarter?"

Judy stopped by a round industrial trash can, jarred. The lights flickered above her, the gray tile floor settling into a blur. She steadied herself by pressing a hip against the trash, one hand on her chest fluttering against the open collar of her blouse. The man in front of her looked unfamiliar, a long face framed by close-cut hair, so full of styling gel it looked like plastic blades of grass. Tiny gold hoops glittered in his ears, set off by blond side-burns that followed the line of his jaw, then bent abruptly into sharp points, like paring knives that tapered toward his mouth. Dark sunglasses, rimmed in gold, rested on the bridge of his sharp, freckled nose. He pushed them back onto his head and offered her a lopsided grin, stuffing fists into the pockets of his rumpled jeans.

"A quarter?" Judy asked, dazed, her hand falling slowly to her purse. Without taking her eyes off him, she fished around in the satiny lining like a crab picking its way through litter. She sifted through gum wrappers, paper clips, crumpled tissues, matches, lipstick, hard candies, bullets.

He was taller, more muscular than she might have imagined, remembering his adolescent body, how thin and hairless he had been, lying in his bed as a boy, waiting to kiss her good night. Now a navy blue V-neck stretched between his pecs, framing a tuft of downy chest hair. And street clothes! She had never pictured him in ordinary clothing — just the saffron robes he'd left in, although she'd heard he was different now, had become a theater teacher at an elite school just outside the city.

"Here." He laughed and stepped forward, not to hug her but to grab her purse. He frowned as he dredged the pockets. "What is all this shit?" he asked, then pulled out her tube of lipstick, squinted at the label, and said, "Christ, Judy, are you still wearing Cherry Fire? Girl, you need a makeover."

She laughed, a low hiccup of a laugh, almost a sob, then took her purse back, tucking it under an arm.

"Ma, Ma." Carson draped an arm over her shoulder. "Let's have none of that." He braced her firmly against his body, cupping her elbow in the palm of his hand.

"My youngest son" was all Judy said, trying not to gulp, conscious suddenly of her car-rumpled skirt and blouse.

He stepped back, delivering a soft punch to her arm. "Awww, you still call me that?"

Judy cocked her head to the side and dabbed at the corners of her eyes. "What do you mean? Of course I still call you that."

"Okay, whatever — you never call, you never write. You know, you Glides are odd folk." He shrugged and spun around on a corduroy slipper, then crossed back to the flower machine, scrounging change from the depths of his pants pockets.

"I'm sorry," Judy said.

"You should be," Carson said without turning. He squatted to dig around in the vending machine's hatch for his loot, then pulled out a single rose — deep red, encased in a tube of plastic.

"Here," he said, grabbing her hand, enveloping it with his strong fingers. "We'd better see what's going on in room twelve twenty-four. Last time I checked, she was still pushing." Judy let him lead her toward the elevator, feeling like a small child in his grasp, and when the doors closed she cried silently all the way to the twelfth floor, hoping he wouldn't notice or mind too terribly much.

She wasn't sure what she had expected, but she hadn't expected this — all of this, in one night. Now it was already a new day, the baby still on its way, and here she was cruising up in the elevator with her own longlost boy.

In the waiting room, Sunny and Klaus were fast asleep, Klaus in his makeshift bed of chairs, Sunny curled up in a corner, still wearing her muumuu, head resting on her big gold leather purse.

"God, who is that and what is she wearing?" asked Carson, giving a little snort. "Mom, don't tell me you know these people."

"They're the other grandparents," she whispered, shaking her head.

"Shit," Carson said, grinning lopsidedly at her. "No wonder Dad begged me to come."

"He begged?" Judy asked, pulling aside two chairs for them by the window. Through the glass, the glow of a new dawn was be fore them, pink light resting on the treetops.

"Well," Carson sighed, "mainly there was a long pause, then he said, 'Please.'"

"And?" Judy pressed.

"Then he apologized for not calling sooner and asked what I thought about meeting you down here at the hospital."

"I didn't know he even had your number. Did he say where he was?"

"I didn't think to ask." Carson shrugged, rocking back on the chair legs and wrapping his sunglasses around one thigh. "I was too stunned. But it sounded like people were moving around with dishes in the background."

"Hmm." Judy gave a little shrug. "I'm sure he'll be back here at some point."

"I doubt that," Carson said.

Judy eyed him, taking in his sideburns, his sharp profile, the way his bottom lip curled out, the same as Rusty's.

"I told Dad I'd only come if I didn't have to see him," Carson said flatly, fiddling with the Velcro strap of his watch.

"Oh," Judy said.

"Henry's on his way, too."

Judy tried to follow Carson's eyes out the window, to see what he was looking at, but it was too hard for her to focus on anything. Her lids felt heavy, the back of her mouth cottony. "I need some shut-eye," she said. "I've been through a trial you don't know the half of."

He touched her shoulder. "I'm sure you have, Mom. I'm sure you have."

*   *   *

When she awoke, Judy sat up, dazed and sore from sleeping sideways in the chair with her head against a wall. She rubbed her eyes. Carson was thumbing through a magazine. It hadn't been a dream. And there next to him, with his shirt off, was Henry, the eyeball pendant around his neck gleaming in the sunlight.

"This is a historic event, man," he was saying. "You're lucky you get to be the one to document it."

A young man Judy had never seen sat next to Henry, scribbling intently on a notepad. He stopped to chew his pencil, then asked, "So, Ransom, how does it feel to be reunited with your brother here, Carson Glide?"

"Rad, man," Henry was saying. "This tops opening for Megadeth in eighty-seven."

Judy closed her eyes again. Sun from the window felt warm on her legs.

"How does this affect the Brother of Carson Glide? The image? Your next tour?"

"It's going to change everything, man," Judy could hear Henry saying. "Plus we got my sister's little one on the way, and that's way cool, too. We're a family again, you know, and that changes you. It changes your core, man."

"And that's your mother over there?"

Judy felt a hand on her wrist. She opened her eyes as Henry stooped to wake her, a hank of dark hair obscuring half of his face. The eyeball around his throat glowered at her. "Ma," he said. "Writer here from the *Chicago Reader* is doing a story on the band. You want to talk to him? We're all here, we're all together again."

Judy forced out a weak smile. "Hello," she nodded to the writer, a short little man with no hair and glasses so tiny they looked like wings pressed to his nose. "Someone just tell me if I'm a grandmother yet." She yawned, wrapping her arms around the purse in her lap. "Is it here? Did I miss it?"

"Long road," Carson piped up. "Nurse just came out and says it's crowned."

"Crowned," Henry said slowly, reaching around to scratch his shoulder blade. "Good word, man."

"Can I get a shot of the two of you with your mother?" asked the journalist.

"Group shot," Carson sang. He and Henry crouched down beside Judy's chair, their chins brushing her shoulders as the flash went off. Judy asked, "The nurses let everybody in here?"

"It's a hospital," Carson said with a shrug. "They don't care. It's like a mall for the ill."

"Mall for the ill," Henry repeated. "That sounds like a song."

The writer scribbled away, his pen audibly scratching against the page. Then he flipped his notepad over, recrossed his legs, and continued scribbling.

At 1:17 PM, Ray appeared in the door of the waiting room, ashen and elated-looking, the veins in his neck and forehead throbbing visibly. Henry and Carson had ventured down to the cafeteria to scrounge up some lunch. Klaus and Sunny had disappeared, maybe in search of the doctor, or maybe they'd gone home to shower and change clothes. Judy was the only one left in the waiting room, leafing through a dog-eared copy of *Newsweek*.

"He/she's here," Ray said, closing his eyes dramatically. "Mother and baby are fine." He put his feet together and bowed to her from the doorway.

Judy felt a wave of relief. "Oh," she cried, "can I hold it?"

"Absolutely. Gretchen's just finished nursing."

Judy's legs wobbled as she rose, following Ray down the hall and into the dim cocoon of the birthing room, where two corner lamps were on low, only the tiniest rays of sunlight seeping in around the curtains. A nurse was packing up an IV. Gretchen was sitting up before a lunch tray, hungrily wolfing down what looked like green Jell-O. And there, in her other arm, was something wrapped in a black blanket.

Speechless, Judy kissed her daughter's cheek and peered around her shoulder at the little face. "Who is this?" she asked, her voice suddenly high. "Who is this precious bundle?" Even in its scrunched state, she saw something she recognized. The baby had Ray's dark hair, a shock of it that formed a widow's peak, and when Gretchen unwrapped its hands from the blankets, Judy saw tiny versions of Gretchen's long, delicate fingers.

Gretchen beamed, wan though she was, and passed the baby from her arms to Judy's. "Here's your granny," she whispered, then looked up at her mother with a wide smile. Judy cradled the baby in her arms and roamed slowly around the room, cooing.

"We're going to wait a few days to name him/her," Ray said, padding over to Judy. "We're pooped. I can't even think straight."

"Sure," said Judy, "sure."

She gazed lovingly down at the face, the puckered eyelids, the milky dark eyes, the tiny lump of a nose, and faint eyebrows. "He/she's lovely," Judy said, just as she'd practiced. She caught Gretchen and Ray exchanging smiles. "I love whatever it is."

"Not an 'it,' Mother," Gretchen said.

"Sure," said Judy. "Sure."

"Where's Dad?" asked Gretchen between sips of orange juice. "Where are Sunny and Klaus?"

"It's been a crazy night," Judy wanted to say, but instead she said, "I imagine they'll be by soon."

Judy was still holding the baby when Henry and Carson knocked, sticking their heads in around the door. "Is this the magical suite?" asked Carson, grimacing. "Is there room for two weeping uncles bearing roses?"

Judy saw Gretchen's eyes light up. "You came," she said from the bed.

Ray, who had sprawled out on the couch, raised one lid, then shut it again.

The brothers gathered around Judy's shoulders, looking down at the sleeping face, at the dark hair trimmed by the black blanket.

"It looks like a little comma," Carson remarked, slipping away to kiss Gretchen on the forehead and setting the roses by her bedside. "Nice work," he said, taking both her hands in his.

Judy could feel Henry's breath on her neck. She turned to look at him. "You want a turn holding?" she asked.

Without looking at her, he nodded. He'd put his shirt back on. It even looked as if he'd brushed his hair. It was swept back, resting in neat black wings at his temples. The bracelets on his wrist rattled gently as he took the baby from his mother, holding it closely to his chest. He stepped softly away from Judy in his black leather boots and held the baby awkwardly, both elbows cocked out, as he put his lips to its forehead.

Judy sank into the easy chair by the window and watched her children move about the room. How easily they conversed with one another. It was as if they were right in her living room; it was as if they had never stopped speaking to one another. And maybe they hadn't. She had never dared ask Gretchen what she knew and whom she talked to. Until recently, she had been too numb to want to know.

Now their conversation moved over Judy like a soothing tide, then washed away in a comfortable silence. Her mind felt cleansed, eased of worry and wondering. She sat sipping a soda — legs crossed, eyes watching — and just was. As the new baby passed from one set of arms to another, she felt that they were passing a new openness. The future itself. And she was glad no one had put a name to it yet. It was still only to be imagined.

Finally Gretchen sank back into her pillow, eyes glossed over with sleeplessness, and said, "I don't have the energy for another word." She closed her eyes. Henry set the sleeping newborn in the bassinet, giving its forehead one final stroke of affection. Judy smiled to see her eldest son so tender. He even made sure the chain on his wallet didn't hit the side of the bassinet and wake the baby as he turned to go.

As she closed the door to the room, Judy took one final look at Ray curled up on the couch like a snail, at Gretchen on the thin bed, her face serene, her lips slightly parted, her short hair giving off a radiant glow against the white linens. Judy blew a kiss and made sure the door latched with only the quietest of clicks.

In the hallway, she expected to see Sunny and Klaus come barreling around a corner, maybe even Rusty rushing in on his soft loafers, but there was only the man from the *Reader*, flipping through his notes.

"Can I get a quote from you?" he asked Judy as she lifted her sweater off the back of a chair and prepared to go.

"No," she said. "I'm speechless."

Chapter 14

GENTLEMAN CALLERS

I t was raining when Judy finally pulled into her driveway and started up the front walk, stepping gingerly around the earthworms in her heels. She unlocked the front door and sniffed at the foyer, wondering if Rusty would be inside or if he was out tinkering in the garage. She considered not checking, just to have the day stretch out in uninterrupted peace, a perfect breath of a day.

The air in the house smelled stale. Someone had closed all the windows during the rain. He had been here. She dropped her bags in the living room, then checked the bedrooms. All empty.

"Rusty?" she called, wanting him there suddenly, wanting to tell him about the birth and even to thank him — to thank him for bringing her children together.

She crossed the kitchen to the garage door, thinking, *Let him be there. I want to climb into the passenger side and sleep on his shoulder.* But the door opened to emptiness, oil spots on the concrete, a Ping-Pong ball hanging in breezeless space.

She shut the door and went back to his bedroom closet. It was just as she knew it would be. Empty. A single black tie on the floor, like a river fluke. Then she went to the bathroom and opened the medicine cabinet, as if this were one last way to make sure. There stood his toothbrush, but all his other things were gone — razors, comb, even his cologne. Even the soap dish sat empty except for a pool of cloudy blue water.

There was a knock at the front door. Judy ran to it and opened it without even looking through the peephole as usual. Donald stood on the stoop, his green feed cap in his hands, his face drawn.

"Ma'am," he said, as if he were addressing someone he did not know. "I tried to stop him." He shook his head, a swath of ice white hair swinging loose from his neatly gelled swoop.

Judy looked down at his square-toed boots and told him to come in. Donald bowed and stepped inside, standing awkwardly in the entryway with his shoulders hunched as if the ceiling might come down. Judy motioned him into the kitchen and pulled out a chair from the table, but Donald raised a hand. He licked his lips and tugged at an ear. "I don't aim to stay. I don't want to be a bother. I told him to at least leave a note." Donald rubbed his hands together. "But he seemed hell-bent to go. I am truly sorry."

Judy went over to the sink and filled the kettle with water. "Donald," she said, looking not at him but out the window to where the feeders swung empty from the boughs of the oak. "I've never been a neighbor to ask much, but I'm asking you now, please stay and have a cup of coffee with me. It's all I ask."

Donald accepted her offer by pulling out a chair and sitting down with his elbows on the table. Judy lit the stove and set the kettle to boil, then lifted two mugs from their hooks under the cupboard and measured tablespoons of crystallized coffee into each one.

"Gretchen had a healthy baby this afternoon," Judy said softly as she set the mugs on the table. She pulled out a chair for herself and ran her hands along the underside of her thighs as she sat down.

"Aw, now that's some good news," Donald said. She could hear something catch in his throat, a question he was about to ask but then swallowed. "I'm real happy to hear that."

"And my boys came back," she said. "Carson and Henry, they were both there."

Donald raised his eyebrows and stuck out his lower lip. "Well, how 'bout that. How are they doing?"

"They looked real good," Judy said. "Everybody looked real good."

Donald nodded, long and slow. His boots scuffed under the table as he shifted. Judy noticed he'd put on a clean shirt to come over. It looked as if maybe he had even just shaved. There was still a little white patch of something on one side of his narrow jaw. He rested his watery blue eyes on her and smiled.

"It was Rusty's doing," she said. "He called them. I never would have." She looked at her hands, which were laid out on the table in front of her like silverware. She moved the salt shaker a little to the left. "That's note enough, Donald," she said. "That's all that needs saying."

When the water boiled, she stood up. She reached for a reindeer mitt and used it to lift up the kettle and pour the water. It ran like a slow shush into each cup. Then she got out a teaspoon from a drawer and stirred circles. "Sugar?" she asked Donald.

"Please." He blushed. "Doctor says I shouldn't, but I know it wouldn't hurt this once."

They sat across from each other with their hands on their mugs, looking quietly around the room. Judy rested her eyes on the knitted covers she'd made for the blender and the toaster and even some of her flour canisters, and she thought now that they looked ridiculous. It looked like her kitchen was dressed for winter. She stood up and yanked them off and stuck them in a drawer, then sat back down across from Donald.

"Good coffee" was all he said.

"I'm glad to think Rusty has you as a friend," she said. "I'm glad you were the one to see him off."

"Something's not sitting right with him," Donald said.

Judy nodded. "I know."

"He'll be back though, I think." Donald rubbed his chin, catching the shaving cream on his thumb. "Can't imagine any place he'd go. No place better than Fort Cloud anyhow."

"Maybe he'll just drive and drive," Judy said, sucking coffee through her teeth. "That's what he likes to do."

Donald nodded. "Got that right."

When he'd finished his coffee, Donald stood up and moved around the table to set his mug in the sink. "Celeste'll be really happy to hear about the baby," he said, putting on his cap and adjusting it with both hands. "And you need anything, you just holler across." He put his fists in his pockets, then withdrew his right hand and extended it to Judy. "We got a deal?"

She shook his hand. He circled back around the kitchen table. "Mind if I just go out through the garage?" he asked.

"Go right on ahead."

The next morning, Judy awoke to a knock at the door. She stumbled into the hall, groggy, feeling sleepless. Expecting Donald, she swung the door open only to find a camera in her face and a microphone up by her mouth, a blonde in a pink suit with boxy shoulder pads pressing in on her.

"Are you Mrs. Glide?"

Judy put a hand on her throat. "What?"

"I'm from Fox News," the woman said briskly. "We're reporting on a group of people out of Chicago who call themselves

Future Parents. Now, your daughter was taken hostage by this group?"

"Hostage?" Judy said.

"Are they dangerous?" the woman asked. "And excuse me for asking, but do you know if they leave the genitals of the children intact?"

Judy tried to catch her breath. "I'm not going to say anything," she said.

"Have you been sworn to secrecy, Mrs. Glide? Is your son Ransom also a member?"

"I don't have a son named Ransom," said Judy. "His name is Henry, that's the name I gave him."

Off to the side, she could see the neighbors all along the street coming out of their houses and standing on their lawns, most of them still in bathrobes. Celeste stood at the base of her driveway, arms folded across her chest, her feet set squarely together in white sneakers.

Judy retreated, shutting the door against the microphone, hearing the wide-shouldered blonde calling, "Mrs. Glide, do you accept this baby as a legitimate grandchild?"

Judy locked the door and waited with her body against it until she heard the woman leave. She went into the living room and drew the curtains, then sat down on the arm of Rusty's brown chair. Through the sheers she could see the news crew packing things into their van, neighbors gathered around — people she'd never seen or didn't recognize anymore. She closed her eyes and remembered the warmth of the baby in her arms. She felt different, settled. She was a grandmother to a child with no name or sex. Yet it was a presence all its own, and that brought her a curious peace she hadn't expected. Gretchen had given birth to a healthy baby, and that's all anyone needed to know.

Later, after she had showered and made herself toast, Judy called down to the hospital. "How's the baby?" she asked when Ray answered.

"Fine," Ray said, his voice hushed. "Not much of a sleeper, though."

"Word seems to have spread," Judy said quietly. "A reporter from Fox News just showed up on my doorstep."

Ray sighed. "Great, just what we need."

"And there was a writer that came with Henry," Judy added. "I'm sorry, Ray, I had no idea. I should have done something."

"It'll blow over." Ray sounded resigned. "Hael won't like it, but we'll be fine."

When Judy hung up, she realized she had forgotten to tell Ray that Rusty was gone. Maybe it was better that way, she decided then. One less thing to worry them. *No commotion*, Gretchen had said. Judy paced the living room, noting the dark stains in the carpet, the faded arms of the couch. The room struck her as suddenly dated and gloomy.

She had a vision of herself wilting against Rusty's old brown chair, cordoned off from her grandchild by a daughter who couldn't trust her, deserted by a husband she'd locked out in the garage. She saw herself growing old in this room, lips paling against the pheasant couch, teeth falling noiselessly into the blotchy shag carpet, her hair growing long and ghostly, rippling over her hips. She'd spend her days staring out the front window at the old woman across the street, both of them waiting for the paper at dawn and nodding off each dusk, laps aglow from the winking light of lonely televisions.

The phone rang. Ray again, exhausted-sounding. "Judy," he said. "We could use you here." Judy was out the door with a new overnight bag before Ray could finish his thought.

Chapter 15

HIGHWAY MAN

Rusty had just crossed into Pennsylvania when the clunking sound started under the hood. He eased the car off the road near some woods and slapped his thigh, remembering that he ought to have packed some tools. On second thought, he was just as glad he hadn't. Let someone else fix it, he thought. He still wasn't feeling like himself, and the last thing he ought to do was crawl around under a damn car, a damn car he didn't even have the papers for, come to think of it. Those were still back at the lot, where he'd called this morning and left a message for the secretary to take the day off. He needed the weekend and maybe more to think things through.

He'd just put up the hood and wait for a passing car to come by and give him a lift to the nearest phone. He'd stay the night nearby, get himself a hotel room this time, not try to camp out in the backseat anymore like some kind of fugitive. Last night, he'd gone down an empty back road and pulled over, expecting to get in a few solid hours of sleep. He'd been exhausted after his rush job packing, playing offense with Donald, and just generally get-

204 • Tenaya Darlington

ting himself out of Fort Cloud. But he'd gotten almost no sleep again. It seemed that empty back road was some sort of trucker hangout. Every hour or so, there'd been a knock on the hood.

Each time, he ignored them, but there was one who wouldn't let up. Rusty finally sat up and put his face to the window, only to see a bearded man chewing on what looked to be a toothpick, with a big smile. "Need company?" the man asked.

"Nope, need sleep," Rusty barked.

"'Kay then."

Rusty had been too tired to move the car elsewhere. He'd pushed some Kleenex into his ears and gone back to sleep. Sometime midmorning, he'd gotten going again, had stopped at a greasy spoon for a plate of eggs that went down easy, although now something in his stomach was awry.

He stepped out of the car into a cool afternoon breeze, popped the hood, and climbed back into his seat to read while he waited. Donald had come over with a tattered copy of *Moby Dick* the day before, wondering if Rusty had ever read it and urging him to take it along. "Toss it in the trunk, along with all the other stuff," Rusty had said.

"You sure you won't tell me where you're headed?" Donald had prodded.

Rusty had shaken his head. "Just got something I've been meaning to do for a while."

"Well, okay then. I see I can't stop you."

Ten minutes hadn't passed before Donald ducked back into the garage again, this time with a waxed bag full of doughnut holes.

"Damn, Donald, what's gotten into you?" Rusty had said, carrying armloads of clothes out from the house to the trunk. "Can't you see when a man needs his peace?"

"I've been eating on these all morning," he said. "Celeste'll have my head if she catches me with them. Why don't you take 'em with you."

"Are they stale?"

"They're pretty good."

"Toss them in on the seat, then," Rusty had said, calling around the side of the trunk.

Now he flipped the pages of his book and was glad for the doughnuts, especially the ones rolled in powdered sugar. He hadn't eaten more than half a dozen when he doubled over in pain, clutching his belly and writhing on the seat. His book fell to the floor and the bag of doughnuts upended all over the dash, sending up little white clouds of sugar.

"Holy Jesus," Rusty cried out, his whole body convulsing. He fought whatever it was that was trying to get out, then banged open the glove compartment, hoping to find the bottle of antacids he'd stashed there earlier. He winced. No bottle fell out. He sat up on one elbow and pawed around through the maps, the other hand still clenching his gut.

The little mirror in the compartment sprang up, and all it took was one glance at his face to convince Rusty that he was going to die. His face was as yellow as the margarine tub. Even his eyes looked like gory dandelions. When had he turned so sallow, and what the hell had come over him?

"I'm being punished," he said, heaving and rolling onto his back. He flopped around like a fish, his whole body locked in a painful spasm. "Dear Lord, I beg you," he cried, flipping over onto his stomach and drawing his knees up under his chest. There he heaved again and again, purging his body of all he had consumed that day and the day before. It filled the car with a smell so noxious that he found the wherewithal to yank open the driver's side door and lunge forth, sputtering for breath and wiping his face of the sour spittle that ran all down his front.

He lumbered along the dirt shoulder a few yards, then collapsed in a heap, his insides still smoldering, his lungs gasping for air. God, this was a horrible way to go. In between painful seizures, he saw back into those mornings when Judy, newly pregnant, had begged him to pull over along the road so she could throw up. He'd been so glad then that he had been born a man, but it all caught up with you. And he remembered the times they'd raced to the hospital, her doubled up with contractions that rendered her speechless. There again, he'd felt spared. Oh, it was all coming to haunt him now. He cursed himself for ever being so smug, for ever thinking she ought to be quieter about it and accept her pains with a little more grace. The Lord would send him to his grave without the least bit of grace, and he supposed he deserved it.

He kicked around and finally rolled off into a ditch, hoping this gesture of submission would encourage the creator to curtail his misery. "I'm ready to go, Lord," he cried. "Just name the time. It's your stinkin' victory." Another wave of pain coursed through him as he closed his eyes and submitted himself entirely to a black place, not unlike the realm of dreams, where, from time to time, he had envisioned his legs spreading to birth a monster.

Chapter 16

BABY X

To Gretchen, it seemed impossible that all she'd been waiting for had arrived. She could remember visiting Hael soon after each of her two births, holding M16, then M64, in the very same hospital. She remembered walking this same floor, hearing babies up and down the hall as they entered the world. Such surreal sounds, those first cries, the mother giving voice to the child's. And to be in that ward and overhear spirits being born — that had been almost wilder than entering the birthing suite to meet Hael and Glyn with flowers for each of their newborns. How could birth be so magical and yet so mundane?

Now here she was with her own little one, and she felt only quiet elation. She couldn't imagine taking her eyes away from its face. It pained her even to blink. Who was inside, she wondered? Each eye like a tiny keyhole, each cry a clue. She surveyed the room from the rocking chair, taking a last look around the birthing suite to make sure Ray and Judy had packed all her belongings. On a shelf, she saw they had forgotten the black candle she'd asked the nurse-midwife to light as soon as the baby's head appeared.

Though she was still exhausted, her body felt light, as if she and the baby were floating. Maybe it was the hours of relaxation exercises Ray had led her through during labor, whispering in her ear, "You're floating in water, let the baby float out of you." And she had pictured this and started to chant the word "floating," laughing to herself now as she remembered how the soft chant had grown into a shrill roar at some point in the night, her voice becoming hoarse as the sun seeped in around the putty-colored curtains.

She said the word aloud now in the room, the afternoon light bent across her knees. The baby blinked, as if in recognition. "Floating," she said. "Would that be a good name for you? Would you like to be a little verb?"

Judy came in, wearing a dark dress, tiptoeing through the room.

"You don't have to be quiet," Gretchen said. "He/she's eyes are open."

"Ray's bringing the car around," Judy said, pressing her palms together and scanning the room nervously. "Have you seen Sunny and Klaus?"

"They were in and out a little bit ago with some lunch." Gretchen smiled.

"I feel terrible," Judy blurted out, kneeling by Gretchen's chair. "I let a guy from the *Chicago Reader* in here after the birth. He was doing a story on Henry's tour."

Gretchen shrugged. "It's okay."

"I know you didn't want any commotion —"

"Mom." Gretchen looked at Judy's shaking hands. "I don't care. I'm so happy, I don't care what anyone knows. Just relax."

Judy forced a weak smile. "I'm a little on edge, I guess," she said. "But, look, I'm wearing all black."

Gretchen nodded approvingly. "You've come a long way, Mom."

Judy grinned feebly. "I'm trying."

*   *   *

They made a dark entourage in the lobby, Judy, Gretchen, Ray —
all of them dressed in black clothing, down to the baby in its onesie. Judy thought she could feel people watching them. *Probably
think we're Amish*, she reassured herself as she helped Gretchen
out of the wheelchair and into the new Volvo Ray had borrowed
from Glyn and Hael. Judy followed closely behind in her Datsun,
terrified whenever anyone changed lanes in front of her or cut too
close to the rear door where the new baby was strapped into its
seat. She couldn't remember being so protective of her own children, but as Celeste had warned her, this was a grandchild, and
grandchildren were different.

Back at Gretchen and Ray's apartment, Sunny and Klaus were
waiting on the stoop in matching blue running suits with gold
piping, sipping smoothies. They raised their glasses in salute as
Ray pulled up to the curb, then came running across the lawn like
Olympians. As soon as Gretchen stepped out of the passenger
seat, people from all down the block crossed leaf-strewn yards to
see the community's newest addition, cooing and whooping.

"Can I hold him/her?" Glyn was the first to ask.

"Let me see!" cried a small child holding a foam blob.

As Klaus helped Ray gather up the bags from the trunk, Judy observed Sunny standing off to the side under an elm. She was smiling to herself, taking it all in. *She knows*, Judy thought to herself,
she knows. But when Sunny finally joined the crowd, it was only to
chat politely about the fall weather and to nod about Gretchen's
bravery and the miracle of birth. To Glyn, who was still rocking
the new baby in his sweatered arms, she said, "I'm just so glad to be
a grandmother. I'm even looking forward to a few nights on the
blow-up mattress so I can help out around the house."

Judy bristled at the thought. Sunny sleeping at the apartment? Sunny within constant range of the baby? What if Gretchen and Ray left the room for a moment? Sunny would be the first to un-snap the onesie and break their confidence. Judy flashed Gretchen a concerned look, but Gretchen only rubbed her still-swollen belly and smiled, her eyes bright against the dark sweater around her shoulders.

From the corner of her eye, Judy caught sight of what looked like a white news van pulling up down the block, but before any reporters emerged, everyone started inside to make supper, leav-ing the yard empty except for a gray foam blob bouncing down the walk.

As late afternoon sagged into evening, Gretchen slipped off to her bedroom with the baby for a nap. Already the day felt like part of a moonwalk. Somewhere between elation and exhaustion, she was still floating. The phone rang, a distant bird trill weaving through her half-sleep. The baby began to cry. She sighed and sat up on the futon, pulling a changing pad out of the diaper bag. The baby fussed briefly, then resumed staring into space. Gretchen looked down at its perfect moon of a head as she unfastened the crotch snaps of the onesie she'd made and began peeling back the diaper's cloth folds. From the living room, she heard Klaus's dry laugh, her mother's birdsong giggle.

It was strange to see the baby naked, even though she tried to make its sex mean nothing. During her pregnancy, she had pic-tured the sex as a sort of blur when her mind dealt with it, but now it surprised her. She found she had to bat away certain thoughts, nicknames, connotations that crept into her psyche. Remaining neutral to these thoughts was more difficult than she had imagined. Some part of her wanted to dash into the hall and show everyone the baby in its pink entirety.

The door swung open, and Gretchen turned quickly.

It was just Ray, but his face was angry. "You didn't have the door locked?" He shook his head as if he couldn't believe this. "There is a lock right here on the door. I could have been Sunny or Judy or Klaus. That would have given everything away." He flung his arms up over his head and spun in place.

"Relax, Ray."

"Relax?" He began to pace, knotting his T-shirt around a thumb, muttering to himself. To Gretchen, he looked like the hairy animal he was, and with two-day stubble on his face, he looked even darker, even hairier. Like an ape, she thought, giggling to herself as she recalled the story Sunny had told about his birth.

"You're laughing at me?" Ray stopped short at the foot of the futon and faced her with a quizzical squint.

"Ray, I was sitting right here. My body would have blocked anyone from seeing the baby."

"Now there you're wrong." He stepped toward her and shook a finger in her face. "You don't know," he said to her eyes. "You don't know. It's us against them."

"Please, Ray." She fussed with the Velcro on a diaper.

"We can't trust anyone — you know that — not for a second, especially with your mother circling like a hawk."

"My mother? How about your mother?" She picked the baby up under its shoulders and was careful to cradle its head. "Listen, Ray, I'll be careful. We'll be careful."

"With your mother letting that reporter nose around, we'll be lucky if strangers don't scale the building and break in through a window to find out the sex."

"That's silly." Gretchen yawned. "You're acting paranoid. No-body's that interested."

"Me, paranoid? Remember the Lindberghs," Ray went on, moving to the window. He stood with his back to her, the muscles of his jaw clenched. "That could be us. It could all come down around us."

"Nothing's coming down around us. Breathe, Ray, breathe." Gretchen leaned back against the pillows with the baby on her chest and began rubbing its shoulders in soothing circles. She studied Ray, his thin hips, the veins pulsing in his arms. The dark cotton curtains on either side of him looked like the opening to a stage, the blue sky through the window a set. At any moment, she expected a pair of invisible wires to carry him up so he could fly away.

He had flown into her life, winged and mothlike, descending around her with his arms the first time she had met him during the performance of her friend's shower. He had invited her back to his apartment for supper — leek soup and bread he'd baked that morning, she still remembered. They had talked late into the night, and she had stayed, falling asleep across his dark hair splayed out on the futon. Fully clothed, they hadn't even kissed. And the same thing had happened the next night and every night after that. It was as if he had literally fallen through the ceiling into her lap, and being with him had felt as natural as breathing. For weeks, they had lived like that, slowly becoming intimate, winding around each other in the night so that she awoke in a kind of cocoon and emerged each morning like a new creature from his moth love.

"Ray," she said now. "Remember how it was in the beginning? The two of us? Those quiet mornings?" Gretchen rolled onto her side. "Let's not get so caught up in this that it ruins us." She could see the lines along Ray's mouth soften. She set the baby down on the bed between two pillows and watched its tiny pink hands fall like leaves around either side of its head. Then she went over to Ray and held him, pressing her belly into his back.

"Oh, Ray," Gretchen whispered. She tightened her hold on him, nuzzling her face into his neck. He relaxed and rubbed her palms with his thumbs the way he knew she liked.

"It's overwhelming, isn't it?" he asked.

"No," she said. "It feels miraculous."

He turned and kissed her. "I was hoping you'd say that."

In the kitchen, Judy helped Sunny with a fruit salad. She used a melon baller to scoop perfect orbs of cantaloupe into a bowl while Sunny sliced peaches, bracelets jangling. After taking a shower, Sunny had changed into white slacks and a gauzy button-down shirt covered with great pink rhododendrons through which a black bra was vaguely visible. To Judy, she not only looked like Florida but carried its fragrance — a salty seaside smell combined with something mushy and floral. There was something frondlike in her movements, her thin arms slicing peaches, her long fingers with their daggerish nails, her wisplike hair fashioned into spikes. And to add to her jaggedness, she wore long, thin earrings made of bone.

"Did you get a chance to visit with the doctor?" Judy asked finally. She had been waiting to ask the question all afternoon, not because she wanted to know for herself, but because she wanted to know where Sunny stood. Judy had made a pact with herself to squelch any further commotion.

"No," Sunny said, eyes on her peaches. Then she turned, her lips tight, her great penciled brows furrowed. "What have you heard from Rusty?"

Judy shrugged and nibbled a piece of cantaloupe.

"You mentioned that he had to take a sudden trip." Sunny paused. "Have you heard from him?"

"No," Judy said. She had decided to keep talk about Rusty to a minimum. She had told Gretchen and Ray that Rusty sent his apologies, that he had been called away on a business trip. She was glad that they hadn't pressed for further information. After all, everyone knew Rusty never took business trips.

"Judy, I don't know whether I should tell you this." Sunny set her knife down on the cutting board. "I have a very bad feeling about your husband." She folded her hands and proceeded carefully, taking her time to find the words. "I get visions sometimes, I think I told you, and for the most part I keep these to myself until I can back them up. But" — she swallowed — "I've had a returning vision, ever since last night, of Rusty lying somewhere in a wooded area." She bit her lip. "He was dead."

Judy felt Sunny awaiting a reaction. Her deep-set eyes seemed to go right through Judy. And to herself, Judy said, *I see right through you, too.* Sunny was just practicing one of her scare tactics, probably trying to sell her on the idea of driving back to Fort Cloud for the night. Then Sunny would be alone in the apartment with Gretchen and Ray. She'd try to get her dragon fingers on the baby, pull back its diaper, peer with great pleasure at its damp, pink flesh, so new, still godlike and innocent. It seemed suddenly grotesque to Judy that parents ever talked about their child's privates to anyone at all.

"Pfff." Judy waved a hand and returned to her melon baller. "Rusty probably just stopped somewhere to take a nap."

Sunny leaned forward on her elbows and looked up at Judy across the counter, her head nodding slowly back and forth, her bone earrings knocking softly against her jaw. "I don't think so," she said, her voice almost inaudible. Then she rinsed her hands at the sink and left the room.

Judy finished the cantaloupe. She was determined not to let Sunny's intimidation techniques affect her. Sunny was wily, that's what she was. She was a saleswoman, and this was one deal she was not going to seal. Butter people up and stick it to them. The whole prepartum party, the fetus muumuus — it had all been part of Sunny's performance. From now on, Judy was going to watch her every move.

That evening, just as everyone sat down to supper, Hael stopped by with a card and some muffins. She stepped through the doorway, looking wide-eyed and ruffled, M16 wrapped around one leg.

"I can't stay long," she said. "Just wanted to say hello before we go."

"Where are you going?" Ray asked, scooting his chair back, the baby over one shoulder, but before Hael could answer, little M16 began jumping up and down and asking, "What's he/she's name?"

Hael bent over and whispered something into M16's ear.

"It's okay," Gretchen said. "We don't have a name picked out yet," she told M16.

A smile crossed M16's face. "I've got a name."

"Yes?" Gretchen tilted her head to the side and smiled at little M16, who was wearing a pair of black overalls and shiny new black clogs.

M16's arms swung in circles; the little mouth grinned a neat row of white teeth. "Barbie," M16 whispered.

"M16!" Hael looked up, embarrassed. "I found one by the front stoop in the bushes," she said, her voice agitated. "And, after a long talk, I let M16 play with it."

A silence fell across the room. Hael looked at the faces gathered around the dinner table and suddenly burst into tears. "I can't take it," she said. "My parents aren't cooperating, and Glyn's angry with me for even calling them. Everything's a mess." She turned and opened the door, scooting M16 into the hall amid her sobs.

It was Ray who leaped from the table. "I'll handle this. You all eat," he said as he passed the baby to Gretchen. He ducked out with an amicable wave.

Supper was quiet. Judy noticed that Sunny hardly ate her food — grilled tofu, Asian slaw, fruit salad. Klaus was the only one who smiled. "Any breakthroughs on a name?" he asked Gretchen as she nursed, leaning over the baby to eat.

"No," she said quietly, then, "Well, we have one, but we'd like to wait for the right occasion to announce it."

"It'd be nice to call it something." He laughed. "What about you, Judy, any word from Rusty?" Klaus met Judy's eyes across the table and popped a melon ball onto his tongue.

So he's in on it, too, Judy thought. "He's still on his business trip as far as I know." Judy smiled extra brightly at everyone around the table.

"Dad doesn't take business trips, does he?" Gretchen asked slowly, shifting the baby to her other breast.

Judy averted her gaze. "No, not usually. This must have been a special circumstance."

"Well, where'd he go?" Gretchen persisted.

Judy looked at her daughter and blinked quickly, as if she could convey something via Morse code. She took her time. "He's in New York," she said. "Yes, New York."

"That's a long way," Gretchen said. "I hope he flew."

"No." Judy looked at her long and hard. "He chose to drive."

"Mom!" Gretchen's voice was shrill. "He can hardly see. He shouldn't be driving that far at his age. And didn't you see him when he was here? He looked terrible. He looked like" — she paused, frowning — "he'd been dieting. I told Ray I thought he looked sick."

"Who'd like another glass of Chablis?" Judy asked, pushing her chair back before anyone could answer. "Just me? Well, okay then."

Ray came in, closing the front door behind him.

"What's the matter? Is everything okay?" Gretchen turned in her chair.

He shook his head at her and sat back down at the head of the table across from his mother. He studied the food on his plate for a minute as if it seemed unfamiliar, his lips pursed. Then he said, "Hael needs to check out for a while. She's headed to a retreat center up in Willard, Wisconsin, and she's quitting the show."

"What?" Gretchen said.

Ray nodded.

"She can't go." Gretchen swung the baby onto her shoulder. "You guys can't dump the show. You've been working on it for over a year."

"I know," Ray said, standing up and turning in a circle by his chair. "She wants to can it. The whole thing down the toilet."

"What's this, now?" Klaus asked.

"Ray's been working on another performance art piece," Sunny informed him. "About his experiences in the intentional community."

Ray rubbed his chin, then put a finger across his lips. "No," he said. "I can't cancel it, I won't. It's in a month."

"I bet you'll sell a lot of tickets if that story comes out in the paper," Klaus piped up, giving a rowdy *har-har*.

"I don't care about the publicity," Ray said. "It's a matter of integrity. Gretchen" — he pointed to her, his eyes suddenly aspark — "you've got to play the female role." He licked his lips quickly, excitedly. "You have to."

"No," she said, raising a hand. "No way."

"I'll condense the part," Ray went on, scratching his head now, tapping a foot. He looked up at the ceiling. "It's mostly my show anyway. Hael played a minor role, and I could easily rewrite her part myself."

"Ray, hello!" Gretchen waved her hand at him across the table. "I've never acted. I am not going to debut after having just given birth. I've got to stay with the baby."

"We could help out," Sunny ventured softly.

Judy, who was listening from the kitchen, froze.

"Let's not discuss this now," Gretchen said, turning back to the table with a long sigh. "Thanks for dinner, everyone." She forced a smile. "It's been a long day. I think the baby and I are going to retire."

Judy stepped out of the kitchen with her wineglass and watched her daughter shuffle down the hall, the baby's head on her shoulder. Just as Gretchen pushed the door to the bedroom open, the baby spit up all down her back.

"Wait," Judy called. "I'll bring a towel." She skittered back into the kitchen, then whisked back to the far bedroom, closing the door behind her. "You've got to be careful," she whispered to Gretchen as she dabbed the back of her T-shirt with a dishrag. "Sunny and Klaus are up to something. They're scheming to find out the sex of the baby."

Gretchen shook her head. "Mom, calm down. Why don't you head home for the night? You've done enough."

Judy licked her lips and put a hand on her hip. "Your father left me," she said.

"What?" Gretchen, who was preparing to sit down on the bed, suddenly stood up. "He what?"

"When I got home from the hospital, all his things were gone. Everything." Judy threw her arms in the air.

The baby whimpered. Gretchen bounced on the balls of her feet and patted its back in a slow, thoughtful rhythm. "Mom," Gretchen said when the baby had quieted, "I don't know what to say."

"It's okay," Judy said. "But if you don't mind, I think I'll stay — at least for the night."

Chapter 17

NIGHT WATCH

That night, for the second time that week, Judy took the insert out of her pump, flipped it over, and dialed the number. Instead of being at a highway rest stop this time, she was at a trendy café with amber walls and mood lighting, couples talking in hushed voices as they toasted marshmallows over small tableside hibachis. After Gretchen and Ray had disappeared into their bedroom with the baby, after Sunny had readied her air mattress in the nursery and helped Judy make up a bed on the couch, Judy had sneaked out. To Klaus, who was washing the dishes and combing the television stations for entertainment news, she said, "I'm just going to go out for a little air."

She'd asked a neighbor where the closest coffee shop was, and he'd directed her down the block. Now she stood off to the side of the cappuccino bar, balancing on one leg, a shoe in her hand.

Carson answered. "I've got a problem here," she said. "Your father's taken off for good, and Sunny and Klaus are up to something. Sunny says she knows what the baby's sex is. She thinks she's psychic."

"What can I do?" he asked, his voice soft on the other end of the line.

"I don't know," Judy said. "I don't even know why I called." She scratched her head, suddenly confused.

"It's all right," Carson said. "You just needed someone to confide in."

"I think Rusty's dead," Judy went on. "I just have this feeling."

A woman drinking a latte at a bar next to Judy flashed her a dirty look. Judy put her hand over the mouthpiece and said, "Mind your business."

"It would serve him right," Carson was saying.

"Yes, I know," Judy nodded.

"This is bad timing, though, you're right." Carson's voice was matter-of-fact. "And I didn't like Sunny or Klaus."

"I'm afraid they'll look down the baby's diaper," Judy said. "Gretchen and Ray are so tired they might not even hear someone break into their room."

The woman with the latte looked at Judy again, then moved one stool to the right with her magazine.

"Oh, God," Carson said, drawing in a quick breath. "That would be devastating for them."

"I know," Judy said. "I just want to do what's best for Gretchen."

"Then you've got to be vigilant." Carson's voice was full of energy. "Mom, this is your chance. You've got to take this in your hands. You're the only one who can."

"Yes," Judy whispered, her voice full of renewed conviction. "I'm going to keep watch all night."

"Good," said Carson. "I can come over in the morning and do the day shift."

"I love you," Judy said.

"Thanks for calling, Ma," Carson said.

*   *   *

Judy stopped by her car on the way back to Gretchen's apartment. She hadn't wanted to resort to this, but it just so happened that she had Rusty's old gun in the trunk from target practice. The question was how to sneak it in past Klaus and into the house.

She'd picked up a double latte and was gulping it in the shadow of some elms when it occurred to her that she could slide the gun down her dress and fake a stomach cramp on her way past the couch. When she was sure no one was looking, she lifted the rifle out of the cello case where she kept it wrapped in a towel, checked the safety, and slid it down against her leg. She held the barrel in place with both hands and went limping up to the front door.

Klaus let her in. "I'm just getting ready to head out," he told her. "Sunny's already found her way to air-mattress land. You okay?" he asked her as she limped through the living room toward the couch. "You look a little uncomfortable there."

"Just cramps, bad stomach cramps," Judy said.

"Sick to your stomach?" He straightened up, his voice now officious. "I'll just wash my hands, then we'll have a look."

"I'll be fine." Judy's voice was firm.

"But we can't have you in pain. After all, I'm a doctor." He started for the sink, humming to himself quietly.

Judy cleared her throat. "No checkup today, Klaus. I'd just like to get some sleep."

Klaus stepped back into the living room, his lips pursed. "Right, then," he said after a moment, tipping an invisible hat. "You know where to reach me." He stuffed his hands into pockets and quietly left the apartment.

The light was on in the hall, but the apartment was still. Judy had time to slide the gun under the couch just before the bathroom door opened and Ray stepped out. He tiptoed down the hall in tie-dyed boxers and peered across the dark living room at Judy. "Henry called," he said, scratching his chest. "He's swinging back through in a couple days for a tour break."

Judy nodded. "Is Gretchen in bed?"

"She and the baby are already asleep. Happy as rabbits," Ray said with a smile.

Judy lay awake, feeling alive. She put her arms over her head and sighed. Then she kicked her legs up into the air and scissored them a few times, letting her dress ride up around her thighs. She didn't care. She got up, let herself out onto the stoop, and leaned against the railing, feeling the breeze in her hair. It smelled cool, of fall leaves and burrowing animals, of French fries and bus exhaust.

A few streets over, she could hear the traffic whining and dogs barking and someone yelling to someone else that he ought to keep his mouth shut. She had grown up in this city and had left it young, but it all came back to her through its sounds, the rush of a place under siege by activity, industry, individuality.

She remembered assisting her father at his store on weekends, helping to stock shoes in the back until she was old enough to assist on the floor, measuring feet and fetching fresh stockings. Customers of all colors and styles came in, and she watched her father, a peaceable man, extend a hand and a cordial smile to all of them.

And sometimes people came in who couldn't afford a thing; they came in just to put their feet into something warm and well made, and he treated them with dignity, letting them prance around on the fine carpet even when all the other salespeople looked on with raised eyebrows. He had been a good man, her father, a lover of people. He'd given everyone a chance, a good-hearted handshake.

Judy laughed to herself and looked to the sky. She hadn't thought of her father in a long time. It seemed like a lifetime ago since he walked the earth, visiting her in the hospital after Henry's birth, shortly before his own death. "A grandchild — that's a sign that there's no such thing as an ending," he'd said. "They change everything. You don't think they will, but they do. They're like a needle. Mends all the loose stitching."

There was a pack of cigarettes on the stoop, half hidden behind a pot of brown geraniums. American Spirits — the wrapper glistened in the moonlight, a pack of matches beside it. Judy picked the pack up, stuck her nose down into the paper, then removed a cigarette. She hadn't smoked since the summer she and Rusty had dated, when he taught her to smoke and drive his little MG. She lit one now and let it burn down a bit, taking the smoke into her cheeks and exhaling a narrow cloud over her knees. It made her cough. She set it beside her on the step and watched it burn down, cinching up on itself, the orange tip like a taillight moving through the dark.

After a while, she went back inside and sat on the couch, Indian-style, and looked out the window, letting the minutes pass, prepared for anything, wanting nothing. She leaned back and stared up at the painting over the couch, the gray orb floating against more grayness, buoyed by the moonlight that filtered through the windows. The painting struck her now as profound, like a meditation on floating, like a commentary on birth consciousness. Judy rested a hand along the waist of her black skirt and felt a brief memory flicker through her, a memory of lying next to Rusty, filled with light.

Several times she got up to look down the hall. The baby woke and fussed, but all doors remained closed. Judy took turns pacing, then sitting, imagining how she'd slide the gun out from under the couch at the first hint of a door opening, how she'd poise herself by the bookshelf, where she could take easy aim if Sunny appeared to be sleepwalking. *Sunny,* she'd say, feeling very Annie Oakley, *this time I've beat you at your game.*

She imagined Sunny's narrow eyes, then Gretchen's stunned face as she drifted into the hall with the baby. Judy chuckled to herself. She still had a few secrets on them.

Eventually, the sun began to rise. Judy was still sitting upright, thanks to her double latte, but her eyes were beginning to softly close as she lingered at the edge of sleep, then opening again. The first glow, a clean slice of white light, took to the edge of the sky, then moved forward over the trees, rising up over rooftops and the sides of buildings until it came right into the room and sat at her feet. It moved up her legs, up her torso, then into her eyes until she had to close them for good. And there, inside herself, she felt as if she had been given a new body, as if she had been anointed by the spirit of life.

Judy was just dozing off when Carson knocked. Only Ray was moving, walking the baby around the room in front of the window so Gretchen could continue to sleep. Judy could hear the two men whispering. "I'm still awake," she managed to say from the couch. "Don't whisper on my account."

She heard them pull chairs out, sit down at the table.

"You're a performance artist, right?" Carson asked.

"Yes," Ray said.

"Actually, I caught your last show, the one about vegetables," Carson went on. "I thought it was brilliant."

"You were at that? The one two years ago?"

"Yeah. I thought you were so in tune with the tomato. That was really something."

Judy smiled to herself. Here was one she hadn't heard.

"You're into that sort of thing, then? You see a lot of shows in the city?" Ray's voice got higher as he got more excited.

"My partner, Ben, and I try to see as much as we can. I teach theater. Ben's mainly into drag." Carson's laugh rumbled.

"Fantastic," Ray was saying. "You do some acting yourself?"

"Here and there. I like musicals. Loved *Hairspray*."

"A classic," Ray said.

"But I'm willing to do anything. I mean, you're talking to a guy who used to dress up in his mother's clothes when she wasn't home and lip-synch to Donna Summer." Carson let out a briny cackle.

"That's fabulous."

"You knew that, right, Ma?" Carson called over to Judy on the couch. "I used to run wild in your turquoise nightie? I used to romp around in your high heels?"

Judy let out a whispery snore. She was completely out.

Chapter 18

RAY'S SHOW

At the end of the weekend, when some of the excitement had died down, Judy drove home to Fort Cloud. She was glad to pull onto Seeley Street, glad to be returning to her own house, her world quiet again. As she neared the driveway, she saw someone bent over in her front yard. It was Celeste. She sat back on her heels and waved a pale blue glove as Judy pulled up. When Judy got out, she saw that Donald's signs from the shower were both planted in the front yard. IT'S A GIRL right next to IT'S A BOY. Celeste said, "I just decided to come over here and plant some bulbs as a little surprise."

Judy smiled. "I thought I might find the house egged after that news van was here last week."

"Oh, goodness, no." Celeste smiled. "When have we ever had a news van pull up to this street? Everyone's excited about the baby. Does it have a name yet?"

"Yep," Judy said. "Only I'm not supposed to say."

"Oh, that can't be," Celeste pushed a lock of blond hair back with her wrist.

"That's the way they want it," she said. "Ray wants to save it for his show."

"The suspense is killing me," Celeste said. "I've already started a little scrapbook. And" — she grimaced — "I'm making some black onesies for our Maggie. Did I tell you she's expecting again?"

"That so?" Judy asked. "Grandchildren are just wonderful."

"Aren't they, though?" Celeste stood, shaking her head, both hands on her hips. "Such a joy, and they really are like little mysteries. There's no telling who they'll be."

"Nope." Judy gazed out across the well-raked yards with a feeling of satisfaction.

"I'll leave you be," Celeste said. "And if you know where we can get tickets to Ray's show, well, Donald and I and some of the neighbors — we'd like to go."

"Great," Judy said. She watched Celeste cross the lawn over to her garage, her garden clogs leaving temporary ovals in the short, dry grass. Next door, Donald was pounding away at something, probably a bird feeder, Judy guessed, or a chair for his newest impending grandchild. Judy made a mental note to pop a box of bootees into the mail for Celeste's Maggie, then thought better of it.

She lifted her duffel out of the trunk and hoisted her cello case over a shoulder. Inside, the house felt cool, empty. Somewhere a door blew shut in the wind. Judy stood surveying the olive cupboards in the kitchen, then pressed her ear to the door that led to the garage. She cracked it and peered out into the dark cavern. Empty, just as she'd expected, the air still saturated with the smell of cigars. She sighed and pressed the button on the wall to raise the garage door, let the wind clean it out.

Then she went down the walk and called up to Donald in his garage. "You want that old brown chair of Rusty's?"

He stopped what he was pounding and came around some saw-horses, taking his gloves off. "What's that?"

"Would you help me move something?" she asked. "I'm set on rearranging a few things in the house."

"Sure," said Donald, stuffing his gloves into the back pocket of his work jeans. "You want to do it now?" He was already across the lawn.

Back inside the house, Judy explained to Donald that she wanted to replace the old recliner with a rocker, and he said that he thought that was a good idea, so they dragged the old brown chair to the curb, where it sat for a few minutes until Donald said he'd go ahead and put it in his garage. "You ever want to sit in it, you just come right over." Donald thumbed his chin. "What else you want moved?"

"Maybe our old bed," Judy said. "Then that'll be it for now."

Halfway across the country, Rusty opened his right eye. His body was floating. There was a bright light overhead, the sun against a pure background of white cloud cover. Then a deep voice spoke. "See if he'll eat something." Rusty closed his right eye and wondered if he was in heaven or hell, and guessed he'd be able to tell by the rations.

"Sir." Someone touched his arm. He opened an eye again, expecting to see a man in robes. Instead he saw a boyish face in blue scrubs, and when he raised his other lid he realized the sky was only ceiling, the sun only an overhead light. He was alive, and there was no pain anywhere in his body.

"I'm in a hospital?" Rusty looked around in awe.

"Well, yeah." The boyish face grinned. "You just had your gall-bladder taken out."

"My gallbladder?" whispered Rusty.

"Yep, that's what it says here." The orderly tapped at a clipboard.

"Was that all they took out?"

There was a laugh. "Were you expecting something else?"

"Oh, no," Rusty murmured, closing his eyes, thinking of his dreams — nightmares, really — and feeling relief flood from his shoulders to his feet. "No, no."

Near the bed, the orderly pointed out a phone and tapped a finger against Rusty's wallet. He said, "You remember what happened out there on the side of the road? You were lucky somebody brought you in."

"Oh?" Rusty scratched his head. "I don't remember."

"We checked your wallet for a driver's license, but there was nothing but an expired library card," the orderly said. "Did you have money in there?"

"I don't remember," Rusty said. "I didn't expect to come back."

"You had a car, though, I assume."

"I don't remember that either," Rusty lied. "I'm just glad to be alive right now."

"Sure." The orderly rested a hand on Rusty's arm. "Sure. I'll check on you again in an hour. You're in Scranton, just so you know, in case you want to call someone around to get you."

Rusty blinked at the spackled ceiling for a while and touched his face with his hands. Everything there seemed to be accounted for. Then he touched his stomach and felt the bandage along his abdomen. "Gallbladder," he said once aloud, as if he were settling on it as an entrée at a restaurant.

After a bit, he pulled the phone closer to his bed and set it on his chest so he could dial without sitting up. He wasn't sure where to begin. How many days had passed? Had Gretchen delivered?

Maybe no one wanted to hear from him. He looped the cord around his thumb and rested his head back against the pillow, re-opening his mind to the fact that he was still alive. In truth, he believed he must have died and that for some reason he'd been spared, brought back to finish something. God only knew why.

Maybe this was his chance to make good, find a new begin-ning — the way each of his children had. For the first time, he ap-preciated the act of disappearing, and he felt that in some small way he understood their sudden departures, the urge to go in search of renewal, refreshment — rebirth.

Judy answered on the first ring. Something about her "hello" sounded different; her voice seemed brighter, yet more serene. "Jude," Rusty said, a name he hadn't called her in years.

Silence. Then, "Where are you?"

Rusty explained what had happened. He could imagine Judy shaking her head, envision her narrow feet on the wine-colored carpet, her earrings dangling just below the line of her hair. She laughed, a low, sweet laugh, and he could see her lips, as red as brake lights, hear her breath moving over the small rows of her teeth. When he closed his eyes for a moment, he remembered the smell of the sweat behind her ears; it evoked a vibrant fern green color in his mind.

"Sunny gave you her Xanax instead of the vitamins," Judy said. "Did you take them?"

"Didn't think to," Rusty said. "I went out for a burger after I left the hospital."

There was a long pause. "I got rid of your old chair," Judy said quietly then, "and our old bed. I'm going to paint the cupboards in the kitchen off-white and get new carpet in the living room, maybe a pale blue-gray or beige." Then she added, "I was hoping you might clean out the garage. That old Christmas tree is still in there." And Rusty knew this was about the closest thing to an invitation home he was going to hear.

"Done," he said.

The question then was just how Rusty would get home. He had no money, was in no shape to drive. Ordinarily, he'd thumb a ride, but in his condition, he wasn't sure he could stand much more adventure. "I might need your help," he said, "if I'm going to get back to Fort Cloud."

"Wait," Judy said. "I'll call you right back." And when she did, she told him that Henry was out in New York and heading back through Chicago sometime soon. Gretchen had told her he had a show in Philadelphia that night.

"Philadelphia?" he said. "Any idea where in Philadelphia?"

"Gretchen's going to try to find out."

"All right, then, Jude," Rusty said. "I'll be home soon." He paused, then asked, "So we're grandparents then?"

"Mmm." Judy purred. "He/she is lovely."

The young orderly knew of the Brother of Carson Glide. "Oh, sure," he said with a laugh, popping his knuckles, "I like that new song of theirs." Rusty promised the boy an autograph if he could scare up some information about the band's next show. And when Rusty finally got through to the ticket desk and then to the box office manager, explaining over and over who he was and answering a million trivia questions about his son, he finally got through to Henry's tour manager and eventually to Henry, who had just been apprised of the situation.

"You going to behave if we come pick you up? It's a little out of our way, you know." Henry's voice was sleepy.

"Behave? Heck, I'll drive," Rusty volunteered.

"Now, Dad, we don't need you to do that. I just don't want you to . . ."

Rusty scrambled to fill in the words, but all he could think to say was "I've got a grandbaby to see."

Henry agreed, but before Rusty would let him hang up, Rusty asked, "You're playing Philly tonight?"

"Yes."

"Would you do me a huge favor?"

Henry sighed audibly, then was quiet. Rusty reached out for his wallet on the bedside. Inside, deep in a leathery corner, there was a piece of photo paper folded twice into a square. He unfolded it on his lap and looked at the face of a boy with freckles and dark hair and even darker eyes. There was a name on the back: *Joe Byrd, age 4.*

Rusty licked his lips. "Would you dedicate a song to a guy back there named Joe Byrd?" he asked quietly.

"Joe who?"

"Byrd," Rusty said. "Joe Byrd."

"Uh, okay. This an army buddy or something?"

"No," Rusty said. "Just somebody, somebody I owe the first of many apologies to. I'll tell you about it sometime when I feel better."

"Joe Byrd," Rusty heard Henry call over his shoulder into the background. "Everybody hear that? We're sending out a song to a guy by the name of Joe Byrd."

"Okay," Henry said.

"Thank you, son," said Rusty. "Thank you, thank you."

Henry's voice was tight. "Pick you up in about thirteen hours," he said. "Scranton General?"

"Mercy." Rusty hung up the phone and closed his eyes, feeling in his heart that he might die from joy.

*   *   *

Everybody on Seeley Street went to see Ray's performance that first weekend in November. Donald and Celeste drove the old woman across the street who nobody had ever met, and they learned her name was Estelle. Donald and Celeste's children even drove down, though none of them knew what to expect from a performance art show. Their eldest son explained that it was kind of like when Letterman or Jay Leno did a monologue, only it went on longer and was somehow a little different. And everybody nodded and thought that would be really interesting. They even made a pact to wear all black, which for some of them meant they had to go out and buy brand-new outfits. Donald figured this would be kind of like a sports event, only artier, and made signs, which he fastened to wood stakes for people to wave. The signs said, WELCOME TO FORT CLOUD, BABY X.

Judy, hired on to do makeup, rode over to the theater with Carson in a cab. She wore a new black pantsuit to camouflage herself against the stage curtains. Carson had told her he'd put a stool back there for her, and she even went out and bought herself a brand-new pair of good shoes — no heel, just soft soles so she could move around quietly if Ray needed her to help with props.

Rusty rode down in the bus with Henry's band, with whom he'd become quite chummy. They'd made him an honorary roadie, part of their autograph-support team. He sat proudly in the passenger seat, next to Rex, their driver, talking on and on about engines. He wore a concert T-shirt — it was black with the silhouette of an infant rising out of a coffin — and he could now hum along to a few of the songs on Henry's latest album. Henry was preparing to launch his Baby in Black tour the following summer. In a surge of inspiration from staying at his parents' house in the interim, he'd written ten new songs while sitting on his old bed in the basement, watching light from the lava lamps play off the walls.

Sunny and Klaus persuaded the doorman from their condo building to come to the show with them, and on the drive there, they got him to commit to buying a food dehydrator from one of their catalogs in the backseat. After the show, they planned to host a reception, and Sunny was excited that she would able to reuse many of her clever prepartum party props. Tonight, she had on her muumuu. Klaus wore one, too.

Gretchen rode in with Ray, the baby fast asleep in the backseat. On the way, Ray listened to zither music to help him stay calm. Due to some recent press in the *Reader,* the show was sold out. The box office had even sold tickets for the aisles. Though Hael was still incommunicado among the Franciscan sisters of the forest, the Figgises told Ray they planned to come with their children and document everything. Glyn volunteered to pass out programs.

Instead of paper, the programs were printed on black onesies with white ink. Gretchen and Ray had sewn them all by hand, along with help from other people in their community. On the front of the onesie, it said, "Maybe Baby." On the back, it read: "A two-man show, by Ray Atwater and Carson Glide, with special help from . . ." There followed a list of names stretching from the neck to the crotch snaps. The last name was "Gray Glide," and in parentheses, "Baby X."

An hour before the show, Judy helped Carson with his hair and makeup, while Rusty stood by with the baby in his arms, talking a constant stream of happy babble, his jowly cheek pressed to its forehead. He wasn't much on the name Gray — even though Gretchen and Ray had explained that it was a combination of their two names — so he called the baby simply "Junior."

"Git on," Judy said to Rusty as he shuffled past with Junior, singing under his breath. "You're breaking my concentration."

She shooed him away from the stool she was sitting on and carefully applied base around Carson's eyes. "Now close them," she commanded.

"Mother," he said, with a little one-note laugh, "I never thought this day would come."

Judy smiled and went on dabbing about his temples with her little round makeup pad, adding some eye shadow. "A baby changes everything," she wanted to say, but she held her mouth. She knew it was more than that. It was many things, a swarm of things. She felt a rush of delight as she uncapped some lip liner.

"This is like heaven," Carson said, more to himself than to her. "You have no idea."

Out of the blue, a word came to Judy's mind. "What's a hermaphrodite?" she asked, picking through her makeup box for a cotton ball.

"An individual with reproductive organs of both sexes," Carson said.

"Oh," said Judy politely.

"Where did you hear that?" He cracked a sparkling eyelid.

"Just around," Judy shrugged.

She leaned over and worked on his top lip, then sat back to study her handiwork. Behind her was a round mirror encircled in small white lightbulbs, like a movie set, a Christmas tree. She caught sight of herself as she rustled around for some mascara, and was momentarily surprised by the reflection. The lights gave her hair a warm glow. It softened all the lines of her face, made her eyes twinkle. It had been a very long time since she had looked at herself, and she had expected to see something horrific, namely a bushy mustache. But it was nothing, a faint shadow.

She leaned into Carson. "See that?" she asked, pointing to her upper lip.

He squinted. "What? That little mustache? You could have that bleached."

Judy smiled and shook her head. "Pucker up like you're going to kiss me," she said. "Here comes the lipstick." He screwed up his mouth and closed his eyes, and before she used her little brush to paint on a new pinkish shade called Sugarplex, she closed her eyes and pecked him on the mouth. More than a peck, it was a press, even a prolonged press, as if they were exchanging a breath. And for an instant, the image that came into her head — as she kissed her son in his girlish costume — was that she had become a man and he a woman, and for one quick, bright second, they swapped worlds.

ACKNOWLEDGMENTS

Thanks to C. Michael Curtis for his simple but beautiful rejection letter, which set me on fire to write this book. Thanks to André and Melissa for giving me a scrumptious niece, which got me scratching my head about babies, and to my old neighbors at Fair Oaks Cohousing, who introduced me to alternative ways of parenting.

This book could not have been written without the support of my parents, Mahlon and Sonja, and my colleagues at *Isthmus Newspaper*, who taught me how to find and unravel compelling stories and gave me the space to do so. Many thanks to Amy Williams, the best agent one could wish for, and to Reagan Arthur at Little, Brown and Company, who took a chance on my manuscript. Oh, honey.

For their driving enthusiasm and the regular use of their ears, I am indebted to Dean Bakopoulos, Heather Lee Schroeder, Heather Skyler, Guy Thorvaldsen, Ron Kuka, Andrew McCuaig, and David Ebenbach. Additional thanks goes to Clint McCown, Alyce Miller, Cornelia Nixon, Tony Ardizzone, Beloit College, and the MFA program at Indiana University.

Much of this novel was written in a little hermitage at the Christine Center in Willard, Wisconsin, where the sisters took great care of me and, what's more, offered terrific specks of insight during our meals together at the great green table. Special thanks to Sister Margaret, Sister Johanna, David, Ingy, John, Mary, Livia, Dexter, and Tom.

Most of all, thanks, Carl.

ABOUT THE AUTHOR

Tenaya Darlington's fiction has appeared in *Scribner's Best of Fiction Workshops 1998*, *Mid-American Review*, and *BOMB*. She lives in Madison, Wisconsin.

MAYBE BABY

A NOVEL

Tenaya Darlington

A READING GROUP GUIDE

A CONVERSATION WITH
TENAYA DARLINGTON

How did you come up with the idea for Maybe Baby?

In the late '90s, my husband and I lived in a cohousing community in Madison, Wisconsin. We were one of five families who shared a garden, childcare, meals, etc. Although we moved out in less than a year to buy our own home, I was really struck by the children who lived there. They played without regard to social roles, they were wildly imaginative, and there was no sense of "boys will be boys and girls will be girls."

It struck a chord with me because many of my friends were beginning to have their first babies at that time, and there were lots of nature vs. nurture discussions in our living room. We also knew people who were very frustrated by the challenge of raising balanced children. And by "balanced" I mean kids who were willing to cross gender lines — to play baseball as young females, or to take up ballet as young males. I kept hearing from these parents that, despite every effort, their children were growing up in more clearly defined gender roles than ever.

But what I saw in cohousing was that kids are a product of their community, and when a community is open to new ideas, the children really develop their own identities. In cohousing, no one freaked out when the nine-year-old boy wore his long hair back in a headband and performed Irish jigs in the driveway. He went on to become the most popular boy at school despite his long blond locks and his kilt. The key was that the community protected his right to discover who he was, and that empowered him to become a leader.

I wanted to write a book that took the notion of gender-neutral childrearing a step further — a book that would be funny and appealing to a wide audience, but that would have a very serious question at its core: Is it possible to raise a gender-neutral child? At a time when parents are able to determine so many factors about their children in utero, I think it's important to ask these questions.

What is your opinion of Rusty and Judy Glide? Were they inspired by anyone you know?

Rusty and Judy are really just an amalgam of people I grew up around in the Midwest. Their house is very similar to the houses in the small-town Iowa neighborhood where I was raised, down to the pheasant-print couch in their living room. From the outside, they appear to be very simple folk, but their inner lives are built around secrets and bitter disappointment. What I like about Rusty and Judy is that they are capable of molting. At its heart, this is a book about tolerance, and I wanted the two main characters to grow new skins and to develop compassion — both for their children and for themselves.

Who are your favorite writers? How do they influence your work?

I'm a full-time journalist — a columnist and editor for *Isthmus Newspaper* in Madison, Wisconsin — so I read a lot of nonfiction. Joan Didion is probably my single greatest influence. I appreciate her attention to detail and mood, but most importantly, I share her thirst for eccentrics. The characters of Gretchen and Ray are very loosely based upon some people I once met while doing a story on a utopian artist village in rural Wisconsin.

I started *Maybe Baby* the night after I saw *The Royal Tenenbaums* in the theater. The idea had been roaming around in my head for about a year as an unfinished short story. Something about that movie — the colors, the tone, the deeply idiosyncratic parents — acted as a kind of incubator. The very next night, I sat down and wrote the first chapter, and because I pictured all of the action very cinematically, the book moved and wrote itself very quickly.

It took me less than a year to finish, and I worked on it mostly at night, writing it all in longhand after work. I was tired, yes, very tired usually, but the characters were so sweet and so earnest — all of them — that I looked forward to meeting them every evening at the end of my long walk home. During that time, I was engrossed in a number of different books, in particular *The Corrections* by Jonathan Franzen and *Middlesex* by Jeffrey Eugenides. I also reread Virginia Woolf's *Orlando* and Paul Auster's *New York Trilogy* — two very delicious morsels.

Do you agree with Gretchen and Ray's choice to raise their baby gender-neutral?

For me, it's not a matter of agreeing or disagreeing. The fact is, when a child is conceived, the first thing on everyone's mind is "boy or girl?" and at some point we have to question that question.

What part of Maybe Baby *was most difficult to write?*

I am a deep lover of beginnings. I could probably sit down and start a new novel every day, so the real challenge for me was breaking out the landing gear. I was terrified by the notion of a final chapter. Luckily, I started the book with the baby's conception, so I had nine months to splash around, and as those months wore on, I became very eager to bring this kid into the world. Right before Gretchen's due date, I hit a wall — I had no idea how to keep the story moving forward, and I was petrified of crashing miserably. I took two weeks off from work and rented a little hermitage from some Franciscan sisters who run a retreat center in Willard, Wisconsin. I spent many of those evenings in their wood-fired sauna, where I literally sweated out that ending.

What is your favorite part of the novel?

I love when Judy becomes obsessed with her mustache. To me, it's the perfect reversal of fortune.

Did you know the ending from the start? Did you ever plan to disclose the baby's sex?

I knew from the beginning that I could never disclose the baby's sex — after all, that's the book's great secret. I always knew, however, that the baby would be named "Gray." It seemed appropriate because it's a neutral shade — a combination of black and white, no less — and also because it incorporates letters from Gretchen's and Ray's names.

Do you have an idea of what happens to the Glides after the story ends?

I don't. I suppose it's too hopeful to think that they all lope toward the setting Midwestern sun hand in hand, but that is what I would like to imagine. Several people have asked me about a sequel — they want to hear the story of Baby Gray. Somehow, though, that would feel like a breach of confidence. In my mind, Gray will always just be wandering around in a little black diaper.

QUESTIONS AND TOPICS
FOR DISCUSSION

1. How does the novel's title, *Maybe Baby*, play off its themes?

2. What were *your* expectations when you first learned that Gretchen and Ray intended to raise a gender-neutral child?

3. Does Gretchen and Ray's experiment seem realistic? What if a family in your neighborhood dressed their newborn in all-black clothing? How do you think people would react?

4. The novel's main characters seem to be more comfortable breaking into one another's homes than they are talking to one another directly. Why is that?

5. How do Rusty and Judy change, both physically and philosophically, in the course of the novel? Is it likely that they will continue to accept Gray once the performance is over?

6. How might the conflicts at the heart of *Maybe Baby* play out differently in another part of the country — in California, say, as opposed to Wisconsin? How does geography play a role in this story?

7. In what ways are Gretchen and Ray similar to their parents?

8. Recent advances in genetic engineering have made it possible for a baby's gender and physical traits to be a matter of choice. How might the novel contribute to the debate over the ethics of "designer babies"?

9. How would you classify *Maybe Baby?* As satire? As humorous fiction? As social commentary?

10. How do Rusty and Judy compare to your parents? How do Gretchen, Henry, and Carson compare to you or your siblings?

TENAYA DARLINGTON'S SUGGESTIONS FOR FURTHER READING

Written on the Body by Jeanette Winterson

Orlando by Virginia Woolf

Middlesex by Jeffrey Eugenides

Gender Trouble by Judith Butler

As Nature Made Him: The Boy Who Was Raised as a Girl by John Colapinto

The New York Trilogy by Paul Auster

Martin and John by Dale Peck

Housekeeping by Marilynn Robinson

Valencia by Michelle Tea

Memoirs of a Geisha by Arthur Golden

Quicksand and *Passing,* two novellas by Nella Larsen

Judge by Dwight Allen